QUICKSILVER RISING

Stan Nicholls has been a full-time writer since 1981. He is the author of many novels and short stories but is best known for the internationally acclaimed *Orcs: First Blood* series. His journalism has appeared in the *Guardian*, the *Independent*, the *Daily Mirror*, *Time Out*, *Sight and Sound*, *Rolling Stone*, *SFX* and *Locus* among many others. Stan has worked for a number of specialist and general bookshops and was the first manager of the London branch of Forbidden Planet. He lives in the West Midlands with his wife, the writer Anne Gray. You can visit his website at: www.stannicholls.com.

Voyager

Quicksilver Rising

Book One of the Quicksilver Trilogy

STAN NICHOLLS

HarperCollins*Publishers*

Voyager
An Imprint of HarperCollins*Publishers*
77–85 Fulham Palace Road,
Hammersmith, London W6 8JB

www.voyager-books.com

This paperback edition 2004
1 3 5 7 9 8 6 4 2

First published in Great Britain by *Voyager* 2003

Copyright © S. J. Nicholls 2003

The Author asserts the moral right to
be identified as the author of this work

ISBN 0 00 714150 5

Set in Meridien by Palimpsest Book Production Limited,
Polmont, Stirlingshire

Printed and bound in Great Britain by
Clays Limited, St Ives plc

All rights reserved. No part of this publication may be
reproduced, stored in a retrieval system, or transmitted,
in any form or by any means, electronic, mechanical,
photocopying, recording or otherwise, without the prior
permission of the publishers.

This book is sold subject to the condition that it shall not,
by way of trade or otherwise, be lent, re-sold, hired out or
otherwise circulated without the publisher's prior consent
in any form of binding or cover other than that in which it
is published and without a similar condition including this
condition being imposed on the subsequent purchaser.

For making a stranger feel a little less alien in a strange land, *Quicksilver Rising* is dedicated to the Brum Balti Boyz – Mike Chinn, Peter Coleborn, John Howard, Joel Lane, David Sutton; and to the Gurlz – Jan Edwards, Sue Edwards, Sandra Sutton. And, of course, to my wife, Anne.

'And the nova cannon?'

'I am in the process of priming it.'

'Good. You have my permission to break formation and attain high ventral vantage over the target.'

'It will be done, archmagos. What is our plan of engagement?'

'The fleet will pin the enemy down,' said Voar. 'And you will kill it.'

A SPACE HULK was more than a material threat. It was an object of religious hatred for the Mechanicus. There were few tech-heresies as grave as xenos ships being melded with Imperial craft. Those Imperial ships had been sacred once, their machine-spirits ancient things before whom tech-priests knelt and begged for counsel. They were vessels of the Omnissiah's wisdom as well as the Emperor's might, god-machines that represented the human race's greatest achievements in conquering the galaxy. Now they were dead and defiled, inhabited by Throne knew what aliens and blasphemers.

Death was the only punishment.

The Fleet Minor broke out of formation and thrust forwards, thousands of engines flaring like fireflies. Countermeasures were launched, bursting in silver fireworks, throwing sensor-baffling filaments everywhere. The *Antithesis* barged forwards, parting the smaller ships in front of it like an icebreaker, swinging to one side to bring its broadside guns to bear. The rest of the fleet moved around it, the Asclepian

Squadron closing in to form a picket around the cruiser.

The fighter squadron carriers, *Sunblade* and *Daggerfall*, platforms shaped like thin cylinders with fighter craft and bombers clustered around them like fruit on the vine, spun through the clouds of chaff to send their squadrons lancing forwards on columns of flame. Electronic warfare ships followed them in towards the enemy, electromagnetic fields crackling between them to form blind spots where the fighters would be safe until they began their attack runs.

The *Constant* rose above it all, protected by its shield of Fleet Minor ships, and blue flames flickered around the barrel of the nova cannon that jutted from its prow.

SARPEDON REACHED THE gun deck. Most of the automated loaders had been reactivated by Lygris's efforts, but plenty of the enormous broadside guns still had to be loaded manually. The Soul Drinkers saluted Sarpedon as he arrived. Sergeant Salk was at the nearest gun, directing his squad to haul the chains, dragging a tank-sized shell into the gun's enormous breech. It was one of a dozen along the steel canyon of an Imperial ship, the *Intolerant*, one of the largest warships in the *Brokenback*'s construction. Sarpedon remembered exploring the place for the first time when the space hulk had first been cleared by the Soul Drinkers. It was amazing that the dead ship's destructive force had been reawakened by Lygris.

'Commander!' called Salk. 'What are we up against?'

'We'll know soon enough. What can I do?'

'Gun eight needs another strong arm.'

Sarpedon glanced down the deck towards gun eight; several Soul Drinkers from Iktinos's command were working it. They were amongst the Soul Drinkers who had lost their officers and chosen to follow the Chapter's Chaplain into battle, forming a flock devoted to Iktinos, who fought with a zeal that bordered on recklessness.

'Then I'll lend them a few limbs of my own,' said Sarpedon. Salk saluted and returned to his gun team. Salk was developing into a very fine officer. He had been new to squad command when the Soul Drinkers had first turned away from the Imperium. Now, he had something new to fight for, and he had become one of Sarpedon's most trusted sergeants. Like the rest of the Chapter, he was learning to strike out on his own.

One of Iktinos's Soul Drinkers was hauling a shell towards gun eight. Sarpedon joined the man, crouched down on his arachnoid haunches and lifted the shell, forcing it the last few metres and into the gun's breech. The other Space Marines slammed the shell home and closed the breech door.

'Ready!' shouted the Soul Drinker crouching at the top of the gun's housing, peering through the targeting reticle that let him see the scene outside the ship. 'Targets! Multiple, small, approaching fast!'

'Lygris,' voxed Sarpedon. 'Who are they?'

'Larger craft supported by smaller,' said Lygris from the bridge. 'They're bringing a lot of interference. Looks Imperial.'

Sarpedon gave this a moment's through. The Imperial Navy would fire on a space hulk if they found one, certainly. Even if they realised there were Space Marines on board, one glimpse of the Chapter's mutations, not least Sarpedon's eight-legged form, would convince them that they were dealing with traitors, and they would redouble their efforts to pound the *Brokenback* to dust.

'Got a good look at one,' continued Lygris. 'It matches one of the marks in the archives, a Sapience-class cruiser. It's the Adeptus Mechanicus, commander.'

'The past is death. But the future is worse still – it is an existence on which order and sanity have yet to be imposed. To fight it, the past is the only weapon we have.'

Daenyathos, *The Armaments of the Soul*

CHAPTER TWO

THE SOUL DRINKERS and the Adeptus Mechanicus had history.

The Adeptus Mechanicus had sought to recover the pre-Imperial artefact known as the Soulspear, so it could be properly studied. The Soul Drinkers, on the other hand, had wanted it returned to them as it was a relic of their Chapter, and, in particular, of Rogal Dorn, the Chapter's primarch, who had given it to the fledgling Soul Drinkers upon their foundation after the Horus Heresy. The rift thus created had been the first in a series of betrayals that had led the Soul Drinkers to break with Imperial authority, become excommunicated from the human race, and ply a new future as a renegade Space Marine Chapter.

The Inquisition, taking responsibility for hunting down the Soul Drinkers, had ordered the Chapter's

name deleted from all Imperial records, so that the danger inherent in the very idea of a renegade Chapter would not imperil the minds of the galaxy's citizens.

The Adeptus Mechanicus did not always follow the dictates of the Inquisition to the letter.

'YOU ARE CERTAIN of this?' asked Archmagos Voar, looking down at the data-slate in his hand. He was seated on the command throne at the top of the pyramid in the centre of the bridge, surrounded by tactical printouts brought to him by the ordnance and sensorium crew. The tech-priest that had handed him the data-slate was from the communications crew, who occupied a section of the library dominated by a monstrous switchboard with thousands of sockets and cables.

'Every piece of data we have is consistent with this conclusion,' said the tech-priest.

'I see.' Voar put down the data-slate and picked up a book fetched by a menial from the rare and sacred books section. It was one of the few copies in existence, since it had been ordered burned by Inquisitorial deletion squads in the great libraries of the Imperium. No doubt not one copy remained in the archives of the Inquisition. A golden chalice was embossed on its cover. It was a military history of the Soul Drinkers Space Marine Chapter. 'You were right to bring this to my attention. Go about the Omnissiah's work, brother of Mars.'

The tech-priest bowed and turned away.

'One moment,' said Voar. The tech-priest halted. 'Summon an astropath.'

The tech-priest hurried down to the pyramid to attend to his orders.

The news he had brought was unexpected, and Voar allowed himself the luxury of a few moments' thought. The Adeptus Mechanicus had a long memory; a grudge lasted a lot longer in a bank of data-medium than it did in a human mind. That memory was not easily erased. The Mechanicus knew the name of the Soul Drinkers and of the rebel who led them, Commander Sarpedon. Sarpedon had killed Mechanicus tech-priests in taking possession of the Soulspear, and had resisted the best efforts of the Inquisition to bring him and his Chapter to justice. The Adeptus Mechanicus, in defiance of the deletion order, had collected all the information they could find on the Soul Drinkers. One such piece of information suggested that the Soul Drinkers were making use of a space hulk named the *Brokenback*, the description of which had set off an alert in the archive of the *Antithesis*.

'This is Voar,' he voxed to the magi commanding his fleet. 'Target identified. No prisoners.'

THE GUNS OF the *Brokenback* roared, and the seeker shells, relics of an earlier age of technology, erupted from the enormous broadside guns, spiralling on columns of fire through the void. Armed with their

own cogitators they sought out targets of opportunity, and drove into the cloud of smaller ships in the vanguard of the Mechanicus fleet. Blossoms of atomic fire erupted and imploded darkly in the vacuum, leaving silvery sprays of wreckage.

On the gun deck of the *Intolerant*, Sarpedon watched them on a grainy pict screen hooked up to the gun's own simple sensors. At this distance, the enemy cruisers were visible as silver darts illuminated by light reflected off the surrounding nebulae, and the smaller craft as sprinkled points of light. Many of them were gone in those first few moments, homed in on by the seeker shells, and blasted into burning dust.

From Sarpedon's position, perched up on the housing of the gun, he could see right down the gun deck. Twenty guns, most of them automated and the rest operated by the Soul Drinkers, roared in unison. Loading cranes swung into action, and the Soul Drinkers began to reload their guns, their forms in purple power armour scrambling over the gun housings to haul the breech doors open and drag more shells into position. Sarpedon made ready to drop to the deck and lend his enormous strength to the task, when he caught movement on the pict screen: a glittering spray of ships approaching fast, wheeling in formation to approach.

'It's a bombing run!' shouted Sarpedon. 'Get to cover!'

Guided missiles sliced down from the weapon mounts of the approaching bombers. Automated

turrets, studding the *Brokenback*'s hull, opened up as they approached, snaring them in a lattice of laser fire. Many were destroyed, sliced in two by the lines of white-hot light, but not before they had released their payloads. Most Imperial Navy craft would have needed to get much closer to strike, but the targeting systems of the Adeptus Mechanicus were superior, and their ordnance streaked into the gun deck of the *Intolerant*.

Sarpedon leapt off the gun mounting. He braced his legs and hit the far wall, his talons finding purchase on the metal. He clung to the wall as the first missile hit home, erupting in white flame at the far end of the gun deck, and shattering the massive structure of a broadside gun. The shock wave hit him, and he clung on as Soul Drinkers were thrown off their feet below him.

The wave of flame was sucked away as the atmosphere shrieked out through the hull breach. Sarpedon's power armour was airtight and could use its own air supply in a vacuum. He still had to hold on, though, as the air ripped past him. Some of the Soul Drinkers below were dragged along by the force of it, grabbing on to loading machinery or grilles in the floor to keep from being pulled through the breach. Silence hammered down as the air was depleted, replaced with the vibrations of the guns, and the space hulk's engines through the metal wall transmitted up Sarpedon's talons.

Sarpedon dropped to the floor and ran for the relative safety of the *Intolerant*'s internal decks. Another missile hit closer, blowing another gun off its mountings and sending the steel tower of the gun barrel somersaulting through the wall. The sounds of destruction boomed through the floor, surreally distant in the vacuum.

The Imperial ship's alarm systems, rigged back to working order by Lygris, were blaring. Sarpedon was in the maintenance decks for the ammunition systems, narrow walkways and corridors slung across steel chasms between the shell hoppers. The loading systems' massive conveyor belts and cranes were clanking along overhead and below, feeding ammunition to the guns that still worked.

'Salk!' shouted Sarpedon into the vox. 'Report! Any casualties?'

'Brother Thoss is down,' replied Sergeant Salk. 'Looks like one of Iktinos's men is dead too.' Over Salk's vox Sarpedon could hear the booming reports of more impacts, scattered with the vibrations from the *Brokenback*'s guns.

'Where are you?'

'Still on the deck. We're regrouping and sounding off.'

'Get out of there.'

'Already on it. We're heading for the cargo decks. We'll put a few hull layers between us and the breach. Salk out.'

Sarpedon switched to Lygris's vox-channel.

'The *Intolerant*'s been hit,' he said.

'I'm tracking the incoming bombers now,' said Lygris. Sarpedon could hear the whirr of cogitators behind his voice. 'They're all over us.'

'Can we take them?'

'Of course. But they're not the danger. They're just spoiling our aim so the cruisers can hit us.'

'How much damage can they do?'

'Ordinarily, a cruiser wouldn't put much of a dent in a hulk this size. But the Mechanicus has plenty of tricks that could hurt.'

Sarpedon knew there were two choices: stand and fight, or flee. The Mechanicus clearly thought they had enough firepower to hurt the *Brokenback*. And the Soul Drinkers would gain nothing from fighting a battle here.

'How long until the warp drives are ready?' asked Sarpedon.

'Another ten minutes.'

'Then get us out of here as soon as you can. The *Intolerant* is being abandoned.'

'Yes, commander. I suggest you and Salk's men go on to damage control. The Mechanicus will get a few free swings at us before we're gone.'

'On my way.'

The *Intolerant* shook as more ordnance hit home. Smaller impacts, like sparks crackling against the hull, were the remains of fighters and bombers scattering against the *Brokenback* after the turrets had done their work.

* * *

THE CONSTANT DRIFTED up out of formation into a high firing angle. The space hulk's guns, formidable as they were, had been too busy fending off the wasp-like attacks of the Fleet Minor to pay the cruiser any mind until it was too late.

Magos Hepsebah aimed the nova cannon. She had designed it and overseen its fitting to the chassis of the *Constant*, turning it from a vessel of the line into a ship-killer. The barrel was so large it gave the cruiser a lopsided look as if it should topple off balance and tumble through space helplessly, but the cruiser's thrusters kept its enormous mass still as Hepsebah lined up her shot.

No single kill shot could be taken against a space hulk. It was a welded mass of dozens of ships, and any one of them might house the bridge, or the ordnance hangars, or the reactors. Hepsebah's duty was simply to do as much damage as possible.

A burning mass on the side of the space hulk that had once been an Imperial ship was ruined and ablaze. There was little point hitting it again. The swollen rearward quarters of the ship were composed of enormous container ships and beetle-like carapaces of massive alien hulks, which looked like they contained little more than empty space and debris. Hepsebah aimed towards the front of the ship, some way down below the reinforced armour of an ancient warship and a forbidding tangle of silvery alien craft. The ships there were many and densely packed, with more chance of important systems surviving.

Hepsebah ordered the firing chamber menials to drag the two enormous hemispheres of radioactive metal together. Hundreds of men hauled on chains, their muscles burning under their skin in the heat of the firing chamber, their taskmaster barking rhythmic orders to keep the hemispheres swinging. The hemispheres clashed, rang like a great deep bell, and released a massive wave of power funnelled by electromagnetic fields into the accelerator formed by the cannon's barrel. The force of it hit the enormous nova projectile, accelerating it down the barrel at impossible speeds.

The nova cannon fired, and, for a fraction of a second, the *Constant* and the hulk were connected by a bridge of burning light.

SARPEDON ARRIVED AT the reactor array of the *Blessed Obedience*, the enormous industrial ship containing many of the plasma reactors that Lygris had got back on-line to make the space hulk warp-capable. The reactor chamber was enormous, close to a kilometre long, criss-crossed with catwalks that gave access to the titanic cylindrical forms of the reactors. The *Blessed Obedience* had carried a dozen such reactors in some previous life as a space-faring refinery, each one powerful enough to fuel a spaceship for decades. Every one of the cylinders contained a vessel full of superheated plasma, locked in a constant reaction that pumped power into the hulk's warp arrays. They were crowned with

spider-like arrays of steel struts, supporting the cables and pipes that provided the reactors with fuel and coolant, and drew off their massive outputs of power.

Sarpedon hurried along a gantry between reactors one and two. Chaplain Iktinos was on a command platform just ahead, along with several of his flock.

'Commander Sarpedon,' voxed Iktinos as he saw Sarpedon approaching. 'I hear on the vox-net that our brothers have fallen.'

'Thoss of Squad Salk, and Renigel of your flock,' said Sarpedon. 'He died when the *Intolerant* was hit. The enemy is going to throw everything he has at us. I am afraid that prayers will have to wait.'

'So it shall be,' said Iktinos.

Sarpedon switched his vox-net to the bridge channel. 'Lygris, I'm at the reactors. It looks like they're holding up well.'

'Stay there,' replied Lygris from the bridge. 'If we lose the *Obedience* then we're done–'

A sound like the death of a world hammered across the reactor chamber. One wall blew in, hurling a hurricane of shredded metal. The nova projectile detonated, and a great gale of fire and shrapnel ripped across the *Obedience*, sending white-hot shards of shrapnel arrowing everywhere.

The shock wave threw Sarpedon off the gantry, slamming him into the wall. His head swam with the force of it. If he hadn't been wearing his helmet he would have been knocked out. Enough of him

remained unshaken to remind him that if he fell, he would probably die. Talons lashed out in a reflex, and dug into the wall of the reactor chamber, halting him as he fell.

The reverberations of the explosion bellowed around the chamber. One wall had been completely demolished, beyond it only a glowing labyrinth of torn bulkheads and decking. A gale of fire howled into the maw of the wound as the air was sucked out through the hull breach.

The explosion had sent shards of shrapnel spearing through the vessels of reactors eleven and nine. Reactor eleven collapsed, its upper half too heavy for the shredded foundations. Deep splits opened up as the reactor's crown fell back into the lake of plasma inside, and raw, white burning plasma looped out in great arcs like solar flares, the massive release of pressure sending it lashing in destructive tongues through the roof of the reactor chamber. Gobbets of it bored through walkways and command platforms. A great torrent burst from the lower half of the reactor and flowed in a glowing flood through the tangle of conduits and cabling that obscured the chamber floor.

Sarpedon was aware of another shape falling towards him: a Space Marine. He stuck out an arm and grabbed the falling Soul Drinker by his shoulder pad. The weight almost pulled Sarpedon off the wall, but he held on. He had caught one of Iktinos's flock, the purple paint on his armour bubbling with the heat.

Sarpedon climbed until he was level with the stub of a walkway. Most of it had been ripped away and thrown into the chamber's depths, but enough of it remained to hold the weight of a Space Marine. It joined the wall at a maintenance entrance. Sarpedon hauled the Soul Drinker onto the walkway, and was relieved to see that he was still alive.

Sarpedon looked across the chamber, trying to see more survivors. He spotted a couple of Iktinos's flock clinging to a precarious length of walkway, making their way towards a command post that had survived mostly intact. From there, they could make it up a ladder into the access tunnels above the chamber. Iktinos himself had been thrown onto the top of reactor three, and was making his way towards the crown of pipes and cables connecting it to the ceiling.

'Lygris!' yelled Sarpedon into the vox. The last of the chamber's air was shrieking and superheated, a terrible sound like a gale of fire. 'Lygris, what in the hells was that?'

Lygris's voice barely swam through the static. 'Direct hit! Commander, give me a damage report!'

'Reactors eleven and nine are breached,' replied Sarpedon. 'Eleven's venting plasma. Nine's about to go.'

'Evacuate the area,' replied Lygris.

The last words had barely reached Sarpedon's ears when reactor nine exploded, the pressure inside too much for its failing structure. A pure white starburst

of plasma erupted, like a caged supernova, and the
structures surrounding reactor nine were obliterated. Bolts of plasma streaked into the nearby
reactors, shearing more maintenance walkways
from their mountings. The sound, just a vibration
transmitted through the wall to which Sarpedon
clung, was like the roar of an escaping giant.

The glare died down. Iktinos was crouching from
the shock wave of the explosion, still clinging to
reactor three.

'Chaplain,' voxed Sarpedon, 'are you hurt?'

'I am not, commander,' replied Iktinos. His voice
was distorted almost beyond understanding. 'But
there is no way off this reactor.'

'There is for me,' said Sarpedon. 'Hold position.
I'm coming for you.'

Sarpedon ran up the wall towards the ceiling. The
whole chamber shuddered as the remains of reactor
eleven collapsed into the floor. Plasma flooded the
lower levels, swallowing up enormous bundles of
cables and drowning the lowest walkways. Reactor
twelve was sitting in a lake of plasma, and was list-
ing as its foundations were eroded. Below the
chamber plasma would be flowing through the rest
of the *Obedience*, looking for ways into the ships
surrounding it. It would melt its way through a
huge area of the *Brokenback*, like a cancer, if it
wasn't stopped.

Sarpedon was above reactor three. He could see
that a spear of shrapnel had punctured the reactor's

side, and plasma was spurting from the wound. The crack was widening, and, every second, the sheet of vented energy grew wider.

Sarpedon ran down a coolant pipe to the top of the reactor. Iktinos was waiting for him.

Iktinos reached up. Sarpedon grabbed the Chaplain's wrist and hauled him off his feet.

Reactor three shuddered and leaned suddenly to one side. Sarpedon glanced up; the conduits were coming away from the ceiling. There would be no way off the reactor in that direction. He spotted a length of walkway hanging from one wall, half-melted away by a bolt of plasma. Sarpedon shifted his grip so that he was dragging Iktinos behind him by the collar of his armour. He crouched down on his back legs and uncoiled, sprinting at full tilt towards the edge of the reactor.

Reactor three split down the middle. Sheets of plasma sprayed out, forming a wall of fire behind Sarpedon as he ran. Metal screamed and heat roared. The metal below Sarpedon's talons became unbearably hot.

Sarpedon reached the edge and jumped with the power of every muscle packed into his arachnoid legs. He reached forwards and his hand closed on the handrail of the walkway. The whole structure bent with the weight of the two Space Marines. Iktinos clambered over Sarpedon, pulling himself onto the walkway, before hauling Sarpedon up after him.

'My gratitude, commander,' voxed Iktinos.

Reactor three split completely in two, a torrent of plasma flooding through the lower levels. Sarpedon got to his feet and followed Iktinos towards the doorway where the walkway joined the wall. Another reactor breached as they ran, sinking into the burning mire and splitting open. A wall of radiated heat buffeted them as Iktinos reached the door and hauled it open.

Beyond was a dark, cramped maintenance space, leading to the cargo ship adjoining the *Blessed Obedience*. Sarpedon followed Iktinos through the darkness as the booming vibrations of dying reactors got louder.

'Lygris,' voxed Sarpedon to the bridge, 'we're clear.'

'I'm shutting down the *Obedience*,' replied Lygris. Sarpedon could hear every alarm on the space hulk's bridge blaring at once. 'Make sure you're well clear. That whole area will be lethal.'

'Can you get us out of here?'

'With the reactors down? I can make it into the warp, maybe.'

'Then do it. Whatever hit us will want a kill-shot.'

'Yes, commander,' voxed Lygris. 'I suggest you hold on.'

'GOT IT,' SAID Magos Hepsebah with relish. Seated in the targeting observatory of the *Constant*, surrounded by the holo-projections of surrounding

stars and spacecraft, she watched another flare of plasma burst from the side of the space hulk. 'Target report!'

Tech-priests' voices from the ship's sensorium filtered back to her through the vox-net.

'Major secondary explosions…'

'Confirm plasma vent. Target reactor breach.'

'Target power levels fluctuating beyond parameters…'

'Arming chamber!' ordered Hepsebah. 'Full recharge! Navigation, line us up for another shot!'

She spun the barrels of the multilaser she carried in place of her left arm. Nothing fired the passions in her like a direct hit: the sum of all her knowledge, brought forth in a single moment of destruction. Such a wonder could only be possible through the Omnissiah's will.

'Magos Hepsebah, excellent damage,' said Voar's voice from the *Antithesis*. 'The Fleet Minor is disengaging. We will coordinate fire and complete the kill.'

'Yes, archmagos,' said Hepsebah. 'The Soul Drinkers, they once did the Mechanicus wrong?'

'Most gravely so,' said Voar.

'Then it will be a pleasure to call in the debt.'

The holo flared red. Indicators around the image of the space hulk showed an enormous power spike.

'Gellar fields active!' came an alert from one of the tech-priests in the sensorium.

'They're hitting the warp!' shouted Hepsebah. 'They're insane. That space hulk's bleeding to death. The warp will swallow it alive.'

'It has survived an aeon in the warp,' said Voar. 'Do not presume to know the capabilities of such an enemy.'

'Hit it with everything we have! Now!'

Most of the *Constant's* offensive power was tied up in the nova cannon, but she still sported plenty of medium-range guns and torpedoes. Every one of them fired, spraying massive calibre fire towards the space hulk, even as the enemy ship was surrounded by a shimmering field projected by what power remained in its wounded reactors. Shots tore through the field and impacted against the hull. The *Antithesis* joined in, and a tremendous broadside hammered against the hulk's side, ripping chunks of spacecraft away, and exposing burning metal innards below. Secondary explosions rippled where stored ammunition detonated, and plumes of vented air burst from the impacts.

Space tore. A slash opened up in front of the hulk, so dark it was blacker even than the void. Power boiled within it, a monumental, malicious reflection of the Veiled Region in another dimension. The space hulk sank into it, explosions still studding its gnarled surface as the rip in space swallowed it up.

The holo blinked, and the space hulk was gone.

'We've lost them,' said Hepsebah. She slammed her multilaser against the observatory wall. 'Damn it! We had them! We had them, and we lost them!' She sat back in the observatory command chair, watching the debris cooling and falling off sensor range.

'Even in the Veiled Region, a wounded space hulk cannot pass without leaving a trail,' said Archmagos Voar. 'We have not lost them for long.'

'Once, I saw the xenos as a terrifying threat, the harbingers of our galaxy's destruction. Now I know them for what they are. Vermin, parasites, suckling at the wounds of a galaxy that belongs to humankind.'

Daenyathos, *War Incarnate*

CHAPTER THREE

'I HAD THOUGHT,' said Sarpedon, 'that no one would find me here.'

The garden of reflection looked like it should have been part of a pleasure yacht, one of the lavishly appointed spacecraft occasionally launched by the fabulously wealthy to demonstrate their superiority to the lesser mortals around them. In fact, it was a part of an Imperial Navy craft, a command ship that had no doubt once served as the nerve centre of a mighty battlefleet. Its captain may have been in command of the most destructive force in the Imperial arsenal – a fleet of battleships that could level cities with their guns – but he still needed somewhere he could be away from the babble of command. The garden's plants were mostly wilted, save for a couple

of extremely hardy flowering vines and the artificial trees that flanked the entrance gates. Its raised stone flowerbeds were barren, and the trees that had once formed a secluded pocket of the spacecraft were now just sprays of withered branches. The corroded steel of the walls and ceiling loomed down over the fountain that fed a now-dry pool.

Techmarine Lygris sat down on the stone bench across from Sarpedon. 'There are few places of solace on this ship, commander. I did not have to look very hard to find you.'

'What is our situation?'

'We were able to enter the warp, but we could not stay there for long. We made it to the nebula, though. If the Adeptus Mechanicus is looking for us then they'll have a damned difficult time seeing anything through the dust clouds.'

'Then we're deeper in the Veiled Region?'

'Very deep. This is unexplored space.'

'Well, at least they're as lost as we are. What about the reactors?'

Lygris had suffered facial injuries earlier in his service as a Soul Drinker that had required the reconstruction of his entire face. It had left him with a mask of synthetic flesh, a good approximation of his features, but without the same capacity for expression. Sarpedon had learned that Lygris could be read by his eyes alone. The techmarine's eyes told him that the news was not good.

'We're down to the dregs of fuel,' said Lygris. 'The last broadsides from the Mechanicus destroyed much of the fuel we took on board at Nevermourn. With the reactors that remain intact and the fuel we have, I can make two more warp jumps. Three would probably kill the reactors entirely. We need more fuel or we will be permanently becalmed.'

'Where can we get it?'

'There are enough working refinery units on board to turn anything from crude oil upwards into fuel. Any civilised world could provide something I could use.'

'Then let us hope we find one.' Sarpedon crouched back on his rear legs, stretching the sinews. The chitin of his spidery limbs was still charred from the plasma fires. His single bionic leg had been warped by the heat and wiring hung from the knee joint.

'You blame yourself,' said Lygris.

'Of course I do,' said Sarpedon. 'Who else is there?'

'The Mechanicus.'

'The Mechanicus wants us dead and they have good reason. They could hardly leave us be when they found us.'

'Then chance, Sarpedon. Fate.'

'No. I am responsible for my Chapter. Gorgoleon and Eumenes challenged me for command, and I killed them both. I cannot take the lives of my battle-brothers to rule this Chapter, and then pretend that I am not at fault when it suffers.'

'The fact that we survive at all is down to you. We could have been wiped out by the old Chapter or the Inquisition years ago.'

'We survive, Lygris? Barely a quarter of our strength remains. I have led us into warzones where we have escaped only at the expense of our dead brothers. Half my brothers disagreed with me so fervently that they rebelled against me and are now dead or fled. This very day, we lost more to the Mechanicus guns. What if we have not survived at all? What if we are in our death throes, wasting away to extinction?'

'If that is what you fear, Sarpedon,' said Lygris levelly, 'then extinction is exactly what will happen.'

'I will not give in, Lygris,' said Sarpedon sharply. 'I will fight until the end of time if that is what I am called upon to do. I would not have decided on this fate if I had been given the choice, but there was never a choice. We could not have fought on as the old Chapter, to pursue our own arrogance at the behest of a corrupt Imperium. When the time came there was no one else to take command, and I will not back down from the role fate has given me. That is why I am responsible for what happens to us, because I have made that choice.'

'Then do not see things to doubt in our situation,' said Lygris. 'The old Chapter sent us technical aspirants to a forge world to study with the tech-priests and learn from them the practices of the Cult Mechanicus. There I learned that a wounded

machine, a smouldering wreck, is not a destroyed thing but the potential for a masterpiece. That is how the Mechanicus can make the things they do, for they see everything as a potential vessel of their Omnissiah. We are not destroyed, Sarpedon. We are not lost. There is in our defeat the potential for victory. We just have to make it right.'

'Then that is my duty. To turn this wreck into a victory.'

'If I could tell you how to do that, Sarpedon, then I would.'

'It is enough that you keep the *Brokenback* spaceworthy, Lygris. Believe me, if you can do that then we will be halfway there.'

Lygris's vox-unit chirped.

'Graevus here,' came the vox.

'What news, sergeant?' replied Lygris.

'The sensorium has picked something up. There's a planetary system nearby, just within the bounds of the nebula.'

'How far?'

'A short warp jump. We're too far away to see much, but the inner planets are close enough to the star to be survivable.

'At this point, sergeant, that will have to do.' Lygris looked up at Sarpedon. 'I am needed on the bridge.'

'Go,' said Sarpedon, 'and if you need my permission to risk a jump towards a planet, then you have it.'

'Yes, commander.'

Sarpedon watched Lygris go. The techmarine had been there from the very beginning, and he had never faltered, not even when Sarpedon had doubted, in the chaos following the break from Imperial authority or the bloody flashpoints at Gravenholm and Stratix Luminae. Even as a student of the Mechanicus ways, Lygris had always been constant in his loyalty to Sarpedon and the new fate of the Chapter.

Sarpedon told himself that he was right. Somewhere in the wreck of the Chapter's situation in the Veiled Region, there was victory. The question was whether Sarpedon had the skill to build it.

THE SYSTEM WAS bordered by a triumvirate of dead planets, as smooth and lifeless as water-worn pebbles, standing silent guard over the approaches to the star. They were perfectly spaced from one another, surely just a fluke of the system's gravity, but looking as if they had been carefully placed to act as dead sentinels. A pair of gas giants orbited lazily beyond them, and past a band of debris and asteroids lay the inner system where the *Brokenback*'s sensors had strained to pick up an echo of life.

The system's star was swollen and reddish, entering the final stages of its life. In its aged light basked the rocky planets of the inner system, and one of them, a grey ball of heavy cloud broken by equally

colourless landscapes, was alive. Sensor waves bounced back off structures that could only be cities or highways.

In high orbit over the planet, space rippled and burst, spilling the necrotic substance of the region's morbid empyrean like gore from an infected wound. The *Brokenback* limped out, still trailing tangles of vented plasma and debris. Its engines flared weakly, as if the hulk was sick. The wound in its hull left by the broadsides and bombing runs against the *Intolerant* still bled.

The hulk settled into orbit over the planet. Through the heavy cloud cover could be glimpsed hints of habitation through the eyepieces and holo-displays of the hulk's various sensors: irrigated fields of greyish crops, and black oceans sprinkled with oil platforms and spindly webs of flood defences. Lygris and the Soul Drinkers assisting him on the bridge interpreted the glimpses of structure and civilisation, and hunted for a city.

Slowly, the clouds swirled and the gaps between them passed over the surface. Eventually, they revealed the edges of a city, a cluttered sprawl of buildings piled up against a natural harbour near the equator. The sensors strained to zoom in and pick out signs of life. The city had all the hallmarks of great antiquity: unplanned and haphazard, cramped tangles of streets giving way to expanses of palaces, and concentric rings of harbour structures radiating out from docks reclaimed from the sea.

Soon afterwards, two of the *Brokenback*'s complement of armoured shuttles was launched.

IT WAS COMPLETELY silent.

That was the first impression that Sarpedon had of the planet. He had been prepared for hostilities, for indigenous humans or xenos to greet the Soul Drinkers with anti-aircraft fire and ground troops, but nothing had come out to see the shuttles land, not even gaggles of fearful spectators.

Sarpedon stepped off the ramp of his shuttle. The stubby, tough little craft had descended through the planet's clouded atmosphere without receiving or intercepting any communications. There should have been something, anything, to suggest the people down there were talking to one another.

'Still nothing,' voxed Captain Luko. Squad Luko, Squad Graevus, Lygris, Apothecary Pallas and Chaplain Iktinos made up the landing party that Sarpedon had selected. Luko had been the first out of the second shuttle, and his squad had spread into a circle to cover the shuttles' landing position from all angles.

'This place is dead,' said Graevus as his squad deployed behind Sarpedon. Graevus flexed his mutated hand, one of the Chapter's more obvious deformities aside from Sarpedon's own, which gave him the enormous strength with which he wielded his power axe.

'Squad, give me a cordon! All angles!' ordered Luko. His squad spread out and took aim at the buildings lining the area.

The shuttles had landed in a city square. Towering habitation blocks surrounded it, all in white or grey stone with dark grey or black tiles. False columns and carved lintels suggested wealth and age. One edge of the square was taken up with a large domed basilica flanked by equestrian statues; the riders were human, which meant that this was at least a human world. A few tattered merchants' stands were scattered around the square. The roads leading away from the square were empty.

There was not one person in sight. There were no birds in the sky. Even the trees were bare. It was as if the city had been drained of life, of sound and of colour.

Sarpedon let his mind reach out. As a psyker, he had enormous power but little finesse, and he could not read minds or extend his senses like some other Librarians of the Astartes. He was still sensitive enough to notice powerful psykers or the chatter of a million minds packed together, though, and, even to his mind, the city was silent.

Graevus's squad, with their jump packs primed and their chainswords drawn, followed Sarpedon and Lygris as they headed towards the closest habitation block. Like the rest of the buildings, the block was monochrome, reflecting the pale greyish sky.

'Nothing on the auspex scanner,' said Graevus.

Sarpedon opened the front doors. Stale air rolled out, dusty and old. Inside, homes led off from a central hallway, with a staircase spiralling to the upper floors above.

'Looks like post-feudal tech,' said Lygris, 'but not by much. They had electricity. One of the structures we saw from above looked like a space port.'

'This city hasn't been abandoned,' said Sarpedon. 'The buildings aren't ruins. There isn't even any sign of vermin.'

'They could have evacuated the city,' said Graevus, 'when they saw us in orbit. There are plenty of cultures where something like the *Brokenback* would be an omen of the end of the world.'

The nearest home was intact. The people of this world favoured latticed windows and ornate archways, with alcoves everywhere for keepsakes. The table was still laid. Aside from a veneer of dust, the place might have been waiting for its owners to return at any moment.

'Whatever happened here,' voxed Captain Luko from outside, 'they fought it.'

Luko's squad had approached the basilica. By the time Sarpedon had joined them, the squad had flanked the main entrance, a pair of brass doors inscribed with images of soldiers marching. Sarpedon saw that the doors and the stone around them were disfigured with bullet wounds. The statues on either side of the doors were

damaged, too, the verdigrised bronze battered by gunfire.

At a signal from Sarpedon, Luko ran at the doors and slammed into them shoulder-first. The doors banged open, and Luko's lightning claws were sheathed in crackling energy as he prepared to fight. His squad stepped in behind him, guns tracking through the basilica's interior.

The interior was a ruin. Once the basilica had been grand, inlaid patterns of black and white marble covering the walls and floor of an auditorium that held court below the central minaret. Wooden benches were in splinters and shafts of pale light fell through tears in the dome.

'No bodies,' said Pallas.

Pallas had been one of the Soul Drinkers that rebelled against Sarpedon at Vanqualis. Pallas had not joined the rebels that had left the Chapter after Sarpedon's defeat of their leader Eumenes. Sarpedon had spoken to him rarely since then; the Apothecary had been key to the survival of the Chapter through controlling their mutations, but he had now withdrawn completely. 'They fought it here, but they were defeated. Then the rest of the city just... gave up.'

'This was somewhere important,' said Iktinos, examining the murals on the nearest wall. They showed stylised humans in debate, or enthroned, or marching in parades through the city's streets. 'An enemy struck here, and when they had finished there was no one left to lead a resistance.'

'And then,' Sarpedon, 'the people were rounded up, and... killed? Taken away?'

'We are assuming,' said Pallas, kneeling to examine the remains of a fallen statue, 'that they aren't still here: either the population, or the people who took them.'

Sarpedon caught a movement out of the corner of his eye. In a fluid reaction, his bolt pistol was in his left hand, and his right was at his back, ready to unsheathe the Axe of Mercaeno he carried strapped to the backpack of his armour.

A tiny black speck clung to the inside surface of the minaret.

'Commander?' said Lygris.

'It's a bird,' said Sarpedon. 'At least there's something alive here.'

The bird flitted down off the minaret. It made a metallic buzzing sound as it swooped down and hovered just above Sarpedon.

It was not a bird. It was an oversized metal insect, held aloft on silver wings, trailing bladed hinged limbs. Tiny red lenses focused on Sarpedon, and its glinting mandibles worked as if in hunger.

The beetle zipped up and disappeared through one of the holes in the minaret.

'Luko!' ordered Sarpedon. 'Get inside and seal the doors.'

'What was that?' asked Pallas.

'I don't know,' said Lygris. 'It looks beyond this world's tech level.'

Captain Luko's squad hauled the doors shut. Two of his Soul Drinkers dragged the remains of auditorium benches over to the doors to barricade them.

Chaplain Iktinos took his crozius off his belt. Like Luko's lightning claws, the crozius was a power weapon, and a blue-white energy field leapt around it. It was a badge of office as well as a weapon, topped with a bladed skull so that Iktinos could swing it like a morning star.

'I can hear them,' he said. 'The voice of the xenos calls us out.'

Sarpedon could hear it, too. A crackling, buzzing sound, deep and resonant, came to them from the grey sky visible through the circular opening in the pinnacle of the minaret. Graevus's squad took up a position in the centre of the basilica around Sarpedon and the officers. Luko's squad held the doors, ready to tear apart anything that came through, with massed bolter fire.

Sarpedon looked up. The beams of sunlight coming through the minaret were cut off.

The minaret collapsed under the weight of tens of thousands of metallic scarabs. They tumbled through the basilica roof in a tremendous metallic avalanche. Sarpedon barely had time to react before they were on him, mandibles chittering as they swarmed over his armour.

Sarpedon yelled, and swung with his axe, shattering a host of the scurrying things. Beside him, Iktinos did the same, clearing the space around him

with wide sweeps of his crozius. Pallas fell to the ground, clawing at a scarab trying to bore its way into his face. Lygris dragged him to his feet, tore the creature off him and threw it to the floor. Pallas stamped on it and began blasting at the floor around him. The explosive bolter blasts shattered two or three scarabs each, but there were always more, swarming everywhere to fill the gaps.

'Flamer front!' yelled Luko over the din of the chittering creatures. 'Vorn! Burn them!'

Brother Vorn, who carried Squad Luko's flamer, stepped forwards from the doors, and hosed the area in front of him with liquid flame. The scarabs caught in the flame convulsed as whatever tiny electronics controlling them were melted by the heat. They spiralled up on burning wings like fragments of ash rising from the fire.

'They're everywhere!' shouted Sarpedon. 'Abandon this place! Make for the shuttles!'

Luko turned to the doors his squad had just barricaded, and squared up to barge them open again.

The doors burst inwards. Luko was thrown off his feet beneath the massive sheet of bronze. A creature swept in through the doorway; a solid rectangular body, longer than a Space Marine was tall, hovered impossibly off the ground. Thick, segmented legs curled up underneath it, and a pair of wicked crushing claws projected from its front edge. A head was mounted on the front, little more than a slab of metal covered in lenses and mandibles. Scarabs

swarmed all over the creature. It managed to be both completely mechanical, and wholly alien.

Brother Vorn turned in time to see the pincers closing around his head. Instinctively, he blasted a plume of fire up against the creature's underside, sheathing it in billowing flame. The pincers closed, and Vorn's helmet distorted, eyepieces popping out under the pressure. The Soul Drinker was picked up off the floor, and the second pincer closed in, clamping around Vorn's arm and tearing his gun arm away to keep him from firing.

The machine's head opened up like a bladed metal flower. Mandibles jutted out and sliced down into Vorn's face. A proboscis punched out through the back of Vorn's skull, and his head burst open in a shower of blood and meat.

Sarpedon faced the machine. Bolter fire was already hammering against its armoured shell, but it looked like it could take a lot more punishment before going down. An aperture opened on the upper surface of its abdomen, revealing a forge, glowing dark red with heat, another couple of scarabs emerged from it to join the swarm.

'Lygris! Iktinos! Get us another way out! Luko, fall back from the doors!'

Sarpedon ran forwards, crunching a scarab or two under his talons, the Axe of Mercaeno in his hand. The spidery floating creature focused its eye-lenses on him, its optics winking through a layer of Vorn's blood. It dropped the Soul Drinker's body. Flame

still clung to it, dripping liquidly from its legs and rippling over its hull.

Astartes from Squad Graevus were following Sarpedon towards the machine, but the scarabs were thick around them, snaring their sword arms and tangling around their feet. Sarpedon was on his own, surrounded by the scarab swarm with the machine bearing down on him.

Sarpedon dropped low, scuttling towards the xenos machine at full tilt. It raised its claws to grab him and tear him apart. Somehow, there was malice in that expressionless face, in the blank lenses and grinding mandibles.

Sarpedon slammed into it just as it began to accelerate at him. Bladed jaws snickered shut just over his head. He powered up off his back legs into its underside, slamming the Axe of Mercaeno into its side. The blade tore through the metal hull and caught there, and Sarpedon grabbed with his other arm and pulled the beast down.

He wrestled it to the ground, forcing it against its anti-gravity motors onto its back underneath him. The legs struck up at him, one catching him hard on the side of the head. Sarpedon's senses reeled and he clung on out of instinct, grabbing a flailing metallic leg and hugging it close to keep it from ripping his head off.

Sarpedon's head stopped spinning. The metal spider beneath him was writhing like a pinned insect, legs kicking out as it tried to right itself.

Sarpedon ripped the axe out of its side, and cut to left and right, hacking off one of its legs. He drove his own legs into the ground on either side of its body, anchoring it to the floor of the basilica. The proboscis, like a bladed tongue, snapped up at him, but Sarpedon's reactions outstripped even the machine, and he dodged back out of its reach.

He grabbed the tongue with his free hand and pulled hard. The machine's head was forced back towards its chest. Sarpedon looked for a moment into its eyes, and saw the hatred there, the arrogance of the soulless machine, without anything human behind it.

Sarpedon's stomach churned. The machine's xenos nature was as clear as could be.

With an effort that even Sarpedon didn't know he could make, he twisted the machine's head right around on its mountings. Wires tore and fastenings snapped. He pulled again, and the head came away in its hands.

The metal spider convulsed as its motor functions went haywire. Half-formed scarabs were spat from its hull. It shuddered, its legs curled up over its upturned body, and it was still.

Sarpedon saw a tide of scarabs approaching from across the city square. Thousands of the machines formed a writhing silver-black carpet over the abandoned buildings. More bulky spiders hovered above them, multiple eyes scanning their targets in the basilica.

Sarpedon hauled the remains of the doors shut, and dragged the dead spider machine in front of them as a barricade. He turned to see how the Soul Drinkers were faring behind him. Scarabs still chittered everywhere, but the main swarm had been scattered or destroyed, and the Soul Drinkers were moving down to the far end of the Basilica. Squad Graevus was close, rushing to hold the doors alongside Sarpedon. A series of explosions hammered from the rear of the basilica, and Sarpedon recognised the reports of exploding krak grenades. Lygris had blown a hole in the rear wall of the basilica.

'I would not like to have to wait for you, commander,' voxed Lygris.

Sarpedon made for the new entrance through which Luko was already leading his squad. Pallas was with them, bleeding from the gash on the side of his face.

'Are you hurt?' asked Pallas.

'No,' said Sarpedon. 'You?'

Pallas did not answer. He ducked through the hole, and followed Iktinos and Lygris after the squads.

Beyond the basilica was a river, its banks heavy with grand buildings of government and commerce. There was evidence of a battle here, too, with bullet scars and claw marks on the walls. Sarpedon imagined that the claws had been those of mechanised spiders, closing in on the city's leaders to butcher them and throw the remains to the

scarabs. A bridge led across the river, and Squad Luko was already securing it. One of Luko's men carried Vorn's body. It was a dishonour to leave a fallen brother behind, not least because the gene-seed taken from Vorn's body would be used to create the Soul Drinker that would replace him.

'A lander is coming down for us,' said Lygris. 'Fast troop ship Jackal-class. We don't have many of them left.'

'Where are they coming down?'

'There's an ornamental garden across the river. It's large enough for a landing zone.'

'Then let's move. Soul Drinkers! Cover and run, fast!'

Sarpedon led the way across the bridge, Luko and Graevus using their squads to keep the forward and rear areas covered with bolters and bolt pistols. Beneath them, the river was choked with debris.

Not debris, bodies... hundreds of them. Their clothes were rich, embroidered togas and military uniforms. Sarpedon had seen thousands of bullet wounds in his life, and he did not see a single one on the bodies that bobbed in the filthy water. The dead had been shredded with blades or chewed up by scarab mandibles. Many of them seemed to have been dissolved away as if by acid, layers of their bodies exposed by some force that eroded skin and bone.

'We found the defenders, then,' said Luko bleakly.

The roof of the basilica collapsed, throwing up a cloud of dust and scarabs. The rear wall fell in under the gouging claws of the spiders. Luko's squad opened up with bolter fire, battering one spider back and shattering the face of another. Scarabs poured out from the ruined building, spilling into the river and scuttling along the bridge. One of Luko's squad had picked up Vorn's fallen flamer, and painted the bridge behind the Soul Drinkers with fire, incinerating the scarabs as they approached.

Sarpedon sprinted to the far end of the bridge. Squad Graevus leapt over him on the exhaust blasts of their jump packs to land in the garden beyond. A willow tree stood at the river's edge, leaves trailing in the water, and ornamental hedges cut into the shapes of fanciful animals stood between flowerbeds and mosaic paths. The flowers were all dead.

Sarpedon saw the contrails of the descending lander. It was Imperial, but of an old mark that its forge worlds had forgotten how to produce, with a blunt brutal nose and downturned wings like those of a bird of prey. Hatches opened up in its belly as it descended.

Twin autocannons mounted on the lander's wings opened up and explosions thundered along the bridge behind Squad Luko. Chunks of masonry and shattered scarabs flew. The bridge shuddered, but it was solidly built and would hold.

'We're coming in hot!' said the vox from the Soul Drinker piloting the lander. 'Xenos are converging from everywhere! Make ready for the pass!'

'How's our landing zone, Graevus?' voxed Sarpedon.

'Clear,' came the reply.

'Then get to the gardens and hold, everyone!'

The Soul Drinkers vaulted over the low walls and kicked through the ornamental hedges. From the pall of dust surrounding the bridge emerged a metallic spider, one of its claws replaced with the barrel of a weapon that spat arcs of lightning as it charged up. Squad Luko studded its hull with bolter fire, but it held firm, and fired.

A bolt of green lightning lanced out from the spider's gun, hitting the ground just behind Sarpedon. Soul Drinkers were thrown off their feet, and earth showered down from the impact.

Its second shot went high, streaking through the wing of the lander. The craft stayed airborne, but only just, swinging precariously as air rushed through the hole in its wing.

Graevus didn't wait for the order. He hurtled over Sarpedon, power axe high, ready to strike. The jets of his jump pack cut out and he landed right on top of the spider. His power axe sheared the lightning weapon clean off the spider, and it rounded on him, its remaining forelimb snapping open ready to slice his head off.

Another of his squad landed beside it, and drove his chainsword into the spider's side, where one of its legs met the hull. The machine flicked a foreleg, throwing the Soul Drinker off in a shower of sparks, but the rest of Graevus's squad was close behind him, and suddenly the machine was surrounded. The Soul Drinkers duelled with the machine, turning its thrashing limbs aside with their chainswords, until Graevus rolled underneath, driving his axe into its underside so hard that the machine's anti-grav units were wrecked and it flopped down on top of him.

Graevus's men hauled the machine to the side of the bridge and pushed it off. They dragged Graevus to his feet, and fell back as the tide of scarabs closed in on them through the dust and rubble.

The lander's engines roared overhead. The craft came in over the gardens and hovered, lowering itself so that the grab-rails around its hatch were within reach of the Soul Drinkers. Pallas and Squad Luko clambered up into the craft, followed by Iktinos and Lygris. Squad Graevus sprinted for the lander, and Sarpedon joined them, leaping up into the belly of the craft as the last of Squad Graevus made it on board.

The ground beneath gave way just as Sarpedon's talons left it. A blast of infernally hot air hammered up at the lander, and it rose up on the swell. Sarpedon's hand closed on the grab-rail. Beneath him, the gardens fell inwards, revealing a great hollow of

black earth that swallowed the stands of trees and topiary hedges that remained.

As if from a nest of insects torn open, scarabs swarmed in the unearthed warren. Spider-machines squatted amongst them, birthing new scarabs from their inner forges.

Sergeant Graevus's mutated hand grabbed Sarpedon's wrist, and, with its unnatural strength, hauled him up into the lander's belly. The hatch slammed shut below him.

'Take us back,' said Sarpedon, 'fast!'

The lander tipped up onto its stern and fired its main engines. It rocketed up towards the pallid sky. Sarpedon saw that the pilot was Scamander, the young psyker, who was the only recruit into the Chapter's Librarium since Sarpedon had assumed command.

'What was it?' asked Iktinos. 'What force has taken this world?'

Sarpedon had no answer to give.

The lander tore through the thick cloud cover, leaving the dead city behind.

'The only enemy worth your admiration is one who has accepted the superiority of mankind and knelt before you to be executed. All others are to be despised. Honour means nothing when it is used to oppose the Emperor's will.'

Daenyathos, *Notes on the Catechisms Martial*

CHAPTER FOUR

ARCHMAGOS VOAR HAD seen the readouts on the bridge, but, in truth, he did not believe them. Perhaps that was just what he told himself, and the truth was really that he wanted to see the anomalies with his own eyes. When the last human parts of him had been replaced with the machine, such moments of weakness would not plague him any more.

The observatory on the *Antithesis* filled a dome blistered up from the ship's upper hull. An array of brass-cased telescopes, carefully inscribed with binary prayers of accuracy, and flawlessness, jutted out from the observatory dome. The inside of the dome was frescoed with images of great discoveries, like Magos Land uncovering lost STC fragments and Tech-Priest Gurvann stumbling upon the principles

of xenos-specific neurotoxins. It was a place of reflection and inspiration. Magos Voar rarely permitted anyone else to enter it.

Voar murmured a prayer to the telescope's machine-spirit and looked into the eyepiece. The object of the strange readings on the bridge hovered in front of him, glowing darkly in the light reflected from a distant star.

It was a world, but it was not a world. It was rather smaller than Terran standard, but possessed a gravity far higher than its size suggested, a suspicious sign if ever there was one. Its surface was as smooth and polished as an ornamental skull, and it had no polar caps or tectonic canyons, not even meteorite craters, which made no sense given its lack of atmosphere.

The strangest feature of the planet, however, was that it was not alone. Two others orbited the same star, precisely equidistant. They were of the same size and mass. They moved, and even spun on their axes, at the same rate. They could not be a natural phenomenon. Not even millions of years of constant gravity could produce such a solar system.

'Sensorium,' voxed Voar. 'Can we be sure the Soul Drinkers passed this way?'

'We've just picked up a plasma trace,' came the reply from the bridge library. 'The hulk dropped out of the warp in the outer system and headed for the inner worlds. It was still venting plasma, so it wasn't hard to follow.'

'Have we found it?'

'We're searching the inner worlds. If they're in orbit around a planet, they'll take a little longer to find.'

'Good. What do we have on the three outer worlds?'

'Nothing new. The Fleet Minor is sending two scouts on a flyby of the nearest one.'

'That is your second priority after finding the hulk.'

'Yes, archmagos. The first scout is approaching sensor range now.'

Voar held up his left index finger, and a dataprobe emerged from the tip. He inserted it into a socket on the side of the telescope housing and interfaced with the sensors of the *Antithesis*. He felt, for a moment, the fleet around it, the bulky presence of the *Constant* and *Ferrous*, the shape of the *Defence of Caelano Minoris* with its hotspots of energy, and the sensor-heavy shoal of the Fleet Minor. He caught two flitting shapes that had broken off from the fleet and were looping into close orbit around the massive dead presence of the planet. Voar mentally commanded the telescope to focus on the first ship. The telescope whirred around on clockwork gears to focus on the tiny glowing dart.

Voar withdrew the probe and looked back into the eyepiece. The scout ship was fast and agile, its slender body loaded with sensor gear. Its small

crew was elite, trained by Magos Khrul in hostile environment operations.

'Khrul here,' came the vox from *Asclepian Gamma*, the ship that Khrul commanded.

'What can you tell me, magos?'

'Mostly metallic crust,' said Khrul. 'No atmosphere.'

'No atmosphere, or minimal?'

'None.'

That was strange. A world of that size should have attracted at least a thin veil of gases around itself. 'Any energy?'

'Nothing geothermal,' replied Khrul. Even across the vox the heavy artificial nature of his voice, piped through his hostile environment chassis, was grating.

'Take them in closer.'

'Yes, archmagos.'

The first craft looped further downwards, the second craft spiralling around it in a double helix dive.

'Wait,' said Khrul, 'I'm syncing the crews' vox.'

'Archmagos! This is Observator Secundus Malian,' said a female voice over the vox. Voar knew that she was nestled in the cramped observatory station of her Veritix-class scout ship, making sense of the masses of data piping in through the craft's sensors, while the pilot crew brought the ship in towards the planet.

'What can you see, observator?' asked Voar.

'It's… It's featureless. Smooth.'

'I can see that.'

'Not just visually. It doesn't even have magnetic poles or a radiation signature. It's totally inert.'

'Then it is not natural.'

'That is not a conclusion for me to draw, archmagos.'

Voar watched the two ships dropping in to skim the surface, so low that their hulls should have been glowing with the heat of re-entry.

'I have a surface feature,' said Malian's voice. A blurry image, juddering as the scout craft's cogitator struggled to compensate for its speed, appeared on one of the pict screens in front of Voar. It was a jagged greenish shape.

'Looks like a crystal outcrop. It wasn't there a moment ago.'

'It is reacting to your presence,' said Voar. 'Magos Khrul, withdraw your–'

'Power spike! Something's lit up down there! Systems... Systems down! We're blind!' Alarms sounded as Malian spoke. 'Our pilot's taking–'

Twin emerald-green lances of light punched up through the planet's crust. Malian's voice was cut off mid-syllable, replaced with a howl of static as the scout craft's vox-net was overloaded, and then silence.

Both scout craft had been vaporised in an instant. All that remained of them were puffs of glittering metal dust dissipating over the planet's pale surface.

'What was that?' snapped Voar. 'All ships, battle stations!'

'Massive energy spike,' said Khrul's voice, almost drowned out by the sudden bursts of chatter over the vox. 'It came from beneath the surface. Fleet Minor pulling back…'

A slab of crust the size of an island was thrown off the planet's surface, trailing chunks of broken rock. Beneath it glinted dull silver and metallic green-brown like corroded bronze. From its hiding place emerged a spaceship the size of a cruiser, shaped like a crescent moon, with a towering pyramid amidships studded with green lights. The tips of the crescent housed projector weapons that were already glowing sickly green as they recharged.

'Evasive action, all craft,' ordered Voar. '*Constant*, fire at will!'

The enemy ship was of a design that Voar had never seen. Aliens, thought Voar poisonously. Heathens. Corruptors of the machine.

'More of them,' came a vox from the bridge of the *Antithesis*. 'Three more, at least. One from the closest world, two from the next. There's a huge power spike on the third.'

'I'm lined up for a shot,' said Magos Hepsebah's from the *Constant*.

'Take it,' said Voar.

The nova cannon on the prow of the *Constant* was wreathed in coils of superheated gas as it charged. The emerging xenos ship seemed aware of the threat, rotating rapidly with main engines flaring to push it out of the weapon's path. Chunks of

jettisoned surface clattered off it as its bulk shifted sideways, but it was too large for quick or subtle manoeuvres.

The nova cannon fired. The *Constant's* engines fired to compensate for the immense recoil. The projectile was hurled from the barrel, streaking towards the alien ship on a column of burning light.

The shot slammed into the upper hull of the crescent ship. The energy of the blast flashed so bright the craft was like a second sun, the nova cannon's power discharging in every direction at once.

Every direction save into the craft. When the glare died down, the crescent ship was intact; its upper surface was scorched and studded with fires, but it didn't look like it had suffered any serious damage.

The crescent ship fired, twin lances of green light playing across space.

'What is it firing at?' demanded Voar. 'Navigation, get me reverse targeting solutions and put us on evasive!'

Alerts flared, projected onto the telescope's lens. The discharge of power was enormous. The Imperial Navy didn't have energy weapons that could compare to those opening up on the xenos craft.

'Khrul here!' came a vox from the Asclepian Squadron. Magos Khrul's heavy metallic voice had enough alarm in it to remind Voar that none of them were free of their human weaknesses. 'We're being targeted! Those were sighting shots! I'm putting us on full evasive, all power to the engines!'

The xenos craft fired again.

Asclepian Gamma disappeared in a flash of violent green light.

Over the open vox-channel, Voar heard Magos Khrul dying, and there was just enough time for the magos to scream before the sound was wiped out in a howling gale of static.

Voar's human mind wanted to reel with the suddenness of the attack, to stumble out of the observatory and seek solace, but that part of him would not win out this day. Emotional suppressant circuits fired and logic implants took the strain.

'Break formation!' ordered Voar. 'Navigation, set a rally point. All craft into the warp, full evasive!'

On the bridge, the navigation crew hurriedly set a location nearby to which the fleet could jump through the warp and re-emerge to regroup, hopefully without the xenos following them.

Voar went back to the telescope. The crescent ship was rapid-firing, spitting fat bolts of green energy that detonated among the ships of the Fleet Minor, and sent its tiny burning craft spiralling through the void. Voar tried to ascertain what xenos race might be flying the enemy ship. Eldar ships were sleek, delicate and graceful, with sails that billowed on solar winds. Ork craft were barely space-worthy collections of junk and salvage. Demiurg factory-ships were stocky, brutal, ugly things that seemed too unwieldy even for the vacuum. The ships of Chaos were corrupted or ancient versions of the

Navy's ships, of debased but recognisably human design. Voar had seen them all, but the enemy was not among them. This was not an enemy he knew. He was fighting blind and ignorant.

Voar ordered the telescope to focus on the furthest of the three dead planets, where the biggest power spike had been detected. The pale surface was blurry for a few moments as the telescope focused; then its machine-spirit found its length and the planet shimmered into view.

Deep cracks were spidering its surface. Chunks of the crust, like fragments of an eggshell, were flaking away into space. Greenish light pulsed below.

A circular mountain range, like a crown of white stone, was forced up. Its centre formed a deep crater that collapsed, and green light flooded out. It looked like a great green eye had opened up, as if the planet was coming alive to look upon the Mechanicus ships as trespassers.

A huge dark shape forced its way out of the third planet. It too was built of crescents, many of them, arranged around a central spire so that the whole craft resembled an enormous steel claw. It was festooned with guns and lights, and surrounded by smaller craft that flitted around it like insects over a corpse. The central spire flared wide towards the stern and barely contained a raging furnace of emerald and crimson fire, an open reactor that bled power out into space. Streams of that power whipped out of the reactor into long trails looping

around the immense craft, and where they touched the ship's weapons they filled up with fire and glowed painfully bright against the void.

It was the size of a battleship. Larger. It was raging with power. It was the most awesome and terrible sight that Voar had ever seen. His logic circuits were at capacity, forcing his mind to contain what he was seeing and not be rendered dumbstruck by it.

'Rally point set!' said a vox from navigation.

'All craft, jump!' ordered Voar.

THE ANTITHESIS LURCHED, its gravity swinging out of kilter as the warp engines accelerated it through the bounds of reality. The *Constant* followed it, Hepsebah reluctantly turning away from its target even as the nova cannon recharged. The orphaned ships of the Asclepian Squadron, then the *Ferrous* and the *Defence*, forced their way through black rents in real space. The Fleet Minor, those spared the fire of the first enemy ship, shifted into the warp behind them. A few stragglers were left behind, thrown out of the wake of the larger ships. The crescent ship closed in greedily, and picked them off one by one with blasts of energy.

The xenos fleet, temporarily free of intruders, gathered on the outskirts of the system. It assembled around the immense mother ship, the smaller craft suckling on the power flooding out of it.

Its drones flitted around the echoes of the rift opened by the Mechanicus fleet's warp engines.

There was just a trace there of the interlopers, a scent of the new races, the upstarts who dared trespass upon sacred worlds.

The fleet did not need to hunt them down. The interlopers could not escape. With a thought, the eyes of the Veiled Region began to open.

PALLAS CAREFULLY PRISED the chitin of Sarpedon's left rear leg apart and used a pair of forceps to remove the crushed remains of a scarab. He dropped it into a medical waste container on the floor of the sick bay beside him. The sick bay had served the Soul Drinkers as an apothecarion for a long time, and was full of the equipment the Chapter had salvaged from elsewhere in the hulk, or from the fleet they had scuttled when they first broke with the Imperium: autosurgeon units fixed to the ceiling, nutrient tanks, transfusion units, racks of medicines and supplies, and even cutting gear and other basic tools for working on damaged bionics.

Sarpedon winced. His abnormal legs were extremely tough, but pain was pain.

'This will heal,' said Pallas, starting to seal the incision in the tough sheath of chitin with a medical laser. He indicated the mangled scarab in the waste container. 'Unlike that.'

Sarpedon's wounds had not been serious, a minor skull fracture and the usual cuts and impact wounds. As a Space Marine, he would heal them all naturally. Apothecary Pallas, however, was skilled at

accelerating the process. Most of the Soul Drinkers that fought at the abandoned city had passed through the apothecarion. Sarpedon was the last.

'I am glad that you remained with us, brother,' said Sarpedon. It was the first time that Sarpedon had discussed the events of the Chapter War with Pallas.

Pallas looked up at him. 'My Chapter is my Chapter. I made a mistake, true, but only a coward would not try to put that right.'

'You had good reasons, Pallas. A mistake it was, but I understand it.'

'You understand treachery?' Pallas looked almost offended by the suggestion.

'I have failed this Chapter many times. I led us to the edge of our destruction. The old Chapter would never have forgiven you, it is certain, but we are not the old Chapter any more and you are still my battle-brother.'

'And I know now that we will continue to die as long as we turn from the Imperium's fold. It is the price we pay for our freedom. When I had to see the dead and wounded from every one of your new dawns, I forgot that. I will not forget it again.'

The laser sizzled against the chitin, and the wound was closed. Sarpedon had removed his armour for the procedure, and the new scar on his leg was just one of many, from the surgical scars from his transformation into a Space Marine to horrible wounds suffered in the First and Second

Chapter Wars and everything that had happened in between. Sarpedon had come perilously close to death so many times that his luck was surely due to run out, every close call ticked off in a snarl of scar tissue.

'We all need to remember it,' said Sarpedon. 'To shy away from following the right path because it will cost the lives of my brothers is to let in the doubt that has led many an Astartes to fall. It is a narrow path to walk, between wasting my battle-brothers' lives and backing away when a victory is there to be won.'

Pallas cleaned up the wound.

'It is one that I do not believe I could walk,' he said. 'Which is why I serve as a sawbones and not as a leader.'

'If you did,' said Sarpedon, 'if fate had put you in command instead of me, what would you do?'

Pallas looked up from the wound. 'Fate did not put me in charge, Sarpedon.'

'Imagine it did.'

'Imagination is not a quality becoming to an Astartes.'

Sarpedon's vox chirped.

'Commander,' said Lygris's voice, 'I need you on the bridge.'

'You are clear to go,' said Pallas.

Sarpedon flexed his repaired leg. It hurt, but it was a good pain. He looked down at the scarab Pallas had pulled from his leg.

'Destroy that,' he said.

'Yes, commander. And…'

Sarpedon paused as he went to leave. 'Yes, Apothecary?'

'I would not surrender to the Mechanicus. If I was leading us, I would not let them take us to some forge world for a show trial. I would die first, and my battle-brothers along with me. That is what I imagine.'

'Good,' said Sarpedon, and left.

THE MECHANICUS FLEET had made its warp jump with minimal planning and no preparation, so in interstellar terms it had only travelled a short distance through the Veiled Region.

The first task had been to count the dead: Magos Khrul and the three hundred men on board the *Asclepian Gamma*, several hundred among the Fleet Minor, and the usual handful of casualties among the menials in the engine rooms and arming chamber of the *Constant*.

The *Asclepian Gamma* had been rather more than nine hundred years old, a fine craft built according to principles that were slowly being lost by the shipwrights of the Mechanicus. The squadron was flying one short for the first time in its history. Its machine-spirit had been bright and aggressive, and it made for a tightly run, efficient ship. Now, it was gone forever. A great tragedy had occurred with the loss of that spirit, for such a thing could never be

replaced. The second task was to mourn it. Incense
candles burned in pools of machine oil, and devo-
tional engines chattered eulogies in machine-code.
Tech-priests led the menials in prayers.

The third task was to find out just what had
attacked them.

Archmagos Voar pored through yet another volume from the shelves of the *Antithesis's* bridge
library. The enemy had been xenos, there was no
doubt about that, but that hardly did much to narrow it down. Several thousand alien species had
been encountered in hostile circumstances since
the Mechanicus records began, and tens of thousands more had been recorded from afar. What
was more, creatures native to the Veiled Region
were unlikely to be recorded, given the lack of
knowledge about the area.

Voar hauled another volume from the shelves
and placed it on the reading table in front of him.
It described the travels of a rogue trader, whose
adventures had seen him skirt the edge of the
Veiled Region before he had headed out to the
western edge of the galaxy. One of Voar's eyes
opened up and a line of green light was projected
onto the open page. Two of his fingers split into
metal armatures that flicked the pages of the book
at blurring speed as the scanner built into his eye
swept across the words written there. Pages of
High Gothic writing streamed into the logic
engine implanted behind his temple and spat

parcels of relevant, filtered information into his consciousness.

There were a few encounters with greenskin pirates, a race of sluggish, primitive creatures on a dying world, and a few xenos mercenaries and traders, operating in the lawless barrens of sparsely populated Imperial space, but nothing relevant.

A lectern-servitor trundled around the corner. The servitor had once been a menial, serving on one of the fleet's craft before it had suffered a crippling wound and been turned into a more useful machine. Its spine was bent over and its back made level to serve as a stand for books, while its lengthened arms carried a stack of volumes it had picked out according to the simple logic routines burned into what remained of its brain. The book lying open on its back was an account of a battle fought by the Adepta Sororitas.

The servitor was accompanied by one of the bridge tech-priests. A hundred of them were working on the problem at that moment, searching through the shelves for hints at the identity of the xenos that had nearly shattered the Mechanicus fleet in a single engagement.

'This may be of use,' said the tech-priest.

'Anything else?'

'Not in all the library, archmagos. The semantic engines have finished their work.'

Voar turned his scanner eye to the tome the servitor carried. It was another minor engagement

where some pious Imperial servants had stumbled across hostile aliens and fought for their survival. The world was known as Sanctuary 101, and the Sisters of Battle, the military arm of the Adepta Sororitas, had fought valiantly against a tenacious foe.

They had also seen a shape in the sky, awoken by the alien warriors that had stormed the chapel they had defended. It was the last sight many of them had seen.

It was a crescent, hanging black against the sky.

Voar froze his scanner and backed up a few pages. His logic engines sifted through the information again, filtering wider and wider until Voar knew all the pertinent details.

He had it. The Imperium had encountered this foe before, not frequently, and rarely with enough insight to understand it, but at least Voar was no longer fighting completely in the dark.

The Omnissiah had smiled upon Archmagos Voar, because now the enemy had a name.

THE BROKENBACK MADE its third warp jump. There had been little to justify exploring the previous world with its abandoned, machine-infested cities. From orbit around it, however, Lygris had located another nearby solar system just visible to the hulk's sensors through the surrounding nebulae. It was close enough for a civilisation like that of the dead city to have colonised, and, now that the

Brokenback was in orbit around the new system's fifth planet, it was apparent that Lygris's instinct had been good.

The planet depicted on the bridge holo-projector was a beautiful green pearl, shining in the light of its sun. Endless forests rolled across its surface, from frozen coniferous valleys around its poles to tropical swamps and rainforests around the equator. Instead of oceans, it had thousands of rivers, weaving across its surface.

'The image is good. Very little cloud,' said Lygris. 'It's a long-range scan, but there's plenty of information. Here.'

Lygris fiddled with the data-slate in his hand, and the image zoomed in to show a low-resolution section of the endless forest.

'That,' said Lygris, 'is not natural.'

They saw a structure as straight as a ruler stretching across several kilometres of forest.

'What is it?' asked Sarpedon.

'An aqueduct,' said Lygris. 'Or maybe a raised highway.'

'So there's habitation there?'

'Definitely. Not much, though, certainly not by the standards of the civilisation that settled it. We'd expect to see signs of agriculture, mass forest clearing and cities. Sometimes cultures in the earlier stages of space exploration set aside a world for their ruling classes, a garden world, to be left unspoiled.'

'Human?'

'The scale's right. Otherwise it's impossible to tell.'

'It may be another xenos lair,' said Sarpedon.

'Or,' said Chaplain Iktinos, who had been summoned to the bridge along with Sarpedon, 'it could be a holdout against the aliens. Certainly the previous world was human. If this one is, humans may still be there.'

'Can we make it there?' asked Sarpedon.

'There, yes,' said Lygris. 'Anywhere afterwards? That is debatable. I can force everything out of the reactors and we can probably get a fourth jump out of them provided it isn't too far. Then I fear we will be running on empty.'

'Better to risk what we have,' said Iktinos, 'than to accept the certainty of failure.'

'I agree,' said Sarpedon, 'but I am not going down there expecting anything other than a hostile reception. Full battle order this time. How many Thunderhawks do we have operational?'

'Three,' said Lygris. He had rendered the *Brokenback*'s Thunderhawk gunships inoperable at Vanqualis to help scupper Eumenes's rebellion. In an act of penance, he had begun repairs on them personally.

'I'm taking a company-strength force down there. It's as many battle-brothers as we can spare, but I will not be outnumbered by whatever we find down there. Bring together what you can to carry them.'

'Yes, commander.'

'And Iktinos?'

'Commander?'

'Prepare the men's souls to battle the xenos.'

'It shall be done.'

'Do not forget,' said Lygris carefully, 'that we are not here to fight aliens. We are here to find fuel for the reactors and get out as easily as possible.'

'The enemy had the better of us at the grey city,' replied Sarpedon. 'They will not do it twice.'

ARCHMAGOS VOAR HAD cleared out a section of the bridge library. The bookcases around him were papered with pages taken from books, copies of diagrams and key passages, hundreds of them. The whole bridge crew had been sent hunting it all down according to Voar's orders. The incident at Sanctuary 101 had been the key to unlocking it all.

The Omnissiah had given Voar all the clues he needed. As a servant of the Machine-God, Voar had dutifully followed them to their conclusion.

Voar sat at the reading desk surrounded by open books and blinking data-slates. He looked up as the magi entered the sanctum he had created.

It went unspoken that Khrul was not with them, but none of them could ignore his absence.

'Archmagos, why have you called us here?' asked Magos Vionel, whose lumbering body barely fit between the bookcases of the archive.

'My gun crew must be supervised in its re-calibrations,' said Hepsebah as tersely as anyone

'It's a tank!' shouted one of the sisters standing guard at a window that had been hurriedly fortified with sandbags. 'It's the size of the chapel!'

One of the sisters before the altar stood up. A cloak trimmed with ermine hung from her shoulders, and her face was studded with golden thorns: a canoness of the Order.

'Sisters Retributor!' she yelled. 'Cleanse it with fire!'

Sister Orpheia shouldered her bolter, and picked up a weapon that had been out of shot at her feet. It was a multi-melta, a twin-barrelled weapon almost as big as Orpheia herself, connected to her backpack by an armoured hose. The metal of its barrels was heavily scorched by years of intense heat. Orpheia patted the gun affectionately.

'This,' she said, 'is the wages of sin.'

Orpheia ran to the barricaded window, and the sister with the picter followed her. An enormous black shape, a slab of darkness with a halo of green lightning crackling around it, could just be seen through the gaps in the half-built walls. It was still far away, but it already loomed larger than the cathedral. It was enormous.

The sisters were taking cover. The canoness stood in the centre of the cathedral, defying the enemy to dare take its best shot.

A bolt of green lightning crashed through the wall. Sisters were thrown off their feet. The picter shuddered violently, and the sister holding it fell

down, the image shifting wildly as it fell on its side. Another sister rolled across the floor, wreathed in green fire. The slam of the lightning echoed along with the screams of the wounded.

'Open fire!' someone yelled.

The Sisters Retributor at the window were silhouetted in the fury of the firepower they poured towards the shape. A heavy bolter hammered. Rockets streamed, sending plumes of exhaust shooting back into the cathedral. Orpheia's multimelta charged for a moment before firing a tremendous beam of red-white heat that seemed to sear reality itself.

The image broke up as gunfire competed with static to create an impenetrable din. It was impossible to make out any coherence among the jumble of images. The sisters were lit by gunfire. Spindly shapes clambered in through the windows. The Canoness was on the ground, a hand clamped over a wound in her abdomen, yelling orders.

The image was moving. The woman carrying the picter was running through the shadowy, half-built chapel. She emerged outside, into the harsh sun of Sanctuary 101.

'Move it! Fall back!' shouted someone. It was a woman again, another soldier. 'They've taken the cloisters! Get to the mausoleum!'

The image broke up and changed, streaked with static. The holo showed the blood-streaked face of a woman: Sister Orpheia. The picter was on her

chest and she was being carried on a stretcher. One side of her face was raw and bloody. It looked like the skin of her face had been stripped away, layer by layer, right down to the bone. Among the sisters carrying her was the young novice that had taken the images from the chapel. The picter was forgotten as it continued to record from the stretcher where it had been dropped.

More gunfire. Orpheia was being carried in a column of sisters moving from the cathedral, which was a burning wreck. Dark shapes, like tall buildings looming over the cathedral, were just visible for a handful of frames. Spindly shapes, skeletal and half-seen, clambered through the ruins. It was impossible to make out any more details of the xenos that had come to Sanctuary 101.

Orpheia was turned around, and the view swept over a graveyard covered in eagle-shaped markers commemorating the lost sisters of the Gilded Thorn, surrounding a grand mausoleum to some heroine of the Order. Sisters were already taking up firing positions among the stones. Many of them were bloody and wounded, chunks of their armour stripped away.

Green fire fell from the sky, fat searing bolts of it. The sisters carrying the stretcher dropped it and took cover. Orpheia fell to the ground and the picter rolled off her.

Lying on its side, the picter's image showed a headstone and a stretch of Sanctuary 101's sky. The

younger woman slumped against the headstone. Her novice's robes were on fire, flaming green. Her eyes were wide with shock and pain. Her face distorted as layers of robe, and then skin, lifted off the side of her face and shoulder. Red, wet muscle gleamed beneath, and then bone, as she was flayed away by the tongues of green flame. She screamed, the sound lost in static, and rolled onto the ground out of frame.

A dark shape hung in the sky above, like a crescent moon, but black.

The image froze. The glow-globes rose again, and the image became dim.

Voar stepped through the image to address his magi.

'They are known,' he said, 'as necrons.'

'I have walked through valleys of sin and oceans of night. I have looked daemons and traitors in the eyes. I have heard the whispers of dark things that wanted my soul. And I have never once encountered anything that struck the fear into me that a xenos would feel if it ever truly understood the resolve of the human race.'

Daenyathos, *Battle Prayers*
XIIIV

CHAPTER FIVE

FROM THE GUNNER'S position on the Thunderhawk, Sarpedon could see the forests rolling out across the planet's surface, streaking past as the gunship descended. Rivers zipped past, bright silver ribbons in the hot sun. Behind him, two more Thunderhawks banked behind the lead craft, arrowing down into the lower levels of the forest world's atmosphere. Two armoured landers followed in their wake. Between them, they carried more than eighty Soul Drinkers. The firing port of the heavy bolter mount gave Sarpedon an excellent view of the planet as its beauty was revealed beneath him.

Trees, hundreds of metres tall, reached up from the canopy, hanging with enormous brightly coloured fruits. Flocks of birds, like columns of

shimmering smoke, swept up from the crevasses and treetops full of nests as the Thunderhawks roared past. Hills tall enough to break the canopy were topped with pastel shocks of flowers.

Sarpedon could see the target in the distance. A pale streak, dead straight, cutting right through the forest. It was the structure Lygris had spotted from orbit. Sarpedon gripped the handles of the heavy bolter mounted in front of him and checked the magazine. The planet was a paradise, but he was working on the assumption that something down there would soon try very hard to kill the Soul Drinkers. Sarpedon was not going to risk getting caught out again. This force was ready to fight.

The Thunderhawk passed over the structure. Sarpedon realised that it was a landing strip, a gash cut into the forest, paved and studded with landing lights. The trees around it had been burned away to keep them from growing back over the strip. The Thunderhawk rounded a hill, and Sarpedon saw that a palace stood at one end of the landing strip.

It had been hidden from the sky by the canopy of trees arching over it, but it was enormous. Several floors of gold and deep red stone were ringed by balconies and raised gardens. Flowering vines draped over balconies like stage curtains. Several grand wings curved around the main body of the palace, dappled with the sunlight falling through the trees, enclosing ornate gardens and artificial pools.

The Thunderhawk made another pass. Sarpedon peered down the sights of the heavy bolter, its bulky body tracking across the palace grounds.

'No targets,' he voxed.

The Thunderhawk swooped around, its exhaust wake stripping the topmost leaves from the canopy, and slowed down as it approached the landing strip. Its nose tilted up as it came down, and its landing gear thudded onto the strip.

'We're down! Clear to deploy!' said the pilot.

Squad Luko jumped from the rear ramp of the gunship as it lowered. Luko was first out, as he always was, already activating the energy field around his lightning claws. Squad Tisiph was next, and Sarpedon followed.

The forest shook with the sound of engines. The second Thunderhawk was coming down. Luko waved his squad into a perimeter, and Tisiph's squad hurried forwards, bolters trained on the forest edge. Tisiph's squad carried several of the Soul Drinkers' heavy weapons, of which the Chapter had very few remaining.

The second Thunderhawk was down. Codicer Scamander and Librarian Tyrendian were with Squads Graevus and Salk.

'Move up for a breach on the building,' said Sarpedon. 'Tisiph, hold here. Luko on point.'

'Yes, commander,' voxed Luko.

Sarpedon watched his force move up towards the palace. Its size was even more apparent from the

ground. Beyond it, Sarpedon could see several sub-palaces, shaped like fanciful castles with delicate spires that just pierced the canopy. Between them were stables and servants' quarters, separated by walled gardens and reflecting pools.

Tyrendian moved up past Squad Tisiph. Tyrendian was the Soul Drinkers' only remaining Librarian aside from Sarpedon. With an aquiline face and a unique lack of scars, Tyrendian looked far too handsome to be a Space Marine.

'Who lived here?' he asked.

'Someone rich,' said Sarpedon. The tension in Tyrendian's words was not lost on Sarpedon. He was assuming, as Sarpedon had, that humans had abandoned the planet. 'Veiled Region's human civilisation probably put this world aside for their leaders.'

'Lucky them,' said Tyrendian.

Scamander was behind them, following Tyrendian. Scamander was the only one of the Chapter's scouts that had remained with the Soul Drinkers after the Second Chapter War. He was a pyrokinetic with a lot of potential, but relatively little control, and Tyrendian had taken him under his wing to train him up as a full Librarian.

Captain Luko ran up to the main doors, his Soul Drinkers stacking up behind him. Squad Graevus moved into position on the other side of the doors.

'No contacts,' voxed Luko. 'The place looks dead.'

'So did the white city,' said Sarpedon.

Behind the spearhead, the other craft were landing. Iktinos had the third Thunderhawk, and the rest of the Soul Drinkers were jumping from the armoured landers. Iktinos was directing them to spread out and advance on a wide front to protect the force about to enter the palace.

Luko breached the gilded double doors by tearing off one side with his lightning claws. The door fell in, and Graevus was over the threshold, his squad-mates following him into the dark interior.

Tyrendian was in next. His particular psychic power was useful at close quarters; a well-thrown bolt of lightning could go a long way to even up a fight. Scamander stuck beside him.

Sarpedon clambered up the outside wall, onto a first floor balcony. The open windows led into a mezzanine floor overlooking the entrance hallway, through which the Soul Drinkers were advancing.

The inside of the palace was as lavish as the outside. Gold chandeliers hung from the ceiling. The walls were red and gold, and the floot was pale stone. The forest had been brought inside, too, with vines winding decoratively up the walls and stands of trees in the corners. A raised pool in the centre of the hallway shone with decorative fish.

'There's nothing here,' voxed Graevus.

Sarpedon headed up the next flight of stairs to the floor above. It was a feasting chamber, pale and elegant, spilling over with lush tropical plants.

He could smell it now. It was unmistakeable. Coming from above, it was a mix of sweet and foetid that would be alien to someone who had not been around as much death as Sarpedon had.

'Head up,' voxed Sarpedon. He drew the Axe of Mercaeno. They would not get the drop on him this time, no matter who they were. 'Graevus, Luko, with me.'

Luko and Graevus were on the upper floor in a few moments, moving up the stairways. Sarpedon followed Graevus, who had his own power axe ready, with the Astartes of Squad Luko filling the cramped stairway behind him.

The stairway was narrow, and it stank. The air was heavy with death. Unaugmented lungs would have struggled to draw breath. Ahead was a solid wooden door that looked well bolted.

'Go,' said Sarpedon.

Graevus kicked the door open and darted inside. His assault squad followed him in, Sarpedon on their heels.

The room stretched the whole breadth of the palace, high and lofty with tall windows drenching it in dappled light. It had once been an artist's studio, with half-finished sculptures and lumps of cut stone standing everywhere.

Corpses hung from the rafters. There must have been well over a hundred of them. Judging from their clothes, they were the nobles and servants of the palace, ladies in their gowns, footmen in their

uniforms and servants in smocks and work clothes. They had been there for some time, and each of them hung above a puddle of corpse liquor, foul and black. Their skin had turned dark and sunken, and their eye sockets seethed with maggots. A few flies, newly hatched, buzzed lazily around their heads.

Sarpedon looked around the room. There were no signs of a struggle. There had been none in the rest of the palace.

'They killed themselves,' said Sarpedon.

'A cult?' asked Luko.

'Maybe,' said Graevus.

'Tisiph here,' came a vox. 'We've got something by the eastern stables. Bodies. Crammed in one of the cellars. Must be fifty of them.'

'Signs of a fight?' asked Sarpedon.

'None,' replied Tisiph, 'and the doors were barred from the inside. Got some gas fuel canisters here. I'm thinking they gassed themselves.'

'Throne of Terra,' swore Graevus. 'What happened here?'

'Whatever was going to happen,' said Sarpedon, 'these people chose death rather than face it.'

'A strange way to kill themselves,' said Luko. 'It's not the quickest or surest way.' Luko climbed onto one of the uncarved stone blocks, and cut down one of the bodies with a flick of his lightning claws. It was the corpse of a footman; the coat he wore had once been bright red, but was now filthy

brown. Luko held up the body, showing the ragged dark hole in the back of its skull. 'Bullet wound,' he said. 'This man didn't hang himself.'

'Commander, Iktinos here,' said Iktinos over the vox. 'I have reached the tower to the north of the palace. There is something here that you might wish to see.'

THERE WERE OTHER bodies. Some had hanged themselves in one of the stable buildings. Others appeared to have weighed their clothing down with rocks and drowned themselves in one of the ornamental pools. In the kitchens of the palace was the body of a man, who had taken his own life with vermin poison. A couple even hung from the trees, high up in the canopy. They must have climbed up there to spend the last few moments of their lives among the birds and insects instead of with their fellow humans. Some of them appeared to have hanged themselves, but others had been killed by other means, usually gunshot, before being strung up. Nothing about the palace or the bodies suggested why they might have been hung up after death.

The riches of the palace were in place: art, gold and silver, even spices and other luxuries in the pantries that must have been imported to the planet. What Iktinos had found in the fanciful tower adjoining the palace outstripped them all in value.

It was a map inscribed in gold and inlaid with precious stones the size of a man's fist. It covered one wall of a chapel. The chapel was not dedicated to the Emperor but to a triumvirate of gods; one was depicted as a warrior, another as a woman with silver fire around her hands and another as a crippled man. Statues of them stood behind the chapel's altar, probably carved by the same hand that had once worked in the artist's studio now hung with rotting corpses.

The map was of a stellar empire. The diamonds were stars, rubies and sapphires were planets. Orbits and space lanes were loops of silver. Two worlds were picked out. One of them was surrounded by a halo of green stones, and bore the heraldry of a sword over a leaf.

'This symbol is over the door of the chapel,' said Iktinos. 'It is probably the planet we are on.'

Iktinos stood before the star map with several of his flock standing guard at the windows and doors. The chapel, like the rest of the palace, looked untouched by conflict, save for being abandoned.

'Then this is a human empire,' said Sarpedon, 'and these are its other worlds?'

'Given our route,' said Iktinos, indicating a fat sapphire, 'this is the world upon which we originally landed, the white city.'

'And this?' asked Sarpedon. He pointed to the second planet that had drawn his eye: an enormous ruby, cut with dozens of facets, surrounded by

diamonds and fanciful loops of gold and silver. 'The empire's capital?'

'It seems more than likely, commander,' said Iktinos.

'I see. Can we use this to navigate?'

'Provided we can match it up with the stellar bodies around us, certainly. Lygris should be able to model a star map using it.'

'The heart of an empire will have space ports, fuel depots. Even if it is abandoned like this place, we will be able to find what we need.'

Sarpedon's notice was caught by a noise outside. It sounded like the drawing of a blade.

BROTHER SKOYLE OF Squad Graevus was alert enough to see the movement, but such was the skill of the infiltrator that it looked like no more than a corpse swaying in the wind.

The body was that of a stablehand dressed in a simple work fatigues and a long leather apron. His face was bloated red and black, his eyes drooping black sacks of ichor and his swollen tongue filling his mouth. He looked like any other body might, strung up from the tree outside the tower and left there to swing for many days.

Beneath those clothes, the skin was slit open and folded over, held together with slivers of metal like steel thread. Its insides had been hollowed out and its chest bulged strangely, the ribs broken and shifted to allow for another pair of arms to fold

over another chest, as if the stablehand had become a coffin for another corpse. All this was hidden by the heavy working clothes the corpse was still wearing.

The swaying had been caused by a hand with blades for fingers, slick with rotten blood, forcing its way out of the hollowed corpse and pinging the metal stitches open one by one.

Black gore dripped onto the ground beneath the corpse. Brother Skoyle heard it again and turned to look at its source. He saw the body moving, and this time it was not with the wind.

Skoyle drew his chainsword. The corpse split open, showering him with rotten meat and blood. It unfolded a second figure from inside. Taller than a man, its slender limbs had been folded up inside it like an impossible puzzle, and it was covered in stinking filth.

It was humanoid in shape, but it was not human. It was not anything that had ever been alive. The gore was crusted over the dull metal of its articulated limbs. A thick jointed spine rose from its pelvis to support a wide chest with thick steel ribs, from the centre of which came a faint greenish glow, the thing's power source. Its long arms ended in blades as long as a man's forearm. Its head hung down in front of its chest, a metal parody of a human skull, with a slit in the thin face in place of a mouth and two green crystals set into deep eye sockets. Sheets of torn skin hung over it, as if this

stylised skeletal creature was still trying to wear the guise of a man.

It landed a metre away from Brother Skoyle, its unmoving face appearing to leer with anticipation as it darted forwards.

Skoyle's chainsword whirred, and he stabbed it at the creature's chest. The metal teeth skipped off the metal of its shoulder, drawing sparks instead of blood.

The thing was on him. Blades as sharp as needles punctured the shoulder joint of his armour and slit up into his torso. Skoyle yelled and threw it to the ground, stamping down on its leg to pin it in place before driving his chainblade down into its chest.

Green light flashed as its power core ruptured. Bladed hands slashed up at Skoyle, cutting chunks from his armour. The alien creature shuddered and fell still, like a machine with the power shut off.

Graevus ran to help him, followed by the rest of his squad.

'Skoyle! What is it?' shouted Graevus.

'Machine,' gasped Skoyle, gingerly testing his wounded shoulder. Blood was running from the joint, black against his purple armour. 'An ambush machine. It was waiting in the corpse.'

Graevus looked around the tower and the palace. There were corpses everywhere, hanging from trees, lying in foetid pools and huddled in storage. Those were just the ones the Soul Drinkers had seen so far. There could be thousands of them.

'Commander, we've been attacked,' said Graevus. 'It was a machine. It's destroyed, but there could be more. They could be surrounding us.'

'All squads!' ordered Sarpedon. 'Pull in close to the tower! Squad Tisiph, stick with the transports and be ready to cover our retreat!'

The metal creature at Skoyle's feet sprang up. The gash in its chest had been covered over with a surface of gleaming new metal. The light inside it was glowing again.

The thing rammed all its blades up into Skoyle's throat. They punched through the ceramite of his helmet and out through the back of his head. Skoyle convulsed and dropped his chainsword, his arms falling dead at his sides.

Squad Graevus riddled the alien machine with bolt pistol fire. It jerked as the bolts impacted it, blasting off an arm, a leg, battering its head into a lopsided mess. It clattered to the ground, turned hazy, and vanished. Skoyle slumped to the ground where the machine had fallen, but he landed on bare earth. The thing had gone.

The alien machines clambered from the upper tiers of the palace, from the belfry of the tower and the cellars beneath the stables, dozens of them, many still wearing the skins of the corpses in which they had hidden. They had hidden among the bodies strung up in the palace's top floor. When Sarpedon had first seen them, when the Soul Drinkers had wondered what fate must have

befallen the inhabitants, the machines had been watching them every step of the way.

Graevus grabbed Skoyle's body and heaved it onto one shoulder. 'Squad! Close guard on the commander!'

Luko's squad ran to the cover of a stable building. They hammered bolter fire up towards the creatures emerging from the palace. Several fell or lost limbs in the first volley, but many more scuttled down the walls and charged towards the Soul Drinkers, moving faster than a man ever could.

Sarpedon could see them emerging from the ground between the Soul Drinkers and the airstrip, hundreds of them, many of them clawing their way out from beneath the soil. These were different, bulkier than the ambushers, and carrying xenos weapons with glowing green barrels instead of bladed fingers.

'Fall back to the tower!' he ordered. 'Get to cover! Defensive positions!'

Soul Drinkers were running ahead of the bloody metallic tide. Sarpedon snapped off a bolter shot and blew the leg off one. Squad Luko's fire cut down several more, throwing shards of gory metal against the palace walls.

When the machines died, they disappeared. They didn't dissolve away or crumble to dust. They just faded away, and were gone.

Sarpedon headed into the tower. Soul Drinkers were gathered around it, sending out disciplined

volleys of fire to cover one another. Iktinos's Soul Drinkers were taking up position at the windows and doors of the chapel at the base of the tower.

Sarpedon headed up the stairway that coiled around behind the altar. It wound up towards the tower's upper reaches. He could hear metal claws clacking against the outer wall, and Soul Drinkers yelling as they forced the doors closed under the weight of robotic bodies. The sound of booming metal filled the tower as the star map on the wall was wrenched down and propped up against one window to barricade it. Gunfire stuttered. Chainblades whirred.

The upper floors of the tower were bedchambers and studies, small personal libraries and reception rooms, all understated but lavish. The floor was marble and the walls were covered in elegantly trained vines.

Silver blood-streaked claws reached over a windowsill. Sarpedon reared up out of the window, and split the alien's head in two with his axe before it could crawl in through the window. A balcony beside the window was already crawling with them. Sarpedon jumped through the window and scuttled along the wall, slashing down at them from the wall above. They cut back at him, blades ringing off his armour, but he cut off an arm here, a head there, and sent the machines falling broken back down to the ground.

They formed a seething red-silver carpet, like a swarm of corroded clockwork insects. They were

climbing the trees beside the tower, too, to jump
from the uppermost branches on to the top of the
tower. Sarpedon fired his bolter, blowing holes in a
couple of torsos. The other machines, the ones with
guns, were in range. When they fired, green flames
played across the walls of the tower, and stonework
was stripped away as if being dissolved. The alien
weapons did not just burn or shatter, they spirited
away the matter of the target, boring through it
layer by layer.

The enemy scouts wore the skins of the dead,
and they had fooled the Soul Drinkers for long
enough to stage an ambush. Their warriors possessed weapons employing technology beyond
Imperial understanding, and they had killed at
least two worlds.

'Tisiph, what is your situation?' voxed Sarpedon.

'Embattled,' came the reply. 'They're coming out
of the trees. Machines. Xenos.'

'Can you bring the transports up?'

'Not all of them.'

'What about a Thunderhawk?'

'Yes, commander. I can do that.'

'Then do it.'

'I can't transport the whole force.'

'Then we'll have to use some imagination. Do
it.'

'Yes, commander!'

Sarpedon looked down at the horde of xenos
assaulting the walls. He could hear chainblades

against metal and bolter fire hammering into machine carapaces.

'See, brothers?' shouted Captain Luko, fighting at the doors. 'Metal dies just as fast as flesh!'

'Graevus, get to the upper floors,' voxed Sarpedon. 'To me!'

Sarpedon ducked back into the tower as the window frame was stripped away by the machines' gunfire. The staircase spiralled up further towards the pinnacle of the tower. He scuttled up it to find a trapdoor leading to the roof. He tore it off its mountings and climbed up.

Graevus was following, the armoured boots of his squad hammering on the stairs. Above the gunfire and clash of metal on metal, Sarpedon could hear the engines of Tisiph's Thunderhawk.

'All squads, hold them!' ordered Sarpedon over the vox-net. 'Stand your ground!'

Graevus reached the roof. 'Your orders, commander?'

'Break the siege,' said Sarpedon. 'Follow me.'

The Thunderhawk hovered low over the tower roof. Sarpedon could see Tisiph in the cockpit. Gunfire hammered from the gunship's weapons, battering heavy bolter and autocannon fire down into the xenos. The roof was battered by the hot, chemical-heavy exhaust from the engines.

Tisiph wheeled the hovering gunship so that the rear ramp faced the window and swung down. Graevus led his squad onto the open ramp, holding

tight to the overhead railings as exhaust wash screamed around them. Sarpedon jumped on to the lip of the ramp behind them.

The horde was growing. For every machine the Soul Drinkers destroyed, another two seemed to drag themselves up from the earth. Fallen robots got to their feet again, wounds closed over with liquid metal.

'Luko, Iktinos, you have to take them apart!' voxed Sarpedon, having to yell over the engines. 'Destroy them completely before they repair!'

'A pleasure!' voxed Luko from below. He loved war, and his love for it was infectious. Even as he spoke, his lightning claws flashed at the door and another xenos was reduced to smouldering components.

'Tisiph!' shouted Sarpedon. 'Take us in!'

The Thunderhawk banked away from the window to hover over the centre of the xenos horde. The machines were crowding forwards, clambering over one another to kill.

'Now!' shouted Sarpedon. He jumped off the Thunderhawk's ramp, the Axe of Mercaeno above his head, ready to strike.

Sarpedon hit the ground hard, letting his legs flex under him and take the impact. Graevus's squad followed, bursts from their jump packs slowing their descent. Sarpedon and Squad Graevus landed right in the heart of the machine horde.

The xenos were swarming forwards, competing for the chance to die, forcing their way into the tower. They were not ready for Sarpedon and Graevus to appear right in the heart of them, and attack.

Sarpedon's axe cut one in half, and Graevus's power axe accounted for another. Chainblades thrust out, and bolt pistols hammered. One Soul Drinker landed right on top of an alien, knocking it to the ground, and wrestled with it down in the dirt. Another landed off-keel and fell, machines swarming over him to cut him up with their bladed hands. Graevus beheaded one of the attackers and dragged his battle-brother out from under them.

They were quick and tough, but Sarpedon had the advantage. A Space Marine never gave that up when he had it. Sarpedon speared them on his talons and butchered them with his axe. He threw them aside and trampled them into the ground. Squad Graevus laid into the machines with similar determination, and soon Sarpedon and Graevus had carved out a clearing in the enemy force, surrounded by a rampart of mangled metal bodies. Some of the machines were intact enough to self-repair and clamber back up, but the Space Marines of Squad Graevus carved them back up or blasted their heads off, and few rose a second time.

'Luko! Lead your men out!' ordered Sarpedon as he tore the arm off a machine and split its metal skull in two. 'Crush them between us!'

'You heard him, brothers!' bellowed Luko to his squad. 'Take it to them! To me, my brothers! To me!'

Luko jumped through the doorway, kicking a machine to the ground as he did so. His fellow Soul Drinkers followed, charging from the doorway or vaulting through the windows. A few moments ago the machines would have swarmed around them, cut them off and dragged them down to their deaths, but now they were fighting on two fronts.

Luko laughed as he cut the machines to pieces in front of him.

Sarpedon led the charge the other way, wading through metallic bodies to close with Luko. Together, the two Soul Drinkers forces split the horde in two, and by the time Sarpedon was side by side with Luko hundreds of the machines were wrecked and broken.

Sarpedon cut at the face of a machine lunging towards him. The axe passed right through it as if it was an illusion. The machine faded out and then was gone completely.

The wrecked machines around Sarpedon's feet were dissolving away, too. The survivors and the destroyed were being teleported away.

'Where are they going?' asked Luko.

'Back to their makers?' said Sarpedon. 'To regroup and hit us again?'

It took only a few moments for the machines to disappear. Even the scraps of broken machinery

were gone, leaving the Soul Drinkers standing alone on a patch of torn earth.

'Either way,' said Chaplain Iktinos, who had fought his way out behind Luko, 'we cannot stay here.'

'Agreed. Tisiph?'

'Commander?' voxed Sergeant Tisiph.

'Good work, sergeant. Land and cover us for embarkation.'

'Understood.'

The Thunderhawk swooped away towards the landing strip. With the noise of its engines fading, the only sound was the wind through the forest canopy and the pinking of hot bolter muzzles cooling.

'These things must have been waiting for survivors,' said Iktinos, looking up at the hollow bodies hanging from the trees. 'When the enemy came to this world they were not willing to leave a single human alive.'

The din of the battle had come entirely from the Soul Drinkers. Other than the clacking of their claws against armour and stone, the enemy machines had been completely silent. Even when they died, they had not made a sound.

Sarpedon did not know what they were, and he had never seen anything like them before, but he did know what the people of this world, and of the white city, had felt when the xenos machines attacked.

They must have believed that death itself had come for them.

'Death? What is death? It is the natural state of all things. It is life that is the aberration. It is life that should be feared, for it can go by with our work left undone, it can be wasted away on failure and indolence. Death is to be embraced.'

Daenyathos, *Nineteenth Sphere of Tactical Apotheosis*

CHAPTER SIX

THE DAMAGE DONE to the *Ferrous* in the opening exchanges with the alien fleet would have been enough to shred a lesser ship. Some energy bolt or wayward Mechanicus torpedo had blown a hole in the underside of the industrial ship's hull, blowing through and depressurising three decks. The *Ferrous*, however, was so old and lumbering that the destruction was wrought only through abandoned decks, with a couple of redundant systems damaged and the usual handful of menials killed.

The Mechanicus fleet had dropped out of the warp in good order, licking its wounds as hundreds of menials and junior tech-priests mounted running repairs and enacted apologetic rites to placate the traumatised machine-spirits. Among them was a gang of menials that attended to the wound in the

underside of the *Ferrous*, which was still bleeding air and debris into the void.

Twenty menials marched through the shadowy, decrepit decks towards the wound. Their skin was almost grey and their faces almost featureless, drooping eyes, tiny black flecks, and mouths, lipless slits that barely ever spoke. Their lives had been spent in space, and they had never seen a blue sky or an ocean, except from orbit.

They pulled on the hoods of their voidsuits as vacuum warnings flickered along the dark corridors, their way lit by chemical lanterns. Walls and decks bowed inwards, crushed by the force of something tearing up through the layers of metal.

The menials were not there to save the decks that had been lost. That ancient metal had been consigned to the void, to be absorbed back into the fabric of the universe so it might one day be wrought again into a work of the Omnissiah. Instead, they were to identify which areas might be salvaged, and seal them off with sheets of tough flakweave and rivet guns. Here and there, they sealed a tear in a wall through which air might yet escape, or a doorway that threatened to give way. Many places were marked as unsafe, to be cut away like diseased flesh when the *Ferrous* was next in dock. It was sombre work, for everywhere hung the necrotic sorrow of the *Ferrous's* machine-spirit.

A section of deck had been torn right through, leaving an enormous cargo hangar sundered and

useless. Hundreds of tonnes of construction materials had fallen out into space. One of the menials,
instead of marching grimly past one of the doorways leading to the condemned hangar, suffered a
spark of initiative and glanced through the frosted
window set into a bulkhead door leading to the
hangar.

'What is that?' he asked.

'Keep moving,' said another. The menials had no
leader, for they were so well-versed in their duties
that they could be trusted to admonish one
another. 'We still bleed.'

'No. This is not right. Come, look.'

More menials crowded around the doorway. The
pane was almost opaque with ice, but they could
still glimpse a great shape of polished silver and
black, like an enormous bullet embedded in the
fabric of the ship.

'It could be unexploded munitions,' said one.

'Or one of the Fleet Minor,' said another.

'Regulations permit us to investigate,' said
another.

'Very well.'

'Let us open it up.'

'And see.'

The menials checked the seals and air supplies on
their voidsuits before two of them hauled the
wheel-lock open. The thin air in the corridor whispered out, and silence fell, broken only by their
boots ringing on the deck.

The object had to be a hundred metres long and perhaps twenty wide, a massive cylinder of black metal inlaid with panels of silver. Its surface was torn from its entry into the ship, but it was still clear that it was not of Imperial design. Where was the tarnish of a hundred years lying in an ammunition hopper, the binary prayers stencilled on the casings? It had a sheen that suggested materials beyond Imperial construction. Towards the upper end, the casing broke up into a crown of drill bits, like a huge snarling mouth that had chewed its way hungrily through the *Ferrous's* hull.

'What is it?'

'It does not matter what it is.'

'For it is not of the machine. It is an intruder.'

'It must be excised! Let us summon work crews! Cutter units! Let the invader be expelled!'

The menials spread out around the ruins of the hangar to see if there was an obvious way of removing the object. Explosives could dislodge it. A craft of the Fleet Minor could pull it out like a diseased tooth, but that would cause further damage to the *Ferrous*. A less violent solution would be preferable, and would require less mollifying of the machine-spirit.

Vibrations sang through the floor. The side of the great cylinder split open. Inside, lights glimmered, green lights, glowing in silver-chased darkness.

The lights were paired, like eyes, and they narrowed as they focused on the approaching menials.

'We should inform the bridge.'

'We should.'

Emerald lights flared. The menials never got the chance to tell the bridge anything.

MAGOS METALLURGICUS VIONEL was touring the industrial base of the *Ferrous*, a series of titanic factory floors and forges running the length of the ship. The purpose of the *Ferrous* was to manufacture replacement parts and refine fuel for a fleet in deep space, allowing the whole fleet to continue operating for long after a conventional force would have needed to return to port due to the attrition of rust. The *Ferrous* was also at risk from the forces of decay, for it was old and the ills of corrosion and weakness had plenty of places to hide among its metalworks and refining halls.

Vionel trudged through the drifts of metal swarf that surrounded the enormous machining floor, raised up on blocks of steel. Thousands of menials laboured there, the hulking machines they served grinding out new components for the factory ship's ailing engines. Vionel's body was a heavily reinforced industrial chassis that clumped loudly up the steps to the machine floor. Overseer Gillard, an older menial, worn into a gnarled lump of a man by years on the factory floor, hurried to greet him.

'Lord magos,' said Gillard. 'Our efficiency targets are well within our sights.'

'But they are not achieved.'

'Regrettably not, lord magos. On a war footing, the energy rationing means that our...'

Vionel held up a huge metal paw to silence the overseer. 'The Omnissiah accepts no excuses. Efficiency is next to godliness. Even in the face of destruction, in the jaws of death, a menial's targets are his sacred duty.' Vionel's vocabulator unit was, like the rest of him, built for ruggedness rather than finesse, and his voice was a relentless monotone grind. 'This is the way of the Machine-God!'

'Blessed be the knowledge He imparts,' said Gillard hurriedly. 'I shall press my menials further, my lord.'

The overseer saluted and returned to the conveyor belt on which the thousands of menials under his command were sorting through heaps of components from the enormous machining unit.

The Mechanicus fleet was in a grave situation. It was pursued by xenos attackers, and its quarry, a space hulk, crewed by Mars knew what renegades and killers, was hostile in its own right. In this rare moment of calm before new orders came from the *Antithesis*, Vionel decided to seek the counsel of a higher power. Vionel let his human mind, one of the few remaining parts of his weak flesh, sink away from his senses, and he felt the mighty ironclad heartbeat of the *Ferrous*.

MAGOS VIONEL, UPON taking command of the *Ferrous* decades before, had installed interfaces with

the ship's ancient machine-spirit in all of its data vaults and cogitators. The ship's machine-spirit had long been considered a curmudgeonly, silent entity that cared nothing for human beings and kept itself to itself. While many ancient ships manifested sophisticated machine-spirits, not all of them were willing to communicate, and these were generally left alone. Magos Vionel, however, knew that this approach was folly. Instead of assuming that a machine-spirit should become more human to allow for it to interface with its crew, he took it upon himself to become more like the *Ferrous*. He transmitted his personality into the information architecture of the factory ship through the interfaces, and forced his human mind into the shape of the machine-spirit's world.

It tasted of rust and the smoky tang of age. It felt warm and creaking, the heat of the factory ship's massive engines and reserves of power caged in the shell of rust.

In the heart of it was the machine-spirit. Vionel's mind was still too human to make of it anything but a murky storm, billowing purple-black clouds of processing power split by the lightning created by rapid calculations. The storm was contained in a great black vault, like some underground cathedral, Vionel's mind making of the physical restraints of the cogitators and data vaults an arching ceiling, supported by thick iron columns dripping with a constant rain of information.

The machine-spirit did not speak to Vionel directly. He had not yet earned that right. He had to interpret the emotions that whipped on information gales, like some fleshly soothsayer interpreting dreams.

The storm roared up towards him, bellowing wordlessly from a darkness at its heart crammed with pistons and flames. Vionel shrank from it, fearful for a moment that it had become angry with him and would devour his mind.

The machine-spirit was simply in pain. Silver webs were climbing across the surface of its clouds as if something was trying to trap the machine-spirit's functions in a net, restrain them and rob it of its power. Beams of emerald light played across the vault, scorching chunks of iron from the walls, which rusted as they fell.

'What pains us?' asked Vionel, turning his thought into streams of machine code. Their zeroes and ones were almost lost amongst the chaos of the *Ferrous's* pain.

The storm boiled away, sucking itself into a tight knot where the compression turned into glowing heat like the heart of a furnace. Vionel felt his mind struggling to hold on to cohesion in the sudden vacuum of the vault. Then the storm burst anew, lightning crackling across the walls, a hurricane heavy with data battering against Vionel. The sound deafened Vionel's mind, and he fought to hold on to his place in the information structures

of the ship. In spite of the burst of energy, the silver web held, shimmering as it stretched around the thunderheads.

Vionel could watch no more. His grip failed, and his mind was shunted back into his body with an impact that made him stumble on his iron-shod feet.

The ship echoed with the machine-spirit's pain. Even the menials could feel it, thrumming through the decks of the *Ferrous* in time with the spirit's screams.

Vionel accessed the ship's vox-net.

'To arms!' he yelled, his metallic voice transmitted all over the ship. 'We are invaded!'

The menials immediately broke out wrenches and shivs, anything they had to hand as a weapon. Overseer Gillard unlocked a weapons cabinet mounted on the side of the machine, and a few menials took shotguns and autopistols from it, simple, ugly weapons, perfect for the sort of close-quarters murder that was typical in a boarding action.

'Bridge!' voxed Vionel. 'Relay to me all reports of intruders. Keep me up to date on damage controls. Tech-guard standby.'

A series of cogitator tones bleeped in response. The *Ferrous* had a complement of tech-guard and trained menials in case of hostile boarders, who were, at that moment, grabbing their flak armour and lasguns and heading through the ill-maintained

mazes of the ship's outer decks to meet the sources of the alert.

'Lord magos,' said Gillard, turning from a bank of readouts on the side of the forge. 'What has happened?'

'The ship is compromised,' said Vionel. 'The machine-spirit has given us warning.'

It might not be enough. The ship was huge. There were thousands of ways attackers could get into the vulnerable factory floors or the processing plants in the ship's rear section, or make their way towards the bridge. The tech-guard couldn't hold them all back.

'They saw me,' said Vionel. 'They know I am here. Their target is the machine-spirit.'

The first he saw of them was a flicker of green fire at the edge of his vision, up among the steel rafters of the machining section. A menial working at the forge reared up in sudden pain and shock. A huge chunk, like a round bite mark, had been torn from his back as if by invisible jaws. One arm was gone, too, flayed down to bloody bones.

Vionel's targeting oculars snapped into focus on the enemy.

'Tech-guard, to my position!' he voxed. 'Enemy sighted!'

They were skeletal machines, animated by the green flame flickering in their eye sockets and chests. They had got in through the maintenance access to the section's ceiling, and they were hiding

among the rafters. They carried elaborate weapons built around glowing green cores, which had projector units surrounded by haloes of electricity instead of muzzles.

Vionel's mind accessed the images from the recording Voar had found in the bridge archives. Hunched metallic skeletons, robotic, relentless: necron warriors.

Vionel pumped all his auxiliary power into his limbs. They were massively powerful, designed to anchor him to the ground and lift enormous weight, but they were also a lot faster than they looked. Vionel ran up the steps towards the conveyor belt even as blasts ripped chunks out of the floor behind him. Cores of metal were drilled out of the deck and flayed to atoms. The few menials with guns returned fire, and flayer blasts fell among them, shredding limbs and flashing away skulls.

Vionel slammed into a section of the conveyor, heavy with machine components. He clamped his enormous metal hands around the edge and ripped a section away. He spun, his torso rotating freely on its chassis, and hurled the hunk of machinery with all his strength.

The conveyor section hit the girders so hard that several of them fell, hammering into the deck with a tremendous ringing like giant bells. Necrons fell, too, some of them crushed against the ceiling by the impact, others buried by the mass of steelwork collapsing on top of them.

Voar's briefing on the new threat had contained most of the intelligence the Imperium had on what its soldiers called the necrons. They were a machine-race, ancient beyond imagining. Their technology was an obscenity of forbidden principles and xenos heresy. They were a corruption of the Machine-God. It was not much to go on, but it was all Vionel needed. He was a forger of the Omnissiah's works, a creator, and his duty was to avenge their destruction.

Tech-guard were emerging from entrances beside the forge, in rust-red body armour with mirrored visors, carrying lasguns hooked up to their backpacks.

'Magos!' called the sergeant. 'At your command!'

'Advance!' said Vionel, projecting at maximum volume.

The surviving warriors advanced or got to their feet, their broken bodies re-forming from liquid metal. Others, shattered beyond repair, disappeared from beneath the wreckage. Even torn limbs and fragments of crushed skull vanished.

The tech-guard, a dozen of them in the squad, ran into the cover of the conveyor belt or the lengths of fallen girder. Lasguns spat. The air filled with the smell of burning and ozone.

Blasts from necron weapons hammered against the machinery with a crackling hiss, as if the metal were evaporating. Vionel stomped through the ruined conveyor into cover, but it was rapidly

disappearing. Menials died, chunks of their bodies stripped away. Others were still returning fire, and a warrior fell, chest blown open. One of the tech-guard stood clear of the wreckage to send a rapid-fire volley into the necrons, but he fell, too, his body armour and half his torso stripped clean away.

The tech-guard sergeant led the way across the chamber towards the necrons entering the chamber to join those who had attacked from the ceiling. The short-range gunfight blazed, red las-blasts and gouts of green fire exchanged through the wreckage and gloom. Tech-guard fell. The sergeant dived to the floor as the cover around him dissolved.

The first warriors were making it onto the machinery floor. Vionel broke cover and fired, sending a volley of rivets through the body of the first enemy he saw. Steel rivets punched through its face and ribcage and it fell. Vionel's next shot shattered a warrior's weapon, and, in a green flash, the gun's energy discharged, the remains dropping uselessly to the floor.

There must have been fifty necrons, and, every time one fell, another seemed to rise up from the ground. Vionel was not afraid. He had not been afraid since that part of his brain had been burned out and replaced with data storage. The chances of survival were not good, but ultimately, that changed nothing.

Necron warriors clambered over the remains of the conveyor. Vionel knocked the legs out from one

and slammed his metal fist down into its body, shattering it so thoroughly that he knew its heathen technology couldn't get it back to its feet. The rivet gun hammered away almost of its own volition, thudding hot metal into the approaching enemy.

The warrior Vionel had disarmed leapt from the conveyor onto his back. Metal hands prised at the cowling of his torso. Vionel tried to throw the creature off, but its hands were inside the plating, reaching for bundles of wires and fragile components, and it wouldn't let go. Vionel stumbled backwards and slammed back into the housing of the machining forge from which the conveyor emerged. The forge was still hammering away, stamping out metal components that spilled out onto the floor with no menials to sort through them. Vionel tried to crush the necron against the side of the machine, but it held on. Bolts of fire burst around him, one shearing deep into his left shoulder and another almost taking his leg off.

Vionel reached up, grabbed the necron around its metal neck and tore it off his back, and threw it into the mouth of the machining forge. The necron scrambled to escape, but it was a fraction too late, and a piston stamped a cog-shaped hole through the centre of its face.

The warriors were still approaching, relentless, their advance slowed by the remaining tech-guard falling back before them and sending las-blasts scoring deep melting furrows across their carapaces.

There were more warriors, too, emerging from access points around the machine floor. Vionel knew he could not fight them all, no matter how much satisfaction it might give him every time a xenos abomination was felled by one of the Omnissiah's rivets. He stomped to the side of the forge. He tore a section of panel away and hurled it, the jagged edge slicing the head off an advancing warrior.

'I require reinforcements!' voxed Vionel. 'Arms-men and tech-guard to my location!'

Across the floor, another tech-guard fell, this time in close combat, his lasgun torn from his hands by a necron, who then jabbed the curved bayonet on its gun into the man's gut. The sergeant blew off the alien's arm in response, but only a handful of tech-guard fought back now, scrambling from cover to cover to fall back to Vionel and the forge.

Vionel hammered with his rivet gun and threw chunks of machinery with his other arm. Fire tore into the forge around him. The forge shuddered and broke down, spewing half-formed components. A warrior clambered, grinning onto the machine floor beside him, and Vionel was barely able to swat the barrel of its weapon away before it discharged a bolt of green fire into him at point-blank range. Vionel hauled the warrior into the air, tore its arms off and threw what remained into another necron approaching with its gun levelled at him.

'We are lost!' voxed the tech-guard sergeant.

'We breathe,' said Vionel. 'We think. We reason. We are not lost.'

Three squads of tech-guard burst in through entrances behind the forge. Las-fire fell as thick as rain, the whole chamber glowing red with it. Vionel crouched down as las-blasts ripped over his head, slicing into necron torsos. Vionel lent his rivet gun to the weight of fire, pinning one warrior to the floor, a very unmachine-like relish firing in his brain as he watched the alien squirming like a pinned insect.

Las-fire was not enough to puncture necron armour on its own, but the weight of it was overwhelming. Twenty bolts might bounce off a necron's carapace, leaving a molten red welt, but the twenty-first might hit a vulnerable spot, or melt a little to far and destroy a critical component. Necrons on broken limbs were easy targets, while others were shot through gaps in their carapaces and fell as they advanced. The tech-guard formed up behind Vionel in a firing line, joined by the survivors of the first squad. One of the tech-guard brought a melta gun to bear, and its superheated beam melted through torsos and metallic skulls.

The necrons fell. Vionel held up a paw, and the firing died down. One of the sergeants yelled the order to cease fire.

The bodies were gone, not those of the fallen tech-guard and menials, which lay in pools of gore

mixed with the swarf from the forge, but the necrons. They simply disappeared when they collapsed. Vionel advanced slowly, wary of necrons self-repairing to attack him unexpectedly.

One necron lay there, quite dead, but without disappearing. It had juddered along the broken conveyor belt and clattered to the floor.

'Magos,' said Gillard, who had somehow contrived to survive hidden among the machinery surrounding the forge. 'Is it over?'

'No,' said Vionel.

More necrons were emerging from the rusting shadows around the machine floor. The first warriors had been the vanguard, and Vionel could tell that the following waves were deadlier, just with a look. Those on foot were broader shouldered with solid, stocky spines to support the weight of their larger gauss weapons, and behind them hovered variants of warriors on flying anti-grav chassis. Metallic beetles scurried along the deck in front of the second wave. Green blasts fell among the few remaining menials, powerful enough to strip them down to gnawed skeletons.

Vionel grabbed the fallen necron warrior and slung it over his back where magnetic clamps, which usually fixed stabilising legs and pneumatic lifters to his chassis, held it firm. 'Tech-guard, we cannot hold this place. Fall back to the dorsal saviour pods!'

A few shouted orders saw the tech-guard units covering one another as they moved back out of the

chamber, maintaining a spattering of fire to keep the necron guns off them for a few seconds more.

Vionel did not follow them. Instead, he ran at full tilt towards the nearest wall. His enormous weight slammed into it, and he tore straight through the wall, his momentum ripping through the bulkhead into the next section. A section of the ceiling fell in behind him. It would hold off the necrons for the few minutes he needed.

Vionel stopped and let his mind sink down again, the artificial parts of his brain banishing the adrenaline from his system so that he could focus. He entered the ship's information structure again, for the next course of action was not his to decide.

All was pain. Even before Vionel reached past the interface protocols, he could feel it. There was fire, but also terrible cold, as if the chill of the void had bled into the soul of the ship. Vionel's mind conjured metallic walls and corridors to represent the ship's low-level systems, but they were decaying, running like water or blemished with biological stains. Banks of datacrystal, which represented the ship's archives, were rotting, or burning to ash in green flames. Vionel did not panic, for such a useless emotion was no longer part of his augmented mind, but the grotesqueness of it still spoke to the weak human parts of him. This was his ship, a thing of ancient beauty and majesty, and it was sick. That sickness manifested turned Vionel's stomach in a very human way.

Vionel sank deeper. The ship was falling apart inside. Glittering conduits of information streaming from the ship's sensors fractured and broke as the *Ferrous* went blind, chunks of raw data raining down like debris in an earthquake. Vionel guided his mind between them, wary that damage to a tech-priest's mind could prove as fatal as damage to the body.

The roaring, thundering presence of the machine-spirit echoed everywhere. Vionel slipped through the next layer, and its anger hit him like a tidal wave. It was hot and vibrant, a shocking, terrible mass of emotion to come from a machine-spirit that had been so quiet for so long. Vionel had known it previously only as a chained storm, its power the potential energy of its great intellect and knowledge contained in the metal shell of the *Ferrous*. Now it was open and raw, all its centuries of existence powering its fury, and its pain.

Waves of pure agony hammered off it. Vionel forced his mind to conceptualise the machine-spirit as it loomed up from the darkness of the ship's higher systems. The storm clouds were angry red, and they rained blood. Fingers of mercury had wormed their way through the walls of the vaulted chamber. Currents of hot, toxic pain flowed around the storm, lashing at it, and the black lightning of pain arced as the machine-spirit raged.

The liquid metal, like thousands of ropes, reached into a spider's web that strangled the

machine-spirit's power. No matter how the storm raged, the silver web tightened, and the storm bled all the more.

'Tell me!' cried Vionel. 'Tell me what I must do!'

A mass of liquid metal welled up, churning like an ocean under the storm. Hands reached up from it, taloned and dripping, and where the lightning struck it the hands grabbed it and dragged it down. Vast reserves of power discharged into that ocean, greedily drained away by the invading force.

The emotion that howled on the gale was not human, but it could not be mistaken. Pain and anger mixed into one, and, in hot desperation, battered against Vionel's mind.

'Please, Lord *Ferrous*! Do not ask that of me!'

There was no reply but the pain. There was no longer enough human left in Vionel to deny it.

The *Ferrous* wanted to die.

Vionel wrenched his mind out of the ship's information systems. He snapped back into his body as it charged and clawed its way down through the outer hull access tunnels towards the lower hull of the ship. The necron warrior fixed to his back was still there, weighing him down with its heresy.

'Vionel to processing!' voxed Vionel.

'Processing here!' came the reply from the overseer. From the sound of explosions and gunfire behind the menial's voice, the necrons had made it into the processing section, too, into the mass of

chemical tanks and fractioning towers that the *Ferrous* dragged behind it.

'Open all the catalyst chambers and inundate with fuel!'

'Magos? That will…'

'I know what it will do! You have your orders.'

The menial paused. Menials had not received the higher teachings of the Machine-God, and were unaugmented and weak. A handful of new tech-priests were promoted from their ranks each year, but the great majority of them would only ever be normal, weak humans, ruled by their flesh and their emotions. Sometimes, they could not be trusted to do the work of the Omnissiah. Sometimes concerns like compassion or fear got in the way.

'Yes, magos,' said the menial. 'It will be done!'

'Fight them,' said Vionel, 'unto death.'

'We will.'

Vionel closed the vox-link. With the ship's information systems falling apart, it was up to the menials remaining in the processing section to do the machine-spirit's will. He could only hope that they would overcome the failings of their human minds.

Vionel reached the emergency hatch that led into an array of saviour pods. Each pod could carry half a dozen crewmen, which meant that one was just big enough for Vionel. The tech-guard was already there, in defensive positions ready to fend off the necrons that might burst in at any moment.

'Abandon ship,' ordered Vionel.

As the tech-guard entered the saviour pods, Vionel opened the hatch of the nearest pod and threw the wrecked necron warrior in ahead of him. He was barely able to get his bulk through the hatch. He had to pull out one of the seats and throw it aside, before he could turn to close the hatch behind him.

The *Ferrous* shook. The necrons had found some critical part of the engines, or their assault on the machine-spirit was forcing the ship to tear itself apart. The end was coming for the *Ferrous*, and Vionel mourned it with the part of his brain that could still feel sorrow.

Vionel mentally commanded the saviour pod's charges to fire. The ring of explosives detonated and fired the saviour pod out through its opening in the ship's hull. The pod, and Magos Vionel, spun away from the dying ship, just as tongues of fire began to run up and down its tortured hull.

ARCHMAGOS VOAR WATCHED the death of the *Ferrous* from the improvised briefing room on the bridge of the *Antithesis*. To him, it was a stream of energy readings spooling across a pict screen, but just as a tech-priest could see meaning in the zeroes and ones of machine-code, so Voar could see the fate of the ship in the jagged lines of the wildly fluctuating power output of the factory ship.

Somehow, even though the Mechanicus had evaded the pursuing ships, the necrons had managed to get at the *Ferrous*.

The *Ferrous's* processing section exploded. The fleet's fuel reserve went up in one titanic ball of orange flame, as bright, for a split-second, as a sun. Nuclear fires tore the factory ship apart, consuming its entire length and ripping the steel of its hull into atoms.

It was beautiful in its own way. Just as everything had to be forged, so everything had to be destroyed, whether by violence or decay. The *Ferrous* was an ancient craft, however, and, with it, died a spirit that could never be built again.

'Archmagos!' came a crackling vox. Voar struggled to recognise the voice through the distortion, but it was transmitted on his personal vox-net, which meant it was from one of the fleet's magi.

'Vionel?' asked Voar. 'You live?'

'But barely, my archmagos. Necrons boarded us. The machine-spirit bade me destroy it.'

'So that was you.'

'There was no choice. The spirit was corrupted.'

The idea was obscene. A machine-spirit, a fragment of the Omnissiah, violated by alien technology. 'Then you have served Him well,' said Voar.

'I am in a saviour pod and have sustained damage. The area is heavy with debris.'

'I will have the Fleet Minor pick you up,' said Voar, 'and take you to Crystavayne on the *Defence*.'

'It is better that I come to the *Antithesis* as soon as possible, archmagos.'

'Why?'

'Because I have something to show you.'

'Brave men die every day, unremembered. Courage receives no prize, but cowardice and dishonour can buy happiness and renown. The brave amongst us must accept their rewards from within, even in the throes of death.'

Daenyathos, *Catechisms Martial, addendum secundus*

CHAPTER SEVEN

THE VEILED REGION became deeper still. The nebula was a bloom of interstellar dust so vast that the solar system could fit into one of its countless whorls. It was lit from within by the fires that burned as the dust clumped together into infant stars. The tides of the nebula heaved slowly, ridges and troughs of dust making for a journey as dangerous as any through the warp.

Micrometeorites, motes of dust from ill-birthed worlds, pattered against the hull of the *Brokenback*. It was heavy going through the nebula, and a smaller, more delicate ship would not have risked it at all. After over twenty-four hours of forging through the nebula, the capital of the fallen empire was in sight, a tiny glimmer orbiting a star that had somehow survived the currents of the

nebula long enough to become fat and yellow like Terra's own sun.

THE BRIDGE OF the *Brokenback* was quiet. Lygris knew better than to take that as an encouraging sign. A hundred warning lights were winking on the various cogitators and readouts, and the reactors could go cold for good at any minute. The ruination of the *Blessed Obedience* was still sparking fires and venting air and fuel, and if Lygris had not disconnected the alarm klaxons the bridge would have been a deafening mass of noise.

'Help us,' said a quiet voice. An unagumented human ear would have missed it entirely. Lygris strained to hear.

'Help us. You must…'

It was there again, almost hidden by the humming of the cogitators. Lygris worked the control panel of the closest cogitator.

The ship's vox-net was clear, so the voice hadn't come from one of the Soul Drinkers. In any case, the voice had sounded female. Lygris searched through the external comms channels, the spectrum of frequencies across which a signal might be sent to the ship from elsewhere.

He found it. It was weak, only just strong enough to stir the cogitator's vocabulator unit. Lygris amplified it and tried to gauge its origin.

'Help us,' the voice said again. It was accented, but spoke recognisable Low Gothic. 'You must

come to our aid. This is Raevenia, last world of the
Selaacan Empire, and we are beset by the stars
themselves.'

ON THE BRIDGE a few minutes later, Sarpedon lis-
tened again to the whole transmission. It was on
a loop, broadcasting constantly, but, with each
iteration, the bridge cogitators were closing in on
its origin.

'The stars themselves?' he mused. 'What can
that mean?'

'Some stellar disaster?' suggested Lygris. Sarpedon and the Techmarine were on the bridge
along with Chaplain Iktinos and Librarian Tyrendian.

'Or our xenos friends,' said Tyrendian distaste-
fully.

'We need help urgently,' continued the signal.
'Weaponry and men, to defend our world. Anyone who hears this, join us in our fight, for more
worlds, more empires than ours face extinction.
Pass us by, and perhaps this doom will fall upon
you next. The choice is yours.'

'Is there any indication that the senders of this
message still live?' asked Iktinos. 'There's no
telling how long it's been looping.

'And where are they?' asked Sarpedon.

'A short jump away.' Lygris examined the screen
of the navigation cogitator. 'Still within the nebula.'

'I don't like it,' said Tyrendian. 'We know where their capital is. We're more likely to find survivors there.'

'Assuming,' said Iktinos, 'that this shadow from the stars did not start with the capital and work its way outwards. The message from Raevenia said they were the last survivors.'

'The bodies at the palace had not been dead that long,' said Sarpedon. 'Whatever happened to this empire happened recently. I believe that we must head for Raevenia.'

'Why?' asked Tyrendian.

Sarpedon threw his fellow Librarian a stern look.

'Because they asked for help,' he said. 'Lygris, can we make it?'

'There and no further. The *Brokenback* will be dead in the void after another jump.'

'Then set coordinates and do it. If we can help these people we can ask for fuel and be on our way.'

'And if we cannot?' asked Tyrendian.

Sarpedon did not answer him. Lygris keyed Raevenia's coordinates into the bridge cogitator. The reactors juddered alarmingly as they warmed up to throw the space hulk through the warp a final time.

'We lost good brothers at the palace and the white city,' said Tyrendian. 'How many more will this jaunt cost us?'

'Do you have a better idea, brother?' snapped Sarpedon.

'The commander is correct,' said Iktinos levelly, stepping between the two Librarians. 'Brother Tyrendian, this is our best chance of saving ourselves. Our pursuers are still out there, and are no doubt closing on us. To do nothing is not an option, and the right choice has been made.'

'I feel their deaths as much as you do, brother,' said Sarpedon, 'but this is not a kind galaxy. Sometimes we must die for our brothers, and no one can say who will die and who will survive.'

For a moment, it looked like Tyrendian would argue. Then his face softened almost imperceptibly.

'You are my Chapter Master and I bow to you,' he said. 'Scamander and I must make preparations for the warp.'

'You have my leave,' said Sarpedon. Psykers were more at risk from the occasional influence of the warp during travel. Sarpedon, being unable to receive telepathy, did not suffer much, but Tyrendian's mind was a little more sensitive, and Scamander, of course, was still learning to control his talents.

Tyrendian left the bridge, and Sarpedon turned back to Lygris. 'If we do find an inhabited world, what are our chances?'

'Assuming they are a space-faring people... reasonable, I would guess. That depends on their being friendly.'

'Then we are assuming much,' said Iktinos.

'We always do,' said Sarpedon. 'Any sign of the Mechanicus fleet?'

'I would tell you if there was,' said Lygris. 'The nebula makes it difficult to know either way. We could have lost them or they could be right on our tail.'

'Then they could follow us to Raevenia,' said Sarpedon. 'We need to move quickly.'

'Very well.' Lygris began to key the coordinates into the bridge cogitator.

'What are your thoughts, Chaplain?' asked Sarpedon, turning to Iktinos.

Iktinos wore, as he almost always did, his full regalia of power armour and skull-faced helm. It was the face he showed to his Chapter, so he did not look like one of them but an impassive judge of their souls. 'I believe that we are on the best course.'

'How will the battle-brothers see it?'

'I will see to it that they understand. We are not answering a distress signal, but searching for civilisation to refuel our ship. This is a mission of survival.'

'They all are,' said Sarpedon. 'You have my leave, Chaplain. The Chapter will need to pray for peace in the warp.'

'As shall we both.'

'Say a word for me, too,' said Lygris as he finished punching in the coordinates for Raevenia.

* * *

ARCHMAGOS VOAR HAD turned his section of the bridge library into a war-room. He had ordered the tech-priests to clear it and bring him everything he needed to appreciate the fleet and its situation: holo-projectors for tactical readouts, a heavy wooden map table with star charts spread out on it still awaiting the first landmarks of the Veiled Region, heaps of books on naval battle-lore, and histories of conflicts with space hulks and alien fleets.

He looked up at the heavy pneumatic footfalls approaching through the library. Magos Vionel emerged into the amber light of the glow-globes.

'Magos,' said Voar, 'I see you have endured close contact with the enemy.'

'Forgive me, archmagos,' said Vionel. Voar was correct. Vionel was effectively naked, although it mattered little given that his body was completely contained within his industrial chassis, with only his half-augmetic face showing. One shoulder was stripped down to the pistons and servos, as if the layers of armour had been peeled away one by one. He was covered in cuts and gouges. He smelled of hot machine oil and torn iron. 'I have come fresh from battle.'

'How badly are you damaged?'

'I require replacement parts. My core functions are largely unaffected.'

'Then what have you to show me so urgently?'

Vionel stomped up to Voar's desk. Voar saw that he had a chunk of wreckage in one fist. Vionel heaved it onto the desk in front of Voar.

'Here,' he said. 'One of them.'

The wreckage was of a robotic humanoid, its limbs hopelessly mangled and its metal skull punched through, robbing it of eyes to go with its lipless mouth.

'A necron?' asked Voar.

'One of their warriors. The basic combat unit.'

Voar stood up and turned over the necron warrior's shattered head.

'There had only been a single exemplar recovered,' said Voar, 'and that was not as complete as this. How did you prevent it from phasing out?'

'I assume it was the damage I caused to it.'

'You were fortunate.'

'The *Ferrous* died under my stewardship. I can see no good fortune in its fate. I hope only that knowledge will flow from my actions.'

'Did the machine-spirit… say anything? Did it have any message before it fell?'

'It could not speak. I believe that destruction was the fate the Omnissiah would grant it. That was all.'

Archmagos Voar knew that sorrow was something that he should feel. He felt its echo. He had grieved before, been sad that some colleague had died, or that he had lost… a friend? He tried to remember the concept of an individual whose

importance stemmed from something other than standing within the Mechanicus. It was there, a trace of grief, and he let himself feel that shadow of bereavement for the *Ferrous*. It did not last long.

'I will take this to my laboratory,' said Voar. 'There may be something I can learn from it.'

'What will you have me do?' asked Vionel.

'Take a shuttle to the *Defence*. Crystavayne will repair you.'

'Yes, my archmagos.'

'And Vionel?'

'Yes?'

Voar looked up from the wrecked necron. 'Can we fight them?'

'In numbers? No, archmagos, we cannot.'

'That will be all, magos.'

Vionel bowed, awkward on his squat chassis, and stomped back off the bridge. He limped as he went, one motivator unit in his hip spitting sparks.

Even with most of its face destroyed, the alien machine seemed to leer up at Voar. It was a gangling ruin, studded with rivets from Vionel's gun and mangled by the machining unit, but the malice it contained was undiminished for all that.

'What are you?' asked Voar quietly. 'Where did you come from?' He picked up the head. The plain black circuit boards in its skull glinted through the wound in its face. 'And if you truly are a machine, who built you?'

Voar paused and took the mask from his robes, the mask that Baradrin Thaal had so foolishly bought as a plaything, and which had led the Mechanicus to the Veiled Region in the first place. He held it up to the ruined warrior's face.

It was the same metal, the same dimensions. The mask was not a part of the same machine; it aped a human face, while the necron warrior's head resembled a human skull in only the most stylised coincidental way. It was, however, a relic of the same empire.

'What news is there of the Soul Drinkers?' voxed Voar to the ship's tactical helm.

'We're still tracking them,' replied one of the many tech-priests who were now taking shifts in monitoring the space surrounding the fleet. 'Their last warp jump was off-course from our calculations.'

'Where are they heading?'

'A system towards the nebula centre.'

'Inhabited?'

'It's possible.'

'Follow them.'

'Yes, archmagos.'

Voar sat down at the desk and shut off the vox-links to give him some peace to think.

'What bargain have you made, Astartes?' he said to himself, turning the xenos mask over in his hands. 'What have they offered you? What will you pay?'

Outside the *Antithesis*, the other ships of the Mechanicus fleet were gathering into formation to

enter the warp, both to stay ahead of the necron aggressors and close in on the Soul Drinkers.

Whether it cost him his fleet, or even his life, Archmagos Voar would find his answers soon.

THROUGH THE DOZENS of sensors on the *Broken-back*, the planet identified as Raevenia was blue-green, glittering and beautiful. Planets like that got rarer every year in the Imperium, as more were settled by billions of pilgrims and refugees, polluted, stripped bare, or turned into smouldering warzones. Raevenia had rings of stellar ice and dust, and several moons, half-formed captive asteroids, orbiting it.

'The source of the signal,' said Lygris, 'is here.'

The planet was shown on the holo-unit that Lygris had set up on the bridge of the *Brokenback*. The Techmarine indicated a point near the equator, on a large continent that fragmented into dozens of islands along its southern edge. 'It looks like there is a city there. Some pollutants and plenty of structures.' Lygris pointed to a pale spot beside the potential city. 'Given that this civilisation is space-faring, this could be a space port.'

'Is the signal stronger?' asked Sarpedon.

'It was. It cut out about three hours ago.'

'Cut out?'

'Just after we broke warp. I've been trying to raise a response on the same frequency, but there's nothing.'

Sarpedon looked more closely at the holo. 'Is there any sign of conflict down there?

'None yet,' said Lygris. 'That doesn't mean it isn't there. More likely, it's another ghost world and the xenos have seen us coming.'

The two Soul Drinkers were alone on the bridge. Much of the Chapter was preparing to depart for the surface of Raevenia, and the rest were positioned throughout the *Brokenback*, manning the sensorium helms and keeping an uneasy watch over the remaining reactors.

'What do you think of it?' asked Sarpedon.

'This planet? It's definitely inhabited, or at least it was.'

'More than that.'

Lygris thought for a long moment. 'I don't like it.'

'No?'

'It's this whole place, the Veiled Region. It feels like it was... waiting for us. It's drawing us further in so it can kill us off bit by bit, as if it is alive and we are a virus to be killed off. Does that sound sane?'

'Stranger things have been proven to exist in this galaxy,' said Sarpedon, 'but as you say, we aren't going anywhere else. It is Raevenia or nothing.'

'I agree. This is our best chance. I only wish that we had some more appetising choices.'

Sarpedon studied the image of Raevenia some more. Here and there, the forests and plains were

stained with dark areas that could be cities, or grey veins that might be roads. North of the possible city was a range of mountains crowned with snow, like white stitches in the planet's surface.

'Whoever is down there,' said Lygris, 'we may have to fight them to take the fuel we need.'

'Then we will fight them,' replied Sarpedon sharply. 'We have done more distasteful things. This is survival.'

'Let us say we do survive. We find a safe berth in the galaxy where we are not hunted. What then?'

'Then,' said Sarpedon, 'we will rule ourselves. That is worth fighting for.'

'Do you think it is possible?'

'Lygris, would I have led you here, would I have led you at all, if it was not? To live free in the Imperium is a fight that might take until the end of time to win, but it is worth fighting. If I believe anything, then I believe that.'

'Freedom?' said Lygris. 'From the Imperium? No one has lived free in this galaxy since the Age of Strife. For my battle-brothers to see it... that is something I would risk my life for.'

'Well said, techmarine,' said Sarpedon. 'It is the Emperor's work. Had he not been betrayed by the tyrants that followed him then we might not have to fight for it like this. Of course, we won't be fighting for anything if we're stranded here.'

'Very well, commander,' said Lygris. 'I will see to it that the gunships are ready for launch.'

Lygris left Sarpedon to contemplate the unspoilt globe of Raevenia. It seemed too beautiful to harbour anything deadly, too natural and pure to threaten corruption.

A Space Marine never let appearances drop his guard, however. If the fates so willed it, there would be plenty of killing on that planet.

THE NECRON FLEET tore the heart out of a star.

It was an old star, fat and red, a lumbering giant that stood as a relic of a time before the clouds of the Veiled Region had gathered. The star darkened, and then collapsed, throwing off outer layers in ripples of radiation millions of miles across. Its remaining substance compacted and heated up, and, for a few final hours, it burned as bright as it had in its youth, spitting violent solar flares and atomic storms in its death throes. Then that energy, too, was sucked out into the void, and the star shrank into a smouldering clump of ashes, burning away the last vestiges of its power.

The star's power fuelled the fleet's alien technologies. The ships hurtled at impossible interstellar speeds, space-time folding through fields of exotic energy, showers of particles that physics determined could not exist streaking across the Veiled Region.

The last echoes of the star's power rippled out as the fleet arrived at its destination. The cold radioactive dust was thrown aside as the necron

necropolis ship tore through it, power crackling off its talons. The rest of the fleet shifted into place beside it, the star's stolen power arcing between them and the necropolis ship. Time and space seemed to complain at the violation that had brought the necrons there, shimmering ripples washing out at the speed of light, echoing off the barren worlds around the dead star.

Tombs, sealed before mankind had evolved, split open, and the lords of the host emerged, hot coils of power burning the patina of millennia from their bodies. They raised their staves, and unliving eyes turned on them. Scarabs swarmed everywhere, fixing the systems that time had undone. Information flickered between the command nodes of the host, between the lords and their master, down to the individual warriors. War machines awoke, too, enormous vehicles like hovering monuments to death, fighter craft folded up in their vertical launch decks like colonies of bats.

To the ships of the sentinel fleet would now be added the armies of necron warriors that had already conquered most of the human empire. Neither the defenders of Raevenia, already whittled down by vanguard units, nor the new interlopers would face any point but elimination.

ARCHMAGOS VOAR HAD kept the laboratory solely for his own use. Not even the other magi of the

fleet had access to this part of the *Antithesis*. Sometimes, solitude was as essential to a tech-priest's studies as his knowledge of the Machine. Sometimes, the things he studied were best kept to his mind, the strongest and best trained, alone.

The laboratory equipment dated back to the building of the *Antithesis*. Its surfaces were brushed steel glowing faintly over the low light. It was attended by a complement of servitors, silver-plated spidery creations with their once-human components hidden from view.

Archmagos Voar placed the wrecked necron warrior on the dissection slab in the centre of the laboratory. An autosurgeon unit swung into place overhead, and a thin beam of white light fell onto the necron, illuminating it in all the fine detail that Voar's bionic eyes could discern.

A pair of mechadendrites uncoiled from Voar's shoulders. They were thin and delicate, quite unlike the crude articulated cables that lower-ranked tech-priests used as additional limbs. Voar's plucked a medical laser and power scalpel from their rack on the autosurgeon, a miniature field of disruptive energy flickering around the scalpel blade.

Voar had been a commander of the Adeptus Mechanicus forces in the field for a long time, too long, perhaps. The purity of pursuing knowledge in this way, information for its own sake

and not as a means to a military end, was like a drug that focused his mind. There was no limit to what a magos could achieve with that focus and the blessing of the Omnissiah upon him. He concentrated on the machine and slowly slit the necron's torso open, heating the alloy with the laser so that it could be slit open by the scalpel.

The vaporised metal did not smell right. It did not glow and deform in the way righteous metal should. Voar had to choke back the sense of disgust. The torso split open, and Voar carefully lifted the two halves apart.

A power core lay beneath, still glowing with unholy radiation with solid black surfaces inscribed with complex patterns in place of wires and circuits. It was nothing at all like the Machine, like the perfection of form as taught by the Omnissiah. Studying it would be taxing on the soul as well as the mind. That was why Voar had to keep it here, in his sealed lab, where it could not infect less well-prepared minds.

'Archmagos,' said a vox from the bridge. It was Magos Hepsebah on board the *Constant*, which was flying in formation ahead of the *Antithesis*.

Voar withdrew the implements from the innards of the dead machine. 'I asked not to be disturbed.'

'They were waiting for us,' said Hepsebah. 'It's all over our scanners.'

'Explain.'

'The xenos. They knew our course before we did. They're here.'

'Anyone outside the fold of the Imperium of Man is an enemy, proven or otherwise, xenos or human. Anyone who lives without the light of Terra walks in darkness.'

Daenyathos, *The Defence of Xall XIX*

CHAPTER EIGHT

SARPEDON SAW THE city first as the lead Thunder-hawk broke through the cloud cover. It was surrounded by a solid defence wall, with grand gates to the north and south, and the city itself was a great crown of decorative stonework contained within those walls. The towers of palaces and civic buildings reached up from sprawling estates and cramped winding streets. Poorer districts domi-nated the south, tumbledown tenement blocks built over the foundations of a once-prosperous district, devolving into ramshackle shanties along the south wall and spilling into the woodland beyond the south gate. The lands around it were carpeted with deciduous forests, rolling up towards a line of hills to the far north. A short distance from the city was the structure that Lygris had correctly

identified as a space port, several rockcrete landing pads surrounding a control tower, all held within its own set of defensive walls studded with fire-points and watchtowers.

'Commander,' voxed Phol from the Thunder-hawk's cockpit. Phol was probably the only Soul Drinker Lygris trusted to fly a Thunderhawk as well as Lygris himself did. 'The Raevenians have come out to greet us. Armed men, several thousand.'

The force had gathered outside the city's south gate. Sarpedon could see them ranked up in regiments, thousands strong, with artillery and cavalry drawn up on the flanks. Banners fluttered in the wind.

'Bring us in, brother,' voxed Sarpedon.

The Soul Drinkers of Squad Luko were strapped into the grav-restraints around Sarpedon. Each one had a pre-battle ritual. Many of them recited passages from the *Catechisms Martial*, the Soul Drinkers' philosophy of war as written by the Chapter's legendary warrior Daenyathos. Others performed wargear rites to prepare the spirits of their weapons and armour, although in truth it was their souls they were preparing.

'Luko,' said Sarpedon, 'we are not going to war. The people down there will decide if our guns and blades are loosed.'

'Is that why you chose my squad to ride along with you?' asked Luko with a smile. 'So you could make sure I stayed my trigger finger?'

'Just make sure your battle-brothers have calm heads on their shoulders,' said Sarpedon.

The Thunderhawk made its final descent, vertical engines grinding as they cushioned the craft into a landing. The trees lining the road leading from the city's south gate shuddered in the choppy gale from the engines. The gunship settled onto the ground.

'Deploy us, Brother Phol,' voxed Sarpedon.

The Thunderhawk's ramp swung down. Sarpedon breathed his first lungfuls of Raevenian air, clean and cool forest air tinged with gun oil and sweat.

The army arrayed outside the gates was huge and magnificent. Its soldiers wore iridescent body armour, gleaming like the carapaces of beetles. They were armed with rifles and machine guns, solid projectile weapons behind Imperial technology, but not by much. The regimental banners were embroidered in silver and gold, and below them stood drummers and trumpeters, and officers resplendent in gold brocade. Behind the army were dozens of artillery pieces manned by gun teams, and a regiment of cavalry armed with sabres as well as rifles.

At the head of the army, standing in the car of a gilded chariot, was a woman in the armour of a soldier and the robes of a monarch. Her black hair was tied back severely, and her strong, handsome face adorned many of the banners flying behind her. Her eyes were a sharp green.

Sarpedon could feel the troops withdraw when they saw him. A Space Marine was monstrous

enough, huge compared to a normal man and wearing enough power armour to turn him into a walking tank, but Sarpedon was a literal monster. The spider legs replacing the lower half of his torso were an obscenity that would warrant immediate execution on most Imperial worlds. Any right-thinking, Emperor-fearing citizen would consider Sarpedon an abomination.

Squad Luko emerged from the Thunderhawk behind Sarpedon. The guns of his troops were not aimed at the army in front of them, but in a split second Luko's battle-brothers could be ready to fight.

Sarpedon stood before the woman in the chariot. He was taller than her in her chariot, but even so she seemed able to look down on him with both curiosity and disdain. Sarpedon had seen many humans recoil before him, spitting curses or running in fear. The queen did not.

A soldier hurried forwards. He looked older than the men around him, the polished plates of his armour inscribed with flowing script in gold.

'Her Majesty Queen Dyrmida of Astelok,' he said in accented Low Gothic. Evidently introducing herself was a task beneath the queen. 'Regent-general of Raevenia.'

'Commander Sarpedon of the Soul Drinkers.'

For a moment, there was only the sound of banners flapping in the breeze, and the engines of the Thunderhawk warming down.

'What are you?' asked Queen Dyrmida. Her voice was as strident as the rest of her.

'A Space Marine,' said Sarpedon. 'A warrior from the galaxy beyond, from the Imperium of Man.'

The men in the ranks were jostling nervously. Officers threw angry glances to quiet them down. Even the horses of the cavalry were disturbed by the sight of Sarpedon, straining at their reins.

'The Imperium?' asked the queen. 'What manner of empire is this? One embattled, like our own? Brothers and sisters in this fight?'

'They are no brothers to you, or to me,' replied Sarpedon.

'Then, no empire moves to assist us? In spite of our calls for help, our begging, we see nothing but you and your men? This is the deliverance we abandoned our pride to plead for? How many do you bring with you?'

'Two hundred and fifty,' said Sarpedon.

'Two hundred and fifty! What difference can you make to us? The Undying are upon us. They will care nothing for your presence unless each of your men is worth a thousand of mine.'

'They are,' said Sarpedon levelly.

The silence was broken only by the sound of banners and trees in the wind.

The queen looked past Sarpedon to the Soul Drinkers of Squad Luko behind him, and the landed Thunderhawk beyond. Two more Thunderhawks were circling overhead. Sarpedon

couldn't imagine what she must make of the Soul Drinkers with their mutant leader, their massive statures and purple armour, their exotic wargear like Luko's claws and Sarpedon's force axe. The fear was clear in the eyes of her soldiers, for they must have thought they were looking on creatures of legend. The armies of many non-Imperial worlds had crumbled at the sight of Space Marines in the past, civilisations, who thought themselves enlightened and advanced, bowing down to worship the terrifying warriors that dropped into their midst from the sky. Whole worlds had fallen to Imperial tyranny in the past by exactly this method.

Queen Dyrmida was made of sterner stuff. Without her, the army might well have melted away, there and then, without a shot being fired, or they would have attacked the Soul Drinkers at the first sight of Sarpedon. Instead, they followed their queen's lead, and stood firm.

'You are not here to help us,' said the queen. 'If you are as mighty as you claim then you would think my world beneath you. Why are you here?'

Sarpedon settled back onto his back legs. The queen was right. If the *Brokenback* had not been crippled, his Chapter would probably have bypassed Raevenia completely, and ignored their pleas for help. 'We can depart, your majesty, and leave you to these Undying. Or we can give you the chance for survival that you currently lack.'

'My city will soon be under siege by the Undying. If you wish to fight, fight. Otherwise, leave. There is no more to be discussed.' Dyrmida turned to he charioteer. 'To the gates!' she ordered. The chariot wheeled around, and the troops parted as it was driven towards the city.

'All squads,' voxed Sarpedon to the Soul Drinkers in the Thunderhawks overhead. 'Come in to land. Do not open fire on the Raevenians. All weapons silent.'

The troops were falling back, rank by rank, to accompany their queen into the city. Captain Luko held his position behind Sarpedon as the banners receded.

'Perhaps we should have come armed with a diplomat,' said Luko.

Sarpedon turned to him. 'Next time you sharpen your claws, captain, try dulling your wit as well. Take command of the squads as they land and set up a position closer to the walls.'

'Where will you be, commander?'

'In the city,' said Sarpedon.

LYGRIS REACHED THE bridge just as Brother Feynin was shutting off the alarms. Feynin was one of the Soul Drinkers left on the *Brokenback* while Sarpedon led the rest to Raevenia. Lygris knew that, while they would not say so, they all wanted to be at Sarpedon's side, fighting whatever battle the planet might throw at them.

'What is it?' asked Lygris.

Feynin looked around from the bridge cogitator. A couple of other Soul Drinkers were on the bridge, examining pict screens or spools of printouts. Warning lights were flashing and the klaxons still echoed through the deck.

'Contacts,' said Feynin. 'In-system.'

'Contacts? From the warp?'

'There's no warp breach. I don't know where they came from.'

Lygris took over Feynin's position at the cogitator. If the bridge viewscreen had been repaired he could have had an overview of Raevenia's system in seconds, but had to make do with the streams of figures flickering down the pict screen in front of him. He stopped them and flicked through a few different screens.

'They were hiding in Raevenia's rings,' said Lygris.

'Queenings?' asked Feynin.

erals saluted as she ranks of ice and rock. A ship table. She had been wore simple blue- old to avoid any sen- holstered at her they-' loose. She looked. Lygris, leafing generals. Here, the

'Your report gine's General H

Lygris switch nnel. 'Commander?'

'Lygris?' said Sar news from orbit?'

[torn paper fragment overlapping text reads:] figures being spewed different and far enormous reserves of to face before the chains that old there be

'The last few reports have come in,' he said. 'None is less than three days old.'

'Do any agents still live elsewhere on Raevenia?' asked Dyrmida.

'It seems unlikely, your majesty. The last information we have is from one of our scouts near Fornow Harbour. He reports the Undying there in great numbers, and war machines converging on the city. Undying scouts were closing on his position when he transmitted. Quite possibly, he fell to them.'

'That puts them within a few days of Astelok,' said the jowly, powerfully built Damask, a general of the army, who had ridden with the cavalry in the wars that had been fought decades ago between Astelok and her fellow city-states of Raevenia. 'With Fornow fallen there won't be anything to stop them forcing one of the mountain passes.'

'What of elsewhere?' asked Dyrmida. 'The Lovinian Principalities? Krassus City?'

'Nothing,' replied Heynan, 'not since the Principalities reported the invaders coming from the sky.'

'I see,' said Dyrmida. 'Then the last of Raevenia's cities have fallen. We are alone. We, the people of this city, are what remains of the Selaacan Empire.'

A few of the less tactful generals exchanged looks.

'Do not pretend,' said Dyrmida, 'that we have not known this all along. When Selaaca fell silent, we knew it could come to this. We know that many worlds have fallen and we cannot assume any

others have been spared. Much as it pains us to accept it, much as the death toll must be beyond our understanding, it is the truth. The empire's last stand will fall upon us. The Undying have exterminated all the rest.'

Damask banged a fist on the map table. 'Then we will give these aliens the battle of their lives! The Undying will pay for every brick and cobble of Astelok! I will man the barricades myself and fight them until the last breath! I and my men will–'

'You will give us all glorious deaths, general?' interrupted Dyrmida. 'You accept the loss of Astelok and all who dwell in her?'

Damask did not answer. He glanced around the table for support, but none of his fellow officers spoke up.

'I intend,' said Dyrmida, 'to fight the Undying here, but, unlike General Damask, I do not intend to lose. I am willing to sacrifice Astelok, but not her people. We must evacuate the population to the space port and get them off the planet.'

'No army scout has returned from the Bladeleaf Glades for weeks,' said Heynan. 'That is less than half a days' march away from the road to the space port. We know there are Undying in the Glades, definitely their vanguard, maybe their main force.'

'There is no way,' said General Slake, another veteran of army command with a deep scar across his lips, 'that we can get the people down that road to the space port. Mustering the army to greet the

newcomers was risk enough. It would take a day at the very least to move the people to the space port, and the Undying could ambush at any time. Your majesty, it would be a massacre.'

'General Slake's words come belatedly,' said Damask grimly, 'but they are true. Give your people good deaths, your majesty. Do not let them die running.'

Dyrmida rose to her feet.

'We have all left it too late,' she said, 'to do what is right. We were afraid to flee our world, for our fellow Raevenians were standing and fighting, and we would not be the cowards who dared to survive. We feared the ignominy of limping back to our world after the Undying had been fought off, but now that will not happen. The Undying have won, and our world will fall. We have no choice over that, but we can choose whether our sons and daughters, our friends and loved ones, are on Raevenia when it happens. General Damask, I will not believe that any death, while denying the Undying their victory, is a bad death.'

Damask sat back in his chair. Only Heynan had little enough concern for his position to speak up.

'How, your majesty? How will we buy our people enough time to reach the space port?'

'Fight the Undying in the city,' replied Dyrmida. 'Draw them in. Force them to commit their main force to our streets. And keep them fighting long enough to get the people out.'

A few frustrated exhalations were just audible as the generals digested this. Dyrmida, ignoring them, stood and leaned over the map of Astelok.

'Here,' she said. 'As soon as we know which direction the Undying will take, we barricade the streets, and funnel the Undying into the Cemetery Quarter. Force them to fight us in the avenues between estates and basilicas, where their numbers cannot be brought to bear. Collapse buildings if need be. The good deaths you plead for, Damask, will be given to every soldier in the city, and you are welcome to join them at the barricades. The population will make it out while the Undying are tied up in the city.'

'Hear, hear!' said some of the generals, eager to show their loyalty even to the last.

'You expect much of the army,' said Heynan.

'Do you say our men cannot do it?' demanded Slake.

'I am saying their deaths may not be enough!' retorted Heynan. 'No one knows how many the Undying can bring to bear! Two hundred thousand men held the walls of Krassus City, and it fell overnight!'

'Then what would you do, Heynan?' demanded Dyrmida. 'How would you face the Undying?'

The words died in Heynan's throat. Any answer he had, withered away under Queen Dyrmida's gaze.

A commotion sounded at the back of the room. The generals and their officers turned to get a better look. From the dim doorway at the far side of the

map room stumbled a soldier, who had been posted there as a guard, clutching his arm. His gun was not in his hand and he lost his balance, scrabbling along the floor.

'I believe,' said a voice from the darkness, 'that the queen's plan is sound.'

Sarpedon emerged from the shadows, the spotlight surrounding the map table catching on the massive plates of his armour and the glossy chitin of his spider legs. The closest generals started out of their chairs, and weapons were drawn, aides pulling out rifles and pistols.

'Stay your weapons!' ordered Dyrmida. She stood up and addressed Sarpedon. 'You! How did you get in here?'

'Your men,' replied Sarpedon calmly, 'showed more enthusiasm than skill in trying to stop me. Fear not, I haven't killed anyone yet.' In one hand he held the rifle he had taken from the guard at the door. He cast it onto the floor. 'My Soul Drinkers, on the other hand, can do things your soldiers cannot.'

'Can you hold the city, Lord Sarpedon?' asked Dyrmida. 'Can you fight the Undying to a standstill, long enough for my people to escape to the spaceport?'

'We can.'

'Then I will ask you again. What do you want from us?'

The two locked stares across the map table for a long moment. The officers had not let their guard

down, and a dozen guns were still aimed at Sarpedon.

'Fuel,' said Sarpedon.

'Then you are stranded here,' said Dyrmida, 'and if you fight, you hope we will give it to you.'

'That is correct, your majesty.'

'Then why not simply take it by force?'

'Because,' said Sarpedon, 'we are not invaders. We are not murderers or thieves. We have our honour, too.'

'Good,' said Dyrmida, 'because if you had decided to simply take it, you would have incinerated yourselves trying to get through the defences. When my people are safe in the space port and the first ships are leaving, then we will give you the codes. Is that satisfactory?'

By way of an answer, Sarpedon walked closer to the table to get a better look at the map of Astelok. Having seen the city from orbit, the cemetery hills, spire-topped palaces and southern slums were familiar to him, not as works of architecture or places to live, but as playing pieces in the strategic game that would ensue if the city was invaded.

'A sound plan, your majesty,' said Sarpedon. 'These Undying will have to commit a massive force to break a determined force in the city's centre. Without my Space Marines, it will not work. With them, your people have a chance of deliverance.'

'Then you will fight?' asked General Heynan. 'You will help us?'

Sarpedon looked at him. Heynan shied away from the Space Marine's gaze.

'Both sides will help themselves,' said Sarpedon. 'We have the same objective, to escape this planet. The Undying stand in our way. Fighting them together is the only course that makes sense.'

'Then I have made my decision,' said Dyrmida. 'The Undying will be fought in the city, and held there so that the civilian population can be evacuated. Are there any further objections, my generals?'

A few of the generals exchanged looks. Most of them, however, kept their eyes on the mutant Space Marine that dwarfed them all.

'Good,' said Dyrmida. 'To your duties, men. Your queen has spoken.'

'What is fear? Fear is the absence of duty. Fear is what fills our minds unbidden when our thoughts turn from our obligations to the human race.'

Daenyathos, *Hammer of the Heretics*

CHAPTER NINE

'Perhaps I always knew,' said Queen Dyrmida, 'that it would happen during my reign.'

The entire city was visible from the graveyard upon the hill. Sarpedon saw how it had been built nestling between the hills at first, a fortified town whose walls still existed amid the palaces and monuments at its heart. Astelok had grown large and prosperous since. In the pre-dawn light, the movement of people was obvious, draining like blood through the veins of the city towards the gates to the south.

Queen Dyrmida sat on an old grave slab, some of her retainers and courtiers waiting a short distance away. She had called Sarpedon up here to organise the last few details of the coming battle.

'How could you be sure?' asked Sarpedon.

'Every monarch before me has believed the same thing. We must always be prepared for the death of that for which we are responsible. It is our way.'

'I have seen worlds die,' said Sarpedon. 'Too many people for me to imagine. Not one of them really believed that death would come for them. I do not think you can ever be truly prepared to see such destruction.'

'That, Commander Sarpedon, is because you were not born on Raevenia,' said the queen. 'A man's life does not mean anything if it is not married to a death of equal merit. A hero can be rendered a nothing and buried in a pit outside the walls, if he does not die a hero's death. A poor and worthless man can be buried up here, amid all its finery, if he dies well enough.'

'And a queen?'

Queen Dyrmida considered this.

'It is unlikely that I will be buried at all,' she said. 'That is a bad death indeed. Only if I am remembered can I expect to be anyone in death.'

'Dying on Raevenia must be an exacting task,' said Sarpedon.

'What of your people? How do they die?'

'In great numbers and ignorance.'

'They sound like bad deaths,' said the queen with a shake of her head.

'They are. That is why the Soul Drinkers no longer fight for the Imperium.'

Dyrmida looked out across the city. Units of Raevenian troops held several crossroads, ready to

slow down the advance of the Undying. The Soul Drinkers were concentrated around the centre of the city, where the relatively open spaces of parks and forums would funnel the Undying towards them.

'Your Soul Drinkers will bear the brunt of the battle,' said the queen. 'The majority of my army must secure the route to the space port.'

'Those are the kind of battles we were created to fight, your majesty.'

'You have not returned to your spaceship and abandoned us,' continued Dyrmida. 'You could have done so at any moment. I am not ignorant of that fact.'

'Being becalmed here is not an option for us. If you require us to fight if we are to escape, then we will fight.'

'There is more than that, Soul Drinker. The galaxy has failed us. It has failed you, too, and made you renegades. You claim to fight only for survival, but I think you are trying to prove something, too, even if only to yourself.'

'Do not be so certain, your majesty. We learned what happens when we fight to better the lot of the Imperium, and it did not end well for us.'

A messenger rode up on a horse, carrying a sheaf of reports. 'Your majesty. Dawn breaks and Imnis has sounded the forlorn hope.'

'Very good,' said Dyrmida. 'Commander, to your positions. I must deliver my people.'

Dyrmida was rapidly surrounded by her retainers for the short journey to the south gate, where tens

of thousands of people were now thronging. Sarpedon turned towards the north, and the battle for
Astelok began.

THE NORTHERN GATES of Astelok were opened just
before dawn. They were shod with brass that had
withstood sieges before, scarred by cannon and battering rams. They would not withstand this one.

The Queen's Own Cavalry galloped out. Led by
General Imnis, they were splendid with banners
and mirror-polished armour. Favours streamed
from the banner each wore on his back, embroidered with each man's personal heraldry. They were
composed of fifty volunteers. Far more had come
forward for the duty, but this death was denied to
most of them.

Imnis stopped his horse and raised his sabre, bellowing a challenge to the trees and undergrowth
covering the hills outside the city.

There only answer was wind and birdsong.

Imnis shouted again, cursing the cowardice of the
Undying and promising them dismal, forgotten
deaths that would condemn them to nothingness.

He heard nothing in return. Imnis galloped up to
the tree line, spitting curses.

A lance of emerald light leapt from the hillside
and skinned him alive in a split second. His flesh
was pared off him, layer by layer, leaving the front
half of his body a wet red mess stripped down to
the skeleton. He toppled from his saddle, and his

horse, a good chunk of its flank stripped away too, galloped wild in pain.

A shape rose from the trees. It was an Undying warrior, but it was not like the skeletal creatures the Raevenians had witnessed before. Its lower half was a slab of metal thrumming as it kept the warrior aloft. The warrior had one arm, the other, a cannon glittering with emerald fire. It fired again, and this time the beam punched right through the horse of one of the cavalrymen. The horse fell, dead before it hit the ground, and pinned the rider's leg under it.

More of the flying warriors rose above the trees, criss-crossing the clearing in front of the gates with blasts of green energy. Warriors stalked out of the tree line, a silent rank of them matching step as they advanced.

The cavalry charged, those at the front lowering their lances and those behind snapping off rifle shots. A warrior fell, face ruined. After a moment, it stood up again, falling back into step.

The first riders clashed with the warriors. Blue light burst where the power blades of their lances made contact, the energy fields tearing through metal. Automatic fire rattled into the Undying, and cascades of bullet casings rained down around the horses' hooves. An Undying warrior was carried up into the air, impaled on a lance, green fire bleeding from its chest. Others were trampled under hooves. A power sabre lashed out and cut a machine's head from its shoulders.

Green fire flashed. Men and horses fell, stripped to the bone so quickly that their bodies took a moment to start bleeding.

The ground shook. The charge faltered. The trees on the hillside began to fall, toppling as a great bulk forced its way through them.

One of the cavalrymen, in command after Imnis's death, called out for the sons of Raevenia to rejoice and die well.

A hundred Undying stepped in eerily perfect formation from the trees, grinning skulls reflecting the glowing power fields of the cavalry's lances. Bullets rained down into them, but fallen Undying simply stood again, and, those that did not, disappeared, replaced a moment later by another metallic warrior striding into the open.

The ranks of Undying opened fire as one. The cavalry disappeared in a mess of flayed flesh and bone. Horses, stripped in half, screamed out their final breaths as organs spilled out onto the bloody ground. Men died before they hit the ground, insides scooped out, reduced to fluttering scraps of skin and uniform.

Given the circumstances, they had died the best deaths they could hope for. The Raevenians watching from the walls took comfort in that.

Thousands of Undying followed the front ranks out of the trees. More flying warriors flanked them, and glittering scarabs scuttled through the grass around their feet. A great crashing could be heard,

and trees fell, scoring a deep line through the forest canopy, as something huge and powerful made its own path towards the northern gate.

Astelok prepared to die well.

'THE NORTHERN GATE just fell,' said Phol's voice over the vox. 'The Undying have massive infantry strength, thousands of them. They have flying support units, too, and something big with them, maybe a siege engine. The cavalry didn't even slow them down.'

Sarpedon glanced up. The Soul Drinkers' Thunderhawks were in the air, among them the one piloted by Brother Phol, acting as the Soul Drinkers' eyes as well as lending fire support.

Sarpedon was stationed with the majority of his Soul Drinkers towards the centre of the city. He was holding an intersection of two of Astelok's grandest streets, lined on each side by mansions and monuments like a canyon of marble. The Soul Drinkers were set up behind makeshift barricades in the street, or in the windows of the buildings. Sarpedon's post was in a semicircular war memorial, inscribed with thousands of names lost in some war between the cities of Raevenia, and crowned with statues of weary soldiers, on the corner of the two streets.

'Tell me when you can see this xenos machine,' voxed Sarpedon, 'and keep me appraised when you have a clear idea of their numbers.'

'Yes, commander. I'll stay over your position. By the hand of Dorn!'

'Trust in your bullets and blades, Brother Phol!' Sarpedon took stock of his command position. Squad Luko had taken up firing positions between the doleful statues, and the rest of the squad crouched in cover nearby, behind makeshift barricades across the street or in the doorways of mansions.

'What do they want with this city?' asked Scamander, who was stationed with Squad Luko where the short-range firepower he kept in his head had the best chance of coming into play. 'What is there on this planet they can't have got enough of?'

'They are machines, Brother Scamander,' said Sarpedon. 'They do not want anything, not as we do. They just conquer.'

Scamander was inexperienced, and he had stained his honour by siding with Eumenes in the Second Chapter War, but he had a quick mind, and he had dedicated his efforts to redeeming himself with the Chapter. His armour carried the gilded insignia of the Chapter Librarium; Scamander was a psyker, and Sarpedon could see his potential as living artillery.

'Targets in the city!' said Phol's voice over the vox. 'The first barricades are falling! The Raevenians are retreating to their second lines. The Undying are pouring in.'

'Lend your guns, Brother Phol, but do not risk the gunship. Soul Drinkers! The enemy is within the gates!'

A pall of smoke was gathering to the north: gunsmoke, burning buildings and the dust of collapsing buildings. Explosions rumbled as booby traps erupted among the abandoned buildings around the gate.

To Sarpedon, the sounds of war were as familiar as his own breathing, but he had never before heard thousands of footsteps, metal against cobbles, stamping through the city in perfect time.

TENS OF THE thousands of Undying made it through the Raevenian fire from the walls. They streamed through the northern gateway into Astelok. The crossfire that met them was terrific, thousands of Raevenian rifles and machine guns opening up as one. The first ranks of Undying were shredded beyond even their capacity to self-repair, but the Undying did not care about losses. More marched forwards, choking the gate with wreckage. A few moments later, the Undying war machine breached the walls.

It was shaped like a titanic metal-shod beetle, pulling itself along on its belly with thousands of legs that writhed along its sides. Its head was a huge maw, ringed with steel teeth, with power glowing in its throat. Scarabs crawled all over its surface, and behind its long segmented tail it left a deep furrow

in the ground as it drove forwards, flanked by the march of the Undying.

The machine's enormous bulk pushed down one of the gatehouses, and tonnes of rubble were sucked into its maw. The useless matter was siphoned off and spewed from vents along its sides as clouds of choking dust.

Men died in its path. The gate district was barren, the forums strewn with half-dissolved bodies and abandoned barricades. A basilica collapsed, detonated to slow the Undying advance with rubble, but the machine just dragged its bulk right through the ruins.

A few Raevenians, who had been wounded or who had run out of ammunition, had been cut off by the rapid Undying advance, and had not been able to give up their last few moments fighting. The Undying turned and herded them towards the giant machine. Some of them threw themselves on the bayonets on the Undying's xenos weapons. Others stumbled ahead of them into the machine's path. They disappeared into the machine's maw, sucked down into its throat.

They were denied the good deaths suffered by hundreds of other defenders. A death in defence of his home, upon the orders of his queen, was a worthwhile goal for a Raevenian's life. There were better, of course, but few men would ever have the chance to even witness them. Plenty of soldiers had asked for the honour of manning the front lines.

Plenty of them received their wish in the first few minutes of the battle for Astelok, stripped to the bone by lances of green fire, or chewed into pulp by hordes of scarabs.

Some of them did not die. A man dragged himself along the street, his leg a bloody length of sinew and bone. Another held in the wet heaving mass of his chest, gasping for breath and bracing his gun one-handed for a few more shots. Another curled into a ball to keep the scarabs off his face, howling as their mandibles burrowed through his back.

The machine harvested them too, as the Undying threw them into its throat, or it simply rolled over them as they tried to crawl out of its way. More good deaths went begging.

The dust began to fill the city like fog. The Undying marched through it, into valleys of apartment blocks that had previously been crammed with refugees. Raevenian sharpshooters aimed through the windows, and sniper bullets punched through metal skulls. A flying warrior fell, sheared through the spine, its anti-grav unit cutting out, sending it tumbling into the gutter. More flyers fired their cannon up at the buildings, boring through walls and the men sheltering behind them. Warriors sent fire spattering up, not missing a step as they advanced.

ONE RAEVENIAN SNIPER shot down a flying machine, plugging it clean through the head. He fell back into shelter, as return fire from the warriors chewed away

at the wall below the window he had used as a vantage point. He was a veteran, his aim honed by sniping birds and stags in Raevenia's forests. The inhuman march of the Undying had not fazed him. He had been raised to kill, and whether it was prize game or alien machines did not make any difference in his mind.

Another soldier ran into the apartment behind him. The place was still scattered with furniture and belongings, the refugees having abandoned anything that could not be carried in a backpack. The soldier was tattered and bloody, wounded by the Undying fire streaking up into the buildings.

'We've got to get out of this building,' said the veteran. 'Keep moving. I'll be right behind you.'

The soldier didn't reply. He slumped against the doorframe. The veteran ran to support him and took the man's weight on his shoulder.

'We'll get you out,' he said to the wounded man. 'You can't die yet. Queen's orders, eh?'

The wounded man turned his head to look at the veteran. His face was a ruin of torn skin. His eyes were lit from behind with green fire. His face split open and bloodstained metal leered through it.

The veteran fought to get out of the machine's grip. Metal claws slid through the dead soldier's skin.

The veteran's scream was lost in the roar of the harvester as it ground through the streets below.

* * *

FROM THE WINDOW of the southern palace, Queen Dyrmida watched another pall of dust billow up above the city. Another building in the north of Astelok had collapsed.

The Undying weren't just killing her city. They were dismembering it before her eyes.

'We have to go, your majesty,' said Lieutenant Kavins beside her. 'The civilians can't be held here any longer.'

He was right. The refugees cramming the southern half of Astelok were beginning to panic as the Undying approached. Most of them had never seen the Undying, and had built them up as ghosts or daemons from the underworld, inhuman and unstoppable, who inflicted fates worse than death on their victims. Those who had seen the Undying, in the fall of cities and settlements scattered across Raevenia, had terrors of their own, memories of green fire eyes and skeletal killers that never stopped. Religion came quickly to people watching their world being devoured, and plenty of the refugees whispered that the Undying had been sent by the gods to punish Raevenia for her people's impiety.

The southern gate was the largest in the city walls, flanked by memorials to the Raevenians that had died to defend Astelok in ages past. People thronged the thoroughfare in front of it, and soldiers on the battlements had their guns trained on the crowds ready to fire if they turned violent.

'Then we must put trust in our people,' said Dyrmida. 'Open the gates. Make sure the troops keep them from stampeding.'

'Yes, your majesty,' said Kavins. 'The transports are waiting for you. We should get you out of the city as soon as possible.'

'Wait a while,' said Dyrmida. 'I will not flee my city ahead of my people.'

Kavins signalled the soldiers holding the gate-house, from the palace balcony, and the gates began to grind open. The crowd surged forwards, and soldiers held them back, yelling orders at the crowd. Women and children were weeping, screaming, yelling prayers and spreading rumours of the Undying closing in.

These were the people for whom Queen Dyrmida was responsible. It was a great burden to bear. If she failed them here, they would die, all of them.

The first columns of citizens were moved through the gates. Some were old or infirm, and were left behind. Others bulled their way forward and were clubbed with rifle butts to keep them in line.

The sound was terrible: thousands of voices tinged with panic and desperation. It would take almost nothing to send them boiling over: a stray shot, a glimpse of the Undying, even just a wrong word shouted in fear.

It had to be this way, however. An hour before, the chances of the Undying ambushing a convoy of fleeing refugees were too high. Now, it was less, still high, but low enough to give them hope. That hope had been bought with the lives of Raevenians dead and yet to die, and Dyrmida had no choice but to grasp it and let it play out until the end.

'My people!' she called from the balcony. 'We will be delivered! Trust in me and in our soldiers! Believe, and be calm!'

Eyes fell on her. She recognised the fashions of many other cities amongst those of Astelok. Some of them had been enemies of Astelok in times past. Now, there were no cities. There was just Raevenia.

A tremendous roar went up from the north. Dyrmida saw the spires of the Dawning Palace falling, clouds of white marble dust swallowing the pinnacles where Dyrmida had once held court. The Dawning Palace was close to the centre of the city, and it was one of the most powerful symbols of Astelok's culture, of its past. With the Dawning Palace fallen, the rest of Astelok could not be far behind.

'Fear not!' shouted Dyrmida as panic rippled through the crowds. 'They will not reach us! This I swear!'

* * *

SARPEDON SAW THE first of the towers falling. The palace just ahead was perhaps the grandest in the city, its slender towers of rose-coloured sandstone defining Astelok's skyline. Now one of those towers collapsed across the road ahead, spilling hundreds of tonnes of rubble into the streets. For a moment, some of the palace's finery could be glimpsed: torn tapestries, gilded portrait frames, painted wood furniture. They all disappeared in the churning mass of stone.

'Salk!' yelled Sarpedon into the vox. 'Fall back! Fall back!'

'On it,' replied Salk briskly. Sarpedon could see Salk's tactical squad sprinting across the street as the palace behind them collapsed. One tower fell towards them, fracturing as it piled into the street. Hunks of broken stone slammed into the street a few metres behind Salk's squad, and the Soul Drinkers were swallowed by the tremendous flood of dust erupting from the palace's torn foundations.

'Phol,' voxed Sarpedon. 'Where is their siege engine?'

'Still heading right for you,' replied Phol from the Thunderhawk overhead. 'I'm losing a visual on it. There's too much dust.'

'Soul Drinkers!' yelled Sarpedon. 'Guns up!'

A couple of Raevenian soldiers, fleeing the destruction, ran between the wings of the mansion that made up one part of the crossroads. Their

shapes became dim, and then disappeared, as the bank of dust rolled over them.

'Brothers, the siege engine is our target!' ordered Sarpedon. 'If we are to hold the Undying in this city, we must strike at the heart of their attack! Let us see how these xenos fight when their enemies do not flee before their war machine!'

'Nothing like the spirit of improvisation, commander,' said Captain Luko.

'Take the enemy's strength and turn it into their weakness,' replied Sarpedon. 'These were the words of Daenyathos.'

The dust rolled over Sarpedon. The crossroads and the war memorial became a pit of shadow. Even to a Space Marine's enhanced eyes the dust was impenetrable.

'Commander, I've lost you,' voxed Phol from above.

'Keep circling,' said Sarpedon. 'Keep low. Don't give them an easy target. They might still be able to see you.'

'Novitiate!' said Librarian Tyrendian, who was sheltering in the memorial alongside Squad Luko. 'To my side. Prepare!'

'Yes, Librarian,' replied Scamander. 'I am ready.' Scamander's gauntlets were glowing, ruddy in the murk, and Sarpedon could feel the heat coming off them.

Sarpedon heard the tramp of metal feet on stone. The ground groaned with the weight of the

war machine. A few voices yelled out, soldiers trying to locate their comrades or crying in pain.

'Coming in on your position,' voxed Salk. 'Hold fire!' Squad Salk emerged from the fog and huddled down in front of the memorial.

Sarpedon looked out over the top of the memorial's wall. He could see a few metres down the street, and then just seething darkness.

Then pinpoints of green fire: Undying warriors, hundreds upon hundreds of them, advancing down the road, between the mansions and across the sculpted gardens.

The war engine bellowed again, throwing out a dark pall of ground-up city that smothered the street in black as if a deeper night was falling. A scream was cut short.

'Soul Drinkers!' voxed Sarpedon. 'We cannot kill all the Undying, but we can hurt them. Our target is the war machine!'

He waited a moment more. He could make out the outlines of the Undying warriors. Their weapons were glowing with pent-up energy as they searched for targets. This window, when the Soul Drinkers could see the Undying but the Undying could not see them, would last only a few moments more.

'Charge!' yelled Sarpedon, and vaulted over the memorial wall.

A lightning bolt leapt over his shoulder and blew a warrior apart right in front of Sarpedon. Sarpedon

didn't have to turn to see it had come from the hand of Tyrendian, whose psychic power took a most direct and destructive form. Sarpedon ran into the gap opened up in the Undying ranks, and slammed his axe through the chest of one of them before its electronic brain had reacted.

The Axe of Mercaeno was a force weapon, tuned in to the wielder's psychic power so that he could focus it into the blade and tear the soul right out of an enemy. The Undying had no souls to destroy, so Sarpedon had to rely on pure strength to drive the axe through them. Fortunately, strength was something he had never lacked.

He struck a skull from its shoulders, and stabbed a leg through the abdomen of another Undying, severing its thick steel spine. Squad Luko and Squad Salk were right behind him, blazing at point-blank range with rapid-firing bolters. Soul Drinkers advanced on either side, and Sarpedon heard the roar of jump pack jets as assault squads leapt over the front lines and into the Undying beyond.

The robotic nature of the Undying was not a strength. It was a weakness. They were tough and fearless, but they had no capacity for imagination. They could not react, except to the commands wired into their machine minds. They had come to this battle ready to fight Raevenians, brave but fallible humans who panicked and ran, who faltered when faced with a wall of metal bodies. They had not been ready for the Space Marines.

Sarpedon was at full tilt, slamming into the warriors and bowling them aside. One of the large floating spiders, the same kind he had dispatched at the white city, loomed through the dust, the lenses studding its head swivelling to focus on him. Blasts of bolter and plasma fire hammered into it from Squad Luko, and Luko himself ran beneath the stricken machine and disembowelled it with a slash of his lightning claws. Sarpedon could see the trails of the jump packs, and hear chainswords against metal as the assault squads went into the fray. There was bolter fire, everywhere, criss-crossing in white trails as they ripped through the pall of dust.

The harvester bellowed. Buildings collapsed in its wake.

'Forward!' yelled Sarpedon. 'Take the war engine! Forward!'

The great dark circle of the maw pushed through the dust. It was bigger than Sarpedon had imagined, too big to fit into the grand street, and it ground its way through the buildings on either side to make passage for itself. It was a monstrous vortex of gnashing metal. It was like the eye of death itself.

'Get onto the rooftops!' shouted Sarpedon into the vox. 'Assault squads, jump! The rest, into the buildings and up!'

Undying warriors were converging in front of the harvester to fend off the attackers. Sarpedon

scuttled sideways to reach the front of a law court that took up one side of the street. The building was already shuddering as the harvester chewed through the far end. Squad Luko was already entering it, shooting out windows and kicking in the main doors. Sarpedon jumped onto the wall, finding purchase with his talons and running up the vertical surface. Undying warriors, bent and fast wielding claws, like the machines from the forest palace, were following him up the wall or emerging from the windows. One of them wore the skin of a dead Raevenian, making for a horrible bloody parody of a human form. Sarpedon paused to take aim, and blew one of its legs off with a bolter shot. Bolter fire from inside the building threw another off the wall.

Sarpedon reached the roof. Deep cracks were running across the walls and roof of the law court, and the whole building leaned under the advancing weight of the harvester. The first Soul Drinkers were emerging onto the roof.

Sarpedon could see the main bulk of the harvester now. It was immense, like a gigantic beetle with a carapace of bullet-scarred metal. It was bigger even than an Imperial super-heavy tank. Power glowed green beneath its overlapping armour plates.

Techmarine Lygris was on the roof.

'Lygris!' shouted Sarpedon over the din of the collapsing building. 'I need you inside!'

'Very well, commander! Open the door!' replied Lygris.

Sarpedon ran to the edge of the roof and jumped. He landed on the hull of the harvester, just behind the lip of its maw. Lygris followed him. Sarpedon, whose legs and talons held him firm to the hull, held out a hand, and caught Lygris's wrist to drag him up onto the upper surface, which was almost horizontal. The harvester swayed and juddered beneath them. Members of Squad Luko were making the jump, too, or crouching at the edge of the roof to grab an edge of armour plate and clamber their way up. Sarpedon saw that Soul Drinkers were making it onto the machine from the opposite roofs, too, and more were on the rooftops up ahead waiting for their turn to make the jump.

'The carapace is too tough,' said Lygris. 'Can we get a plasma weapon up here to blast through?'

'Allow me,' said Scamander. The Librarian had climbed across from the buildings opposite. Tyrendian was still on the roof behind him, shattering an Undying warrior with a well-aimed lightning bolt. Scamander knelt on the hull and put both his hands on one of the armour plates. His gauntlets glowed, and, as they drew heat from the rest of him, ice crystallised on his backpack and the armour of his legs.

The armour plate glowed as Scamander poured psychic heat into it. The edges and the areas beneath his palms began to run molten. Scamander

pulled, and the plate came away, the half-melted metal stretching like sinews. Lygris and Scamander grabbed it, too, and between them they pulled it clear and threw it aside.

The hole Scamander had opened up was big enough for a couple of Soul Drinkers to enter. The cross-section of the hull was riddled with glowing green filaments, humming with the power they channelled around the machine. Sarpedon could see enough room, inside, among the pulsing machinery and power conduits for a Space Marine to move.

Sarpedon led the way in. The Soul Drinkers gathering on the hull followed him, or lined up behind Scamander as he went to work on another armour plate. Many of them covered the machine's hull, sniping at the Undying trying to clamber up at them, or spearing the many scarabs on its back with combat knives.

Sarpedon wiped away the dust that had caked around his eyes. It was cramped inside the harvester, but he could move if he crouched down on his haunches. He pushed between a pair of humming power conduits and saw the chamber opening up before him.

Hundreds of humans, Raevenians, hung from racks on the walls of the cylindrical hull. Their faces were covered by silver masks, like stylised, expressionless faces. A walkway led between the racks of captives. Undying, bigger than the warriors with

reinforced spines to take the weight of their enormous cannon, patrolled the interior to fend off boarders.

'Now?' asked Lygris behind him.

'Now we kill it,' said Sarpedon.

'We are born naked and defenceless, save for a shield around our souls that all humans are honour-bound to maintain. That veneer of disgust, that armour of hate, is all that stands between us and the endless death of corruption.'

Daenyathos, *The Artemesion Campaigns*

CHAPTER TEN

Another ship of the Fleet Minor exploded, a brief nuclear flash sucked dead by the cold of the void. Glittering debris rained out from the place where the troop ship had been. Among the debris were the charred bodies of the tech-guard who had been stationed on the ship.

Asclepian Alpha was trailing ruined hull plates attached by blackened strings of vented plasma, one side of its hull stripped down to the personnel decks by the massive ordnance fired at it by one of the necron cruisers. Half its crew were dead, dissolved away in the blast, or thrown out into space when the decks decompressed. A skeleton crew and the escort ship's machine-spirit were all that were keeping it going, and it shuddered along on a wayward course as if its mind was crumbling, along with its hull.

The Mechanicus fleet was down three major ships and a few dozen of the Fleet Minor. The only equipment salvaged from the *Ferrous* was that contained in Magos Vionel's body, and, without the factory ship, the Mechanicus fleet lacked the capacity to refine fuel and produce spare parts in an emergency. With every auxiliary ship that died, the fleet became a little blinder to the space around it.

Magos Crystavayne, transferred by shuttle from the *Defence of Caelano Minoris*, entered the bridge of the *Antithesis*. The specimen vials hanging at his waist like a soldier's grenades clinked as he walked, and the caduceus embroidered on the hem and cuffs of his robes designated his role as a magos biologis. The command throne at the pinnacle of the bridge was empty, so Crystavayne reported to the makeshift briefing area where Voar had presented what little intelligence he had on the necrons.

Several tech-priests and senior menials were working in the briefing area, poring over countless tactical maps with compasses and quills, or flicking the stones across abaci to perform long strings of calculations.

'Where is the archmagos?' asked Crystavayne.

One of the tech-priests looked up from his map, on which he had already inscribed a web of arcs and angles. 'The archmagos has retired to his laboratory.'

'His laboratory?' retorted Crystavayne. 'We are at battle stations!'

'Nevertheless, magos, he has left fleet command with the bridge. He has requested the magi assist in maintaining evasive manoeuvres.'

'This is intolerable.' Crystavayne waved an impatient hand, its fingers tipped with syringes and the tip of a retracted bone-saw glinting in his palm. He was about to say more, but he bit back his words. A magos criticising a superior was on shaky ground as it was, and doing so in front of an inferior would certainly result in punishment. 'Then I shall assist him in his laboratory.'

'The archmagos has requested that he remain undisturbed, and has refused in advance any offers of assistance.'

Crystavayne, who was equipped to be the finest laboratory researcher in the fleet, fought down words of frustration again. 'Then what am I to do?'

'You have an enhanced logic centre,' replied the tech-priest. 'We lack computing power. We need your help.'

Crystavayne picked up the map the tech-priest had been working on. The locations and paths of the fleet's ships were plotted out many hours in advance, and notes on possible enemy movements were scrawled in every available space.

'What are the archmagos's orders?' he asked.

'Full evasion,' said the tech-priest.

'Not to attack?'

'No, magos.'

Crystavayne looked at some of the other routes being plotted by the tech-priests and menials. The machine-spirit of the *Antithesis* was working on it, too, as evidenced by the metres of printout being carried by menials.

Crystavayne visualised the position of the Mechanicus fleet, the formations of the remaining Asclepian escorts, the *Defence* and the *Antithesis*, the *Constant* and the swarm of the Fleet Minor.

Then he added the necron ships. They were faster and more agile than their size suggested, but the cruisers moved in a stilted, repetitive pattern, turning on exact axes and in unchanging increments of degrees. The biggest necron ship was slower and lumbering, with the huge turning sphere required to bring its main weapons to bear. The second part of the necron fleet, the one that had emerged from behind the planet's moon, was faster, capable of sudden manoeuvres beyond any Imperial ship, but they were predictable, and in any mathematical system that predictability could only lead to one conclusion.

Crystavayne drew a long quill from his robes. He grabbed a sheet of parchment and began to draw on it: tiny annotations in machine-code and ruler-straight lines intersected by perfect arcs. The solution was a ballet, something pure and beautiful. The necron fleet was more dangerous than the Mechanicus fleet, but its only objective was to

destroy the Mechanicus. That forced it into certain manoeuvres, for it had to bring its weapons to bear. The Mechanicus fleet, meanwhile, had only to survive. That gave it far more options. It also had the Fleet Minor and the Asclepian escorts, which, in terms of cold mathematics, were expendable.

Crystavayne had plotted an impossibly complicated pattern in a few moments, his logic engine covering the parchment in geometric shorthand for a tight helix of movement. The Mechanicus fleet would present its least valuable ships to the enemy guns, and then turn in on itself, diving through its own wake before the necron gunners could respond. Any individual ship's course would appear to be a series or random loops and twists. Taken as a whole, it was breathtaking. It only existed in the data medium of Crystavayne's logic implant and in what remained of his human imagination, but it would work. That was certain. It would buy the Mechanicus more time than any Navy general or xenos pirate could squeeze from the approaching necrons.

'Here,' said Crystavayne. Sweat was running down his face, and, for a moment, he cursed the symptom of human weakness. 'Get this to the fleet captains. Execute immediately.'

The tech-priest looked down at the dense geometry of Crystavayne's plan.

'Right away, magos,' he said, and began barking orders to the other tech-priests and menials to turn

the plan into a series of manoeuvres and transmit it to the rest of the fleet.

Crystavayne's pride died down. Emotions were subsiding faster and faster since his last cortical implant. He wondered if he would miss them.

One remained: a faint anger, mixed with frustration, that the fleet's commander had not attended to this crucial matter himself.

'Whatever task takes so much attention, archmagos,' muttered Crystavayne, 'I pray only that the Omnissiah's work is being done.'

LIBRARIAN TYRENDIAN FURROWED his brow, and thrust a hand at the Undying advancing along the war engine's main chamber. Caged lightning arced from his fingers. Shards of hot metal and shattered exoskeleton flew. Green crystal shattered, loosing more bolts of light, emerald this time.

Imprisoned bodies fell, torn from the walls by the discharged power. The walkways along the centre of the chamber buckled, spilling the Undying warriors into the machinery below.

Tyrendian leapt from the gantry above onto a remaining walkway. A squad of the Undying stood before him, bracing themselves as they levelled their cannon at him. Tyrendian yelled, and power crackled around him, blazing from his eyes and grounding off his fingers. He hurled lightning like a javelin, blowing the walkway apart. Undying bodies flew. One cracked against the wall, bringing

down a few human captives with it. Another was impaled on the twisted guardrail, green sparks spitting from the wound.

An Undying clambered back onto the walkway behind Tyrendian, its ruptured torso self-repairing, green fire blazing in its eyes. With its free hand, it brought its double-barrelled gun up and aimed it at Tyrendian's back.

The Undying bent backwards as its spine glowed dull red, and then bright cherry. The heat spread to its chest and neck, and then to its skull. Enormous heat glowed inside its head, and its skull split down the middle, exposing the circuitry of its xenos mind.

Tyrendian glanced back to see Scamander behind him, his armour caked in ice crystals, and his breath misting white. His gauntlets were glowing hot and hissing.

'Good kill,' said Tyrendian.

Soul Drinkers were leaping down to what remained of the walkways. Sarpedon scuttled along the wall, pausing to examine one of the prisoners. Its face was obscured by the alien mask, and tubes snaked into its veins and under its skin. It was a man, in clothes suggesting it was a farmer or a hunter.

Ahead of the main chamber was a section crammed with machines that sorted out whatever was swallowed by the harvester's maw, and either added it to the prisoner racks with long articulated

arms, or threw it into grinders to be spewed from the war engine's vents. There was nothing that way.

The other end of the chamber was the destination of the thick glowing power cables leading from the capacitors beneath the walkways.

'There,' said Lygris as Sarpedon climbed down the wall beside him. 'Lots of power headed that way.'

Tyrendian looked around from the smouldering remains of the final Undying.

'More Undying will be upon us soon,' he said. 'They know we are here.'

'Can you bring this monstrosity down?' Sarpedon asked the Techmarine.

'If there's a cogitator here,' said Lygris, 'I can interface with it and do what damage I can.'

'And if there isn't?'

'I always have faith in explosives, commander.'

'Commander!' said Sergeant Salk's voice over the vox. Salk was up on the hull of the harvester, guarding the makeshift entrances Scamander had opened. 'The Undying are sending their quick ones, the climbers! They're coming in fast!'

'Hold until they're close, and fall back inside,' said Sarpedon. 'You're buying us time.'

'Yes, commander!' Bolter fire drummed away over the vox as Salk's squad levelled another volley at the Undying.

'On me!' cried Sarpedon, and led the Soul Drinkers over the edge of the walkway onto the capacitors filling the lower half of the chamber.

They thrummed with power, the note low enough to vibrate the breastplate of fused ribs in Sarpedon's chest. A few chains of bolter fire rattled off as repairing Undying rose up from between the capacitors, and the ruined Undying phased out as they hit the chamber's curved metallic floor.

Tyrendian was just behind Sarpedon.

'You did admirably back there, Librarian,' said Sarpedon.

'My duty done is its own reward,' replied Tyrendian. 'The new boy is proving his worth.'

'I just wish these damnable things had souls,' said Sarpedon. He was the most powerful of the Chapter's Librarians, probably the most powerful the Chapter had ever possessed, but his telepathic assaults were worthless against the alien machines.

'I am grateful,' said Tyrendian, 'that they do not.'

Lygris forced open a hatchway guarding the way into the next chamber, towards the harvester's tail. Thick power conduits curved around him, blinking with emerald pulses of energy. Beyond it, a powerful greyish light shone and the chamber was thrown into extremes of light and shadow.

Lygris, bathed in light, stepped forwards to stand before a huge cube of crystal suspended in a spherical chamber ahead of him. Light crackled off it, but the crystal itself was pure black, as if

light could not escape its surface, creating a sur-
real silhouette in the centre of the glare.

'This is the device that runs the war machine,' said
Lygris, 'Its data medium. I can interface with this.

Sarpedon could see glints of silver behind Lyrgris
as the fast-moving Undying skirmishers ran down
the walls, leaping between the captives as bolter fire
burst around them.

'Firing lines!' called Captain Luko. The Soul
Drinkers knelt down in regimented firing lines
alongside Sarpedon, ready to pour volley fire into
approaching attackers.

'Do it, Lygris,' said Sarpedon, 'and quickly, if you
please.'

Lygris placed a hand on the surface of the black
crystal. The darkness seemed to seep into him, covering him in shadow. A dataprobe in his palm
pierced the crystal, and the techmarine's body
jerked as power and information ricocheted around
his mind.

'Keep talking to me, Lygris!' shouted Sarpedon.
'Stay with us!'

Luko yelled an order, and dozens of bolters
opened up. Undying on the walls were blown
apart. Some fell, phasing out before they hit the
ground; others clung grimly to the caged prisoners,
ducking down amongst them to self-repair. A terrible rain of body parts fell as the captives were struck
by fire. A few whole bodies came loose and clattered down among the machinery.

The prisoners were dead, Sarpedon told himself, or as good as. Even if there was still some life left in their minds, they were better off with that spark extinguished.

Or, at least, he hoped so.

'I'm in!' came a cry from Lygris, strangled as if in fear.

Lygris fell limp as the black crystal pulsed. Tongues of black light licked off it.

'Close order!' shouted Sarpedon above the gun-fire. 'Rapid fire!'

Volley after volley of bolter fire poured into the shadows between the capacitors. Undying fell and rose up again, some struck down three or four times before they phased out. Sarpedon snapped shots upwards, shooting down the skirmishing Undying skittering along the walls. One dropped into the midst of the Soul Drinkers, and Tyrendian drew his power sword, spinning into a reverse thrust to drive the blade through the alien's chest. Another, one of its blade-arms blown off, clattered to the ground. Sarpedon reared up over it, and stabbed the talon of his bionic front leg through its skull.

'Lygris!' voxed Sarpedon. 'Talk to me, brother!'

The only sound from Lygris's vox was rapid breathing.

Squad Salk was fighting its way down through the ruined walkways. Salk himself cracked an Undying in the jaw with the butt of his bolter, jabbed the

barrel into the alien's midriff, and blew its spine out of its back with a burst of fire. He threw the remains off the walkway, and jumped down after it, the rest of his squad following him.

'Commander!' voxed Salk. 'We cannot stay long. The aliens are converging on us. They're diverting their main force to protect this machine.'

'Then the plan is working,' replied Sarpedon. 'Brother Lygris! We have no time. Whatever you are doing, do it quickly!'

Sarpedon risked a glance back to the chamber. Lygris lay at the foot of the crystal, one hand attached to its surface by the dataprobe. He was convulsing. Blood was running down his chin.

'Brother Lygris! Techmarine, answer me!' There was still no answer. Sparks burst around the dataprobe in Lygris's finger, and power flashed behind his eyelids.

'Damnation!' Sarpedon switched to the vox. 'Salk! Melta-bombs on the capacitors, long fuse! We will bring the fire to them!'

'Yes, commander!' came Salk's reply.

'Captain Luko!' ordered Sarpedon. 'Hold the line!'

'A pleasure!' said Luko, his voice distorted by the hammering of gunfire over the vox.

Sarpedon turned away from the gun-line and ran into the crystal chamber. Lygris was still shuddering. Blood was bubbling between his lips and the skin around his eyes, and the collar of his armour

was burning. Sarpedon grabbed Lygris's wrist and yanked the dataprobe out of the crystal.

Lygris gurgled an incoherent cry, blood slopping down the front of his breastplate.

'Apothecary!' voxed Sarpedon. 'Where are you?'

'Still outside,' came the crackling reply from Apothecary Pallas. 'There was no way onto the machine. I'm towards its rear. The Undying are everywhere.'

'We're getting off this machine,' said Sarpedon. 'I need your assistance as soon as we are out. Brother Lygris is wounded.'

'How badly?' asked Pallas.

'He's bitten off his tongue.' Sarpedon hefted Lygris onto his shoulder. 'We have encountered a moral threat. I fear the worst wounds are to his soul.'

'Commander! Melta-bombs set!' came Salk's vox from behind Sarpedon. 'Three minutes before the capacitors go up!'

'Luko! Fall back to me and prepare to breach!'

Scamander scrambled into the crystal chamber. His gauntlets were smoking, and ice flaked off the rest of his armour as he moved.

'Allow me,' he said. He planted his hands against the rear wall of the crystal chamber.

Sarpedon noticed the crystal. The previously flawless surface was mottled and dull, as if some disease had taken control of it and spread milky stains like cataracts across its surface. Whatever Lygris had done, the war machine had suffered.

Luko led the Soul Drinkers into a tight line in front of the entrance to the crystal chamber. Beyond them, more Undying were converging. The Soul Drinkers were dragging a couple of wounded battle-brothers; even power armour was vulnerable to being ripped away by the bursts of green fire raining down from the Undying. Many other Astartes around Luko were missing chunks of armour, cores bored from shoulder pads, or greaves stripped down to bloody flesh.

Wires shorted around Scamander as the rear wall melted.

'Novitiate!' shouted Tyrendian. 'Stay your power! You will kill yourself!'

Scamander stumbled backwards. Tyrendian ran forwards and caught Scamander before he fell, lowering him to the floor.

'Someone take him,' said Tyrendian, the pure white light of a lightning bolt forming in his fist.

One of Squad Luko dragged Scamander onto his shoulder. Tyrendian turned to the half-melted wall, and hurled the bolt right into it. The flash was so powerful that even a Space Marine's augmented eyes were blinded for a split second. When vision returned, the wall was gone, the melted mass blown outwards by the force of the lightning. Through it could be seen the dust-choked gloom of the streets outside.

'Good work, Librarian,' said Sarpedon. 'Soul Drinkers! Fall back and out of this place!'

The Soul Drinkers charged out of the harvester. The Undying were on every side, but if there was one thing that Daenyathos had taught the old Chapter millennia ago, it was how a Soul Drinker could turn retreat into attack. Tyrendian hurled another bolt that blew an Undying off its feet, and Luko led the rest of the Soul Drinkers in opening fire as soon as they were clear of the harvester. The weight of gunfire threw Undying to the ground, and beat the xenos back into the surrounding buildings.

'Thirty seconds, my brothers!' shouted Sergeant Salk.

'Get clear!' ordered Sarpedon. The Soul Drinkers scattered, firing all the time, heading for the cover of half-collapsed buildings along the side of the street.

One side of the Undying harvester swelled up and burst, spewing flame and wreckage. Shards of hot metal whickered around the street, ricocheting off walls. Another explosion blew the tail off, and the blazing cone of segmented metal rocketed past Sarpedon, embedding itself in the building opposite, and bringing the walls down.

Smoke and rubble filled the street. It was denser and blacker than the dust that had heralded the harvester's approach. Everything was darkness and noise, dominated by the ear-splitting howl of the harvester imploding.

Sarpedon looked up from cover. Through the murk, he could make out the burning wreckage of

the harvester. The capacitors, with their stores of power, had been breached, and that power had torn the harvester apart.

Apothecary Pallas and the Soul Drinkers who had been caught outside the harvester approached through the rubble.

'Commander,' said Pallas. 'Let me see him.'

Sarpedon hauled Lygris off his shoulder and laid him at Pallas's feet. Pallas's narthecium gauntlet unfolded into a probe that he inserted into a port on the forearm of Lygris's armour.

'I will do what I can,' said Pallas, 'but our brother is in a grave state.'

Sarpedon nodded, glanced down at Lygris, and turned away to look up at the sky just visible through the smoke. 'Brother Phol, what news of the xenos advance?'

The vox crackled with static for a few moments in reply.

'The xenos are diverting towards you,' said Phol's voice. 'Their forces to the west of the city breached the walls to defend the harvester. The civilians are on their way out of the south gate.'

'Then we are successful?'

'So far, commander.'

'Close in and lend us your fire, brother.' Sarpedon switched to the all-squads frequency. 'Soul Drinkers! On me, my brothers! Let us sell these aliens the streets of Astelok at a price they cannot pay!'

Pallas carried Lygris as the Soul Drinkers grouped up. The smoke swirled in the wash from the Thunderhawk's engines, and the gunship's heavy bolters opened up, stitching explosive fire through the Undying. The Soul Drinkers' fire opened up, too, punctuated by Tyrendian's bolts of lightning.

Cold and fast, just as Daenyathos had once written, the Soul Drinkers sent Undying phasing out on every side as they advanced towards Astelok's south gate.

'The legends, the superstitions of your Chapter, are nothing more than stories to the ears of outsiders. But you know they are the soul of your Chapter, the collective admonishments and inspirations of every battle-brother who has gone before you.'

Daenyathos, *The Borders of Moral Endurance*

CHAPTER ELEVEN

QUEEN DYRMIDA WATCHED from the walls of the space port. Her retinue of soldiers had known better than to dissuade her from putting herself at risk, She had left the relative safety of the command centre to take to the battlements. It was her duty to watch Astelok die, for she had made the decision to sacrifice it.

A dark pall rose over the city. Most of it was dust from the terrible path the Undying war engine had chewed through Astelok's heart, but there was also smoke and flame, and bursts of green light like lightning. Most of the palaces of the city centre were obscured by the dust, but the few she could see were in ruins, their walls pushed in and their roofs sagging.

'Your majesty?' said Kavins, who had been chosen for the duty of accompanying the queen to the top

of the walls. 'The people have asked for you to address them.'

'What can I say to them?' she asked. 'That their homes are destroyed? That the troops that stayed behind are dead? They already know those things. And what of the future? Should I tell them that we will depart for a safe haven that may not exist?'

'I do not know, your majesty,' said Kavins uncertainly.

Dyrmida waved a hand dismissively. 'These are not matters for anyone to concern themselves with save myself. It is my responsibility. Of course I must speak to my people. They must be calmed and reassured. It is the least they deserve from me.'

Astelok's space port was a series of huge rockcrete circles, covered in docking clamps and fuelling rigs, and marked with warning strips corresponding to the landing gear of various types of Selaacan spacecraft. Hangars for equipment and vehicles were dotted around the space port, and a tall multi-spired building contained the command centre, which, in peacetime, saw orbital controllers guiding down trading and passenger craft, welcoming them to Astelok in the name of the queen.

Now the space port was a miserable makeshift city. Maybe three hundred thousand people were making their homes there, sleeping wherever they could or gathering to pray, talk, or simply sit in silence. The soldiers had set up tents everywhere they could, almost covering several of the landing

pads, but there were only enough for the children and the infirm, and some of the women. The men gathered together as if they were soldiers, too, mustering in units, ready to defeat the Undying scourge. Perhaps, eventually, they would have to do exactly that.

The ruse, the sacrificing of Astelok, had worked. Dyrmida's plan had been a success, but she could take no triumph from it. The Undying forces had been focused on forcing their way through the city, where the Soul Drinkers were facing them, and so had abandoned the positions outside the city from which they could have ambushed the columns of civilians making for the space port. The population of Astelok had been evacuated, most of them, at least. Some had refused to leave, or were members of the army that volunteered to fight in the defence. No doubt more than a few, who had no loved ones, or had too many and were always assumed to be with someone else, had been left behind to die. But the soldiers had managed the crushes at the southern gate and at the gate of the space port well enough, and the Undying had not descended on the column of civilians before they could find safety. It was what happened next that worried Dyrmida. Once off the planet, there was no telling if another world would be any safer.

'I need a few minutes to myself. Then I will speak to them,' said the queen. 'I will use the space port's vox-casters, or there could be a crush.'

The soldier's eye caught something by Astelok's southern gate, and Dyrmida turned around to follow his gaze. People were emerging from the southern gate. She assumed they were stragglers, survivors of the devastation, who had banded together and found a way out.

She was wrong. They were armoured in purple and armed to the teeth, bloody and battle-filthy, but moving quickly into the trees and undergrowth that dotted the route to the space port.

The Soul Drinkers, they were alive.

'I WILL GIVE you your voice back, Brother Lygris,' said Pallas. 'It is the smallest honour that can be done.' He leaned over the bed on which Lygris was laid, and finished soldering the voice box into place, a simply metal case that fitted around Lygris's larynx.

One of the hangars in the space port had been set up as an infirmary. The sickly and decrepit of Astelok had been laid on beds, or on the floor when the beds had run out. The dead were covered in sheets waiting to be carried out. Most of the others were silent, asleep or insensible, or staring at the ceiling waiting for a friend or relative to find them. Every now and again, one of them moaned in pain, or in a nightmare.

Pallas had set up in a corner of the infirmary, screened off by sheets hung from the hangar ceiling. The wounded Soul Drinkers from Astelok were

there, tending to their wounds, or lying stripped of their armour, their injuries patched up by Pallas. There were virtually no medical supplies in the space port, and what little the Raevenians had brought with them was inadequate for their own needs, so Pallas could work with only what he carried on him.

Sarpedon stood by Pallas's shoulder. Lygris made for a sorry sight. His right hand and forearm were black with electrical burns, and Pallas had slathered them in antibiotic gel. Lygris had not regained consciousness, not fully, but his eyes were open and unfocused, roving, as if watching something that no one else could see.

'The Raevenians have little augmetic technology,' said Pallas as he soldered flesh to metal around the edge of the voice box 'I was fortunate that their medics had this device. When I get Brother Lygris back to the *Brokenback* I can give him a far more suitable replacement.'

Lygris coughed, and a little blood trickled from his lips. Pallas had seared closed the stump of Lygris's tongue, but still it bled.

'Brother?' said Sarpedon. 'Can you hear me? Speak to me, brother.'

A metallic braying issued from the voice box, a mechanised cry of anguish.

'He should rest,' said Pallas.

'No,' said Sarpedon. 'He saw the mind of the machine. He looked into the xenos soul.'

'One... One of them...' spluttered Lygris.

'One of them?' asked Sarpedon.

'One soul.' The voice was a mechanical drone, devoid of the pain in Lygris's eyes. He still could not focus, and his eyes darted randomly. 'One mind. There is but one mind among them. The time... the millions of years, the mountains of steel... the lord with the eyes of flame...'

The voice broke down into fractured moans. Lygris convulsed again, and Pallas leaned over him to hold him down.

'Think, brother!' said Sarpedon. 'Tell me what you saw. What do these xenos want? Who leads them? How can they be destroyed?'

'One! One mind! The lord with the eyes of flame!'

Alerts beeped on Pallas's narthecium gauntlet. Pallas jabbed a needle into Lygris's neck, and sedatives flooded his system.

'Give him time,' said Pallas. 'His vital signs are fluctuating. He'll burst a heart without rest.'

Sarpedon sat back on his haunches. 'In my training at the old Chapter's Librarium, we were warned of this. To contact the mind of a xenos is to invite madness. Many good battle-brothers have been lost when a human mind touches that of the alien.'

'It is not right for an Astartes to live on in such a state,' said Pallas. 'I can do no more than tend to his physical wounds. Brother Lygris must fight this madness off himself.'

Sarpedon knew that Lyrgris was strong. All Astartes were. Sarpedon also knew, however, that the Undying were not just creatures with alien mindsets; they were not creatures at all. Lygris had seen what the Selaacans had seen at the white city and the forest world, when their skies went dark and the Undying began to march. He had seen death.

IKTINOS WAS WAITING for Sarpedon in the space port's command centre. He was in the observatory, which housed a gigantic telescope that allowed orbital controllers to see spacecraft above Raevenian, and assess any damage they were reporting. It was a grimly industrial place, all greasy metal and shadows, dominated by the telescope, which reached up through the domed roof far above.

A few of Iktinos's flock were with him when Sarpedon entered. They were watching through the telescope's eyepiece or taking readings from the banks of instruments beside it. It was a measure of Iktinos's standing within the Chapter that he had been the Astartes to which those Space Marines had gone to seek leadership, and it spoke of his dedication that he had taken them on as his personal charges.

'Chaplain?' said Sarpedon. 'You asked to see me?'

'The situation has changed,' said Iktinos. 'Most gravely so.'

'Have the Mechanicus tracked us down?'

'More than that. It is best that you observe for yourself.'

The Soul Drinker at the eyepiece made way for Sarpedon, who had to drop down on to the knees of his mutant legs to get level with the eyepiece. He peered through it, and saw the multicoloured mist of the Veiled Region.

Glimmers of light sparkled, darting around like bright fish in a shoal. The telescope focused in on them, and Sarpedon saw that it was a spaceship, shaped like a crescent of dull metal. Slivers of green fire spat from it as it spiralled around a ship of Imperial design.

'Xenos?' said Sarpedon, looking up from the eyepiece.

'So it seems,' replied Iktinos.

'What of the *Brokenback*?'

'It is safe for the time being,' said Iktinos. 'The Mechanicus fleet and the xenos are fighting one another, and it seems they have enough on their minds not to worry about our hulk. That situation will probably not last once the xenos have despatched their enemies.'

'The aliens will win?'

'Oh yes, commander. There is no doubt about that.'

Sarpedon stood back from the telescope. A member of Iktinos's flock took to the eyepiece, making notes on a data-slate. 'Do we know anything about the composition of the xenos fleet?'

'Mostly battleships,' said Iktinos. 'The sensorium crew on the *Brokenback* are assessing their combat potential, but they are far advanced compared to the Imperial ships.'

'I take it, Chaplain, that there is little chance of the Raevenian evacuation making it through the alien fleet?'

'There is none, commander.'

'Then the Raevenians have no chance of deliverance after all. They never did. When their transports leave this space port they will be slain by the Undying fleet as surely as if they had stayed in Astelok and waited to die.' Sarpedon sat down on his back legs, as he usually did when he had thinking to do. 'No matter what we do or how hard we try, Raevenia is dead.'

'Again, commander,' said Iktinos with his customary solemnity, 'there is no doubt.'

'Does there exist in the galaxy, in this universe, a place where enemies do not lie in wait for the Soul Drinkers? Is there anywhere we could look where some enemy does not lurk? If not the Imperium, the mutant. If not the mutant, the alien.'

'Such is the path we have chosen,' said Iktinos.

'That I have chosen. I took on the leadership of this Chapter when I challenged Gorgoleon for it. Everywhere we find ourselves, I have put us there. That is what it means to be Chapter Master.'

'And what will you do?' asked Iktinos. 'Now that we are beset once again. What orders will you give?'

Sarpedon looked up at him. If there had been doubt, it passed in that moment, reflected in the eyepieces of the Chaplain's skull-mask.

'We fight,' said Sarpedon. 'We are Astartes. It is why we were created. We face the enemy and we fight them, and if we fall, we fall. That is the way of Daenyathos. It was the way of the Emperor.'

'Then we will fight the Undying here, on Raevenia?'

'If we flee, the Undying will shoot us down as they will the Raevenians,' said Sarpedon sharply. 'The *Brokenback* is stricken and vulnerable. A man is at his most vulnerable when he flees, for then the enemy can strike unanswered. A Space Marine does not flee. Yes, Iktinos, we shall stand and fight.'

'Then I swear,' said Iktinos, 'that the Chapter's souls will be prepared.'

'I must tell Queen Dyrmida,' said Sarpedon, 'that her people will not escape this world after all.'

'I can do so, if you wish,' said Iktinos.

'It must come from me.' Sarpedon pushed himself back onto his talons. His mutations had made the Raevenians that saw him gasp in disgust, and he knew what they would say when the Undying descended to take the space port and wipe them out. It was the mutant. The monsters. He promised us deliverance, but he delivered us only into the hands of the Undying.

It did not matter what they thought. Nothing mattered now. It was down to duty and dereliction,

to failure and victory, and all else was just chaff to be ignored. It was a strange feeling, to know that the universe was pared down to those extremes. A Space Marine was trained, created, even, to make the right choice. It was, perhaps, something of a comfort. Sarpedon did not need to worry about anything except the fighting. The endeavour of battle was all that remained, and, as every follower of the Emperor understood, endeavour was its own reward.

THE SOUND OF explosions, muffled by the hull, shuddered the walls of Voar's laboratory. Sample jars jangled on their shelves, and delicate components shifted across the dissection table at which Voar sat. Archmagos Voar regarded the noise with more annoyance than alarm.

The guns of the *Antithesis* were firing, countermeasures probably, sprays of chaff and electromagnetic pulse munitions to throw the xenos sensors off as they targeted the Mechanicus ships. If the xenos used sensors the Imperium understood, of course... if they needed to see the Mechanicus at all.

Voar had laid out the components of the dissected necron warrior on the table. Arcane machines were hooked up to it by electrodes and probes. Winking lights lit the dim laboratory, and the only sounds, aside from the dull thuds of the ship's guns, were the hum of the machines and the

clicking of Voar's implements as he worked. The necron's limbs had been broken apart into the many hundreds of struts and servo units that drove them, and lay in neat piles beside the torso. The torso had been carefully carved up, and split open to reveal the circuitry and components clustered around the power unit that still glowed faintly green. The warrior's head had been removed and placed to one side, but it was still connected to the torso by the articulated cable that served it like a spinal cord.

Voar was close. He knew it. The necron's technology was a puzzle, completely unlike anything Imperial or even pre-Imperial that he had ever seen. It had required him to relearn some of the most basic principles of science, of sacred cause and effect. It was unholy, for it breached the basic tenets of the Omnissiah's logic, but it was fascinating. A weaker mind than Voar's could have been seduced by it.

Voar opened up a small unit in the chest beside the power unit. He pared it open to reveal a silvery contact. With precision that a human hand could not match, Voar soldered the end of a wire to the contact. He plugged the other end of the wire into one of the laboratory machines. It was a highly sensitive scanner that could pick out all manner of exotic frequencies and radiation types. It was perhaps three thousand years old, which was how Voar knew it could be relied upon.

Voar carefully watched the readout dials on the machine's brass casing as he cycled through frequencies. The necrons had to be connected to something, some central source of control or power, to account for their abilities and behaviour. When they phased out, they had to go somewhere. Their power units were not generators at all, but capacitors, taking energy from elsewhere and storing it. That power had to come from somewhere.

Someone banged on the laboratory door. Voar looked up, scowling. He had left orders not to be disturbed, even if the *Antithesis* was about to explode. His work was more important than fighting a battle the Mechanicus could not win. It did not matter since the door was sealed with gene-locks that the crew could not access, but any distraction was unwelcome.

The unwelcome guest hammered at the door again. Voar put it out of his mind and continued to search for signals going into or out of the necron. He expected it to be exotic, something the Mechanicus would never normally consider, something as alien as the rest of the heathen creature.

A terrible roar of torn metal filled the lab. The door was ripped clean off its mounts, spilling the remnants of the gene-lock onto the laboratory floor.

Magos Crystavayne and Magos Vionel walked in, Vionel's iron-shod feet stomping on the laboratory

floor. The remains of the door were held in Vionel's huge metal paws.

'Archmagos,' said Crystavayne, 'we would speak with you.'

'What logic compels you to defy my orders?' blared Voar.

'Destruction!' bellowed Vionel, throwing the door to the floor. 'The removal of our knowledge from the Omnissiah's work! All we have done, all we ever will do, will be undone at the hands of the alien, and you hide here in the dark!'

'And what do you know of it?' retorted Voar. 'What cares the xenos whether I command or not? What string of logic will bring us victory against a foe that exceeds us in every way?'

'Your duty,' said Crystavayne, 'is to lead us in the pursuit of knowledge, whatever form it may take and whatever obstacle may stand in our way, even to the point of destruction.'

'But that destruction,' said Voar, 'has not reached us. There has been no suggestion to me that we will be die here.'

'We cannot win this battle, archmagos! You said so yourself!'

'The battle, magos, not the war.'

Vionel stomped forwards, and a floodlight emerged from one shoulder cowling, which was still scarred from the necron fire. The acid yellow light glared off the machines and dissected parts on the laboratory table. 'And this will win us that war?'

'The chances are small,' said Voar, 'but they exist. And they exceed any increase in the likelihood of our survival with me at the helm.'

'Where is your sense of duty?' asked Crystavayne. 'Vionel nearly died on the *Ferrous*. Hepsebah is directing the fire of the *Constant* as we speak. Khrul gave his life!'

'Duty,' said Voar, 'is secondary to logic. Understanding that is the difference between my rank and yours.'

Crystavayne emitted a curse in clicking binary.

'You are a disgrace to the Adeptus Mechanicus,' he said.

Voar's hand went to the ornate pistol he wore at his waist beneath his robes. 'If you intend to challenge me for command, magos, then out with it and let us settle this.'

Vionel stepped between Voar and Crystavayne. His rivet gun cycled, lumps of metal thunking into its chambers.

'Archmagos or not,' he said, 'if you abandon us in this battle, we will take over your office. And if you resist, then I shall balance your equation myself.'

One of the machines chirped shrilly. Vionel turned his floodlight on it. A green light was winking in its brass casing.

'It's found the frequency,' said Voar.

'The frequency?' asked Crystavayne.

'The necron warriors are acting on remote orders. They are only semi-autonomous, and the commands

must come from elsewhere. They need a signal to give them coordinates so they can teleport out when deactivated, too. My studies have suggested that both functions originate at the same location.'

'Where?' asked Vionel, his rivet gun still trained on Voar.

Voar took the power scalpel and activated the tiny power field around its blade. He fiddled with a couple of the controls on the machine and read off the numbers from its various dials and readouts. Then he moved aside one of the necron's dissected arms and scratched a pair of intersecting lines into the surface of the table. He carved a few figures beside it, frequencies and wavelengths, as he read them off.

'It can be triangulated,' said Voar. 'It's barely perceptible. Either this unit is too damaged to pick it up properly or their technology is far more sensitive than ours. It is a miracle we can hear it at all.'

Vionel's rivet gun dropped.

'Where?' he repeated. 'Where is it coming from?'

Voar took a data-slate and keyed in the coordinates he had just generated.

'Take this to navigation,' he said, 'and find out. I must finish up here.'

For a moment, the two magi did not move. Then Vionel took the data-slate from Voar, and they turned to leave the laboratory.

Voar unplugged the probe from the necron's innards and picked up its skull. He turned it over in his hands, looking into its eyes.

'Let us see how you fight,' he said, 'when you are blind.'

'Often we speak of duty unto death, of defiance to the point of extinction. But what does this mean? What work of ours can change the galaxy, if it ends along with our lives? Works of true devotion, acts of true duty, last far beyond our own lifetimes.'

Daenyathos, *The Four Pillars of Sacred Hate*

CHAPTER TWELVE

FOR SOMEONE WHO had just learned that she was going to die, Queen Dyrmida was calm.

She had set up a command centre in the control tower in the middle of the space port, and had ordered the generals and staff to leave while Sarpedon spoke with her. Perhaps she had wanted to make sure the information he gave her was properly controlled, or perhaps she just didn't want to look weak if she received his news with shock. Certainly, she had known from the moment Sarpedon had entered that he brought bad news.

'Why have you told me this?' asked Dyrmida when Sarpedon finished. 'And do not tell me that you are doing the right thing. No one on this planet is doing anything, except what they must do to survive.'

'If we were to flee,' said Sarpedon, 'the Undying fleet would shoot us down. Our ship cannot escape them without fuel. That means that we must fight, and we will have a better chance if the Raevenians fight too.'

'A better chance of what?' Dyrmida's eyes were bright with anger. 'You say, yourself, that there is no chance of getting off Raevenia, and I dare say there is none of defeating the Undying army on the ground. What would you hope to achieve with the lives of my subjects?'

'An Astartes,' said Sarpedon, 'does not kneel for the executioner's bullet. He does not beg for a quick death. Every Soul Drinker will fight on because it is his duty to ensure that his death does not come cheaply to the enemy. And your majesty, I understand something of the Raevenian way of death. Think of the good deaths that would be won at the walls of this space port, lost for monarch and for world. Think of the bad deaths that would be inflicted if the same people tried to flee or surrender. It may not be an easy decision to make, but there is only one decision in the end.'

Queen Dyrmida sighed. Sarpedon realised how much she had aged since the Soul Drinkers had first landed outside Astelok.

'A death means something,' she said, 'only if it is remembered.'

'Then order your people to flee and die, or march out into the Undying's hands. But remember this:

the people in that harvester were still alive. They had not long to live, perhaps, but they were prisoners, not trophies. If nothing else, Queen Dyrmida, that is a fate worth fighting to avoid.'

Sarpedon had nothing more to say. Raevenia was going to die, and nothing he did would make any difference to that. He left Dyrmida alone with her thoughts.

'Soul Drinker,' said Dyrmida as Sarpedon left the command centre.

'Your majesty?'

Dyrmida took a data-slate from a pocket in her fatigues and threw it to Sarpedon. 'Were it not for the Soul Drinkers, Raevenia would already have been lost. Those are the codes for the fuel tankers beneath the space port.'

The data-slate in Sarpedon's hand showed strings of numbers and letters in the Raevenian alphabet, recognisably derived from Low Gothic. 'My gratitude, your majesty.'

'If the Undying truly have this planet blockaded then its value is little more than symbolic. But on Raevenia we honour our debts, even in the hour of our destruction. If any of you survive and the chance to escape presents itself, take it, and take whoever survives of my people with you. Then there will be someone to remember all those good deaths.'

'I will need to organise my Astartes,' said Sarpedon. 'The space port has many weak points in a

siege. It will need a great deal of fortification and planning to hold it.'

'The army of Astelok will do the same,' said Dyrmida. 'If the Undying have any memory, if they have a history of their damnable species, then the last battle for Raevenia will be a part of it.'

SERGEANT SALK WAS waiting at the entrance to the control centre. The Raevenian ships were being fuelled and prepped for takeoff behind him. They were simple, sturdy ships, unadorned and functional. Each one was large enough to hold several thousand people, and more were being brought up on elevators from the hangars below the landing pads. They were enough to carry almost all the Raevenian survivors, minus the infirm and wounded, who would be left behind. No doubt, thought Sarpedon, those ships would be abandoned and hauled back into their hangars once the news broke of the Undying fleet bearing down on them.

'Sergeant,' said Sarpedon, 'what news?'

'The officers wish to speak with you, commander,' said Salk. Salk, like most of the Soul Drinkers, was still scuffed and scorched from the battle on the harvester, and chunks of his armour had been stripped down to bare ceramite by glancing hits from the Undying guns.

'About what?'

'Tyrendian has a plan,' said Salk.

'For what?'

'For everything.'

THE SOUL DRINKERS were waiting in the makeshift infirmary, where Pallas had tended to the wounded Astartes, and helped the Raevenian medics patch up the few wounded soldiers that had made it out of Astelok.

Tyrendian was waiting in the screened off area, along with Iktinos and Luko. Lygris still lay semi-conscious nearby. Together, they represented the surviving officers of the Soul Drinkers. The sight of them reminded Sarpedon just how many battle-brothers he had lost; the Chapter was barely at quarter-strength.

'Librarian,' said Sarpedon, 'what have you come up with?'

'The Adeptus Mechanicus will be destroyed,' said Tyrendian. 'That is certain.'

'It is,' said Sarpedon. 'No doubt you have seen the situation in orbit yourself.'

'And we will be destroyed shortly afterwards,' continued Tyrendian. The Librarian's manner was reminiscent of many officers from the old Chapter: superior and dismissive, somehow conveying a sense of arrogance no matter what he actually said. Sarpedon had come to understand that beneath that face was a dedicated and intelligent warrior without whom the Chapter would be worse off. 'Along with Raevenia.'

'This is true,' said Sarpedon.

'Then we and the Mechanicus are in a similar position.'

'Meaning?'

'Meaning, we send a delegation,' said Tyrendian. 'We make an alliance with the Mechanicus. Lygris has seen much of the information structure underlying the Undying invasion. The Mechanicus have no doubt sought information on the enemy. If nothing else, we could fight together and buy more of a chance than we have now.'

'You propose an alliance with the Mechanicus?' asked Sarpedon. 'They have gone very far out of their way to kill us.'

'True,' said Tyrendian, 'but they won't, not if the Undying get there first.'

'We have our enmities,' added Luko. 'I hate those red-robed freaks, but they're logical, you have to give them that. If we give them a chance to get out of the Veiled Region with their steel hides intact then they'll take it.'

'And what can we offer them?' asked Sarpedon.

'Lygris can answer that,' said Tyrendian.

'Lygris?' Sarpedon walked to Lygris's bedside and leaned over him. 'Brother? What do you know?'

Lygris's eyes opened a little. 'I saw... inside them. Their system. The... the mind that rules them. The lord... the lord with the burning eyes. Millions of years of hate, all burning through

those eyes...' The voice box strained to turn Lygris's slurring into intelligent speech.

'One mind,' said Tyrendian. 'One lord. The Undying are controlled by one intelligence. Lygris saw enough of it in the harvester's data medium to see it. And if we kill it, there will be nothing controlling the Undying.'

'You saw this, Brother Lygris?'

Lucidity sparked in Lygris's eyes. 'Yes, commander. I saw him... it. It watches over everything. It's a spider at the heart of the web. You... you would not believe it. To see it. You would not believe anything could survive in the galaxy but these Undying. We are just... insects. Microbes. Like something on a slide to be... to be ignored, and allowed to wither away. When we have been forgotten in the galaxy there will still be the Undying, and when they rule...'

'Techmarine!' snapped Sarpedon. 'Enough of this heresy! No alien will have this galaxy. It does not matter how long they have waited. Humanity will wipe them out.'

Lygris coughed again, blood running from his lips. 'They... they do not have doubt. They know. They know they will rule.'

Sarpedon glared at Lygris, but Lygris shifted back into a daze.

'The Mechanicus,' said Tyrendian, 'might still be able to find this intelligence and deliver us to it. If anyone in the Veiled Region is capable of inflicting

justice upon it, we are. That is the deal we offer them. They find it, we kill it, and the Undying are halted.'

Sarpedon looked between the officers assembled in the infirmary. Tyrendian and Luko had made their case. Pallas, still tending to the wounds of his battle-brothers, had not spoken up, and Lygris was in no position to offer an opinion.

'Iktinos?' asked Sarpedon.

'I have,' said Iktinos, 'misgivings about an alliance with our enemies. Such a path would constitute a moral threat. But my misgivings about remaining on this world to die, when an alternative tactic might remain unexploited, are deeper still.'

'Our options,' said Sarpedon, 'are to stand and fight, and die; to flee and die, or to risk an alliance with the Adeptus Mechanicus. Like Captain Luko, I have little enough love for the Mechanicus, but given the other two options, the decision is clear. Tyrendian, will you head this embassy?'

'I will, commander, if you wish it of me.'

'I do. The Mechanicus may not tolerate a mutant on their ship long enough to hear our offer.'

'I should go, commander,' said Chaplain Iktinos. 'My experience with dealing with those outside the Chapter exceeds yours. It was one of my duties in the old Chapter. Added to which, I am not a mutant.'

'You will remain here,' said Sarpedon, 'to lead the Soul Drinkers at the space port. The focus of the

Undying must be kept on Raevenia, or there will be little chance of any other mission succeeding.'

'Then the flock will hold this ground,' said Iktinos. 'If you need a force that will not falter, there is little better choice than my faithful.'

'Tyrendian,' continued Sarpedon, 'Phol will take you. He's our best pilot. Soul Drinkers, to your duties.'

The Librarian and the Chaplain headed out to the landing pad on which the Soul Drinkers had stationed their gunships and transports. Luko and Sarpedon remained in the infirmary.

'It is not like you to keep so quiet, captain,' said Sarpedon.

Luko looked around to see that Pallas was on the other side of the infirmary and Lygris was unconscious. 'I must confess something to you, Sarpedon. Not as an officer to his commander, not even as an Astartes.'

'Speak, Luko.'

Luko paused for a long moment before he spoke, as if the words wanted to stay hidden in his throat. 'When... when I found out that the Undying were ready to invade, and that Raevenia had no chance... I was relieved.'

Sarpedon did not answer. He had never seen Luko vulnerable like this. His infectious ferocity, his love of the fight, was one of the engines that fuelled the Chapter's sudden, shock assault form of warfare. It seemed a different man was wearing Luko's armour and lightning claws.

'I was relieved,' continued Luko, 'because it meant that it would be over.'

'Over?' asked Sarpedon. 'You want to die down here?'

'I want peace,' said Luko. 'Just that. Just peace.'

Sarpedon sat back. Luko sat on one of the infirmary beds.

'Everything I do,' said Luko, 'is a lie. Everything. For… for years now. Since before the Star Fort.'

'You fooled us,' said Sarpedon.

'I know. Forgive me.'

'Luko, there is nothing to forgive,' said Sarpedon. 'You are the best officer I have. Without you leading from the front we would all have been lost many times over. How many Soul Drinkers owe you their lives? What evils would have been perpetrated against the people of this galaxy if you had not lived that lie?'

'But that's it, commander. It was a lie. All of it. Every time I joked about the killing or I acted like I was never happier than in battle, that was a lie. What are we fighting for, if not to find some truth in the galaxy?'

'And so you want to die.'

'If that is the only way it can end, then yes, I want to die.'

'You will not get what you want.' Sarpedon stood up to his full height, and he towered over Luko. 'Not here. Not yet. I promise you, Brother Luko, you will never have peace while I still live.'

'I don't know if I can carry on, commander. I have played an Astartes for so long…'

'You are still Astartes. You still know no fear. Nothing has changed.'

'I cannot go on lying.'

'Then stop. But keep fighting. That is an order. Do you understand?'

'Yes, commander.'

'Good. Stay with your squad. If Iktinos is successful, we may have to move quickly.'

'I understand.'

'And captain?'

'Yes?'

'It will end. Maybe it will be here. Probably, even. But we won't fight forever. Either we'll die out here, and it'll happen soon enough, or we will fight until we carve out a chunk of space for ourselves. Rule it like the Ultramarines rule their own roost. Make of it what the Imperium should be. That's the only way we can continue to exist in this galaxy. If we make it, or if we die trying, then our war of survival will be over. If you trust me, Luko, trust me with that.'

THE DEFENCE OF *Caelano Minoris* cut a gallant figure as it burned. The Fleet Minor gathered around it like pallbearers as green fire rippled up its hull, forcing its way in through the tears in its hull. Explosions wracked the laboratory ship as the fire cooked off stores of chemicals and fuel. Saviour

pods escaped, riding on columns of compressed gas. Some of them barely made it beyond the ship, and were caught in flashes of fire, incinerating whoever was inside.

Two necron cruisers closed in. The efforts of the Fleet Minor, which were deploying every countermeasure they had, had spoiled their aim to the extent that they had to close in to deliver a killing blow. Since the destruction of the *Ferrous*, the Mechanicus fleet had been frustratingly reluctant to hang still in front of the necron guns, and the xenos cruisers eagerly took to the kill. The *Defence* had already lost most of its prow and a good chunk of amidships, its few guns abandoned or stripped away from the hull like proud nails.

The two necron cruisers rotated to bring their main weapons to bear on the ship. Arcs of power flitted between the tips of their crescent-shaped hulls as they charged.

The *Defence* carried several containers of highly volatile chemicals. Usually kept in separate lead-cased chambers, they had been piled up in barrels just behind the plasma vessel of one of the ship's reactors, an experimental power source that provided great efficiency in return for considerable volatility. Magos Devwyn, commanding the *Defence* in Crystavayne's absence, had reasoned that the reactor would explode under enemy fire soon enough anyway.

When the burning prow of the *Defence* was pointed at the closest cruiser, Devwyn gave the order. It was relayed to a team of menials that had volunteered to stay on the ship and command the servitors, who were now set on fire and sent striding into the chemical stockpile.

The chemicals detonated, creating a vortex of exotic particles that obliterated the engine section of the *Defence*. Its stern disappeared in a shining white cloud of vaporised metal.

The reactor went critical, its core bombarded with particles. Its mass was converted instantly into energy. The structure of the *Defence* held just long enough to send the energy mass along the length of the ship as it converted into pure yellow-white light and fire.

The *Defence* fired like an enormous cannon, almost its entire mass, including the volunteer menials and even Magos Devwyn, converted into energy. The bolt of power streaked across the void and speared the necron cruiser at the base of one of its crescent wings. The wing was sheared off, and chain reactions rippled along the remnants of the alien ship, spraying bursts of shrapnel from its hull like steel volcanoes.

The second necron cruiser's engines flared, and it tore itself out of a firing position to avoid the titanic chunks of wreckage spinning out of its dying sister ship. Strange technologies, chunks of glowing green crystal, the bodies of broken necron warriors

and sprays of liquid silver poured out of the damaged cruiser's wounds. The lights studding the surface winked out, and the ship drifted dead away from the field of debris marking the site of the *Defence's* sacrifice.

'NO KNOWLEDGE COMES without a price,' said Archmagos Voar.

The wreckage that remained of the *Defence* boiled away in a cloud of dimming silver, glittering on the main viewscreen of the observatory.

'And no price,' said Magos Crystavayne, 'is paid without leaving its mark.'

Crystavayne had been in the observatory of the *Antithesis*, following the execution of his navigational commands, when the *Defence of Caelano Minoris* exploded. It had been spectacular, perhaps as beautiful as such destruction could be, but Magos Devwyn had been a fellow walker on the path of knowledge, one without whom the Mechanicus would never have penetrated the Veiled Region. Voar and Crystavayne mourned him in their own ways, in silence, with an internal prayer of machine-code clicking through their logic centres.

'Preparations are almost complete,' said Voar.

'I want to be with the boarding force,' said Crystavayne.

'Then it shall be so.'

'Can we win?'

'That is a more complex question than it first appears,' said Voar. 'It is possible that we will. Should there be, for instance, a form of communications device without which the necron fleet cannot operate, and upon which we stumble, then we shall succeed. Should we capture their ship and are able to operate it, we may flee intact. There are other routes to success, but they are too unlikely to be considered viable. As they are, the chances of success border on the nominal. They are still, however, greater than our chances should we continue to fight as we do now. To answer your question, by the standards generated by a logic engine such as mine, we can succeed, but by the less exact standards of an unaugmented human, we cannot.'

'It does not matter,' said Crystavayne. 'To take the fight to the alien is its own reward.'

The tech-guard troops had been gathered from the fleet's other ships and assembled on the *Antithesis*. The *Antithesis* had few boarding facilities, being limited to a handful of armoured transports and a single complement of boarding torpedoes. It had not been designed as an assault ship, and to launch the attack it would have to get close enough to the necron mother ship, the target most likely to yield some meaningful success, for the mother ship to stand a very good chance of blasting it out of the void. If it got that far, and if the mother ship did not have some heathen technology to defend against boarders, there were no

doubt legions of necron warriors on board to fight through.

It was, at least, better than sitting back and waiting to die, but not by much.

Crystavayne took out the neuro-sword he carried scabbarded under his robes. Most tech-priests and magi were armed, and Crystavayne's weapon of choice was a blade of shiny black crystal inlaid with silver circuitry.

'I made this myself,' said Crystavayne, 'to make sure I would never be helpless should the quest for understanding become a battle. It will do me little good against an enemy without a nervous system. What do we have left in the armoury that I could use instead?'

'Here,' said Voar. He took a pistol from a holster on the belt of his robes. It was a miniature melta weapon, its grip moulded around its fuel cell. 'Even without this, I am not poorly armed.'

Crystavayne took the gun. It was an inferno pistol, and was probably the single most valuable weapon on the *Antithesis*, including the ship's guns.

'My gratitude,' said Crystavayne. 'When does the attack begin?'

'In thirty-nine minutes,' said Voar.

'I have one question before we deploy.'

'If the Omnissiah so wills, it shall be answered.'

'After you have attained your rank, archmagos, after you have lost so much of the emotional

centres of your brain and replaced them with logic, do you still want revenge?'

'Of course. The desire for vengeance is not an emotion. It is the purest logic of all.'

'Good,' said Crystavayne.

An alert tone chirped in the communicators of both tech-priests. 'Voar here.'

'An approaching craft,' came the reply from the bridge, 'is requesting docking permission. It's Imperial.'

'One of the Fleet Minor?'

'Astartes. A gunship.'

'Astartes?' said Crystavayne. 'The only Astartes out here are the Soul Drinkers.'

'Then logic dictates it is them,' said Voar. 'The two choices we have are to receive them or destroy them.'

'We can achieve the first without ruling out the second.'

'Agreed,' said Voar. 'Bridge, prep a deck to receive them, and do so quickly. They may not survive out here for long.'

LIBRARIAN TYRENDIAN WAS accompanied by ten Soul Drinkers of Squad Salk. They were met by several squads of tech-guard on the launch deck of the *Antithesis*, and the men looked at the Astartes as if they were facing a particularly volatile and dangerous animal.

Three tech-priests approached across the deck. As Tyrendian descended the embarkation ramp of the

Thunderhawk, it was clear that they were senior members of the Mechanicus, heavily augmented, their robes embroidered with symbols of rank. One was an enormous industrial machine, shaped something like a huge metal ape. His head was low between his shoulders, vaguely human with the lower half of his face concealed by a heavy rebreather and vox-unit.

The second was the highest-ranked, although he looked far more human than the first. He was slender and rather taller than a normal man, with shoulder-mounted manipulator units folded over his back and circuitry woven into the skin of his face.

The third was also shaped like a human, but one of his hands had been replaced with a complex medical gauntlet, hooked up to vials of liquid implanted in his forearm. One of his eyes was a bionic, reminiscent of a microscope, which was probably the function it performed.

The first tech-priest stomped forwards, and a round clacked into the chamber of the gun he had in place of one arm. His armour was pitted and battle-scarred, and he more resembled a machine of war than a tech-priest.

The lead tech-priest stepped in front of the war machine and gave a hand signal that caused the assembled tech-guard troops to lower their lasguns.

'I am Archmagos Voar of the Adeptus Mechanicus,' he said. 'This is my ship, the *Antithesis*.'

'I am Brother Tyrendian of the Soul Drinkers.'

'What is your purpose here?'

'To propose an alliance.'

'To what end?' asked Voar.

'Mutual survival,' said Tyrendian.

'There was little survival on anyone's minds at the Star Fort,' said Voar. 'We know of you, Soul Drinkers. The Inquisition tried to delete you from history, but we have long memories. You are renegades and murderers, and among those who have suffered at your hands are members of the Mechanicus. What promise can there be that you will not betray us? That you are not even working in concert with these xenos?'

'The xenos are the enemy,' said Tyrendian sharply, 'of any human, renegade or not. And they will destroy us as surely as they will destroy you if we cannot find a solution between us. If you wish to die out here, archmagos, without ever having possessed a chance of survival, then reject us.'

Voar paused only for a moment to consider this, but there was little doubt that logic engines in his head were whirring through banks of data.

'What can you offer us?' asked Voar.

'We have information on the xenos machine-spirits. We know of a single intelligence that rules them,' said Tyrendian. 'In addition to which, you will find no better assault troops than two companies of Astartes. What can you offer us?'

'We know where they are,' said the third tech-priest, the medical specialist. The archmagos glanced at him, but said nothing.

'Where?' asked Tyrendian.

'Does it matter?' asked Voar.

'We know who we are fighting,' said Tyrendian. 'You know where it is. Take us there and we can kill it. The Undying operate under the control of a single intelligence, and, if it is slain, we will buy ourselves our only chance at victory.' Tyrendian indicated the tech-guard. 'With these troops you can do nothing against an Undying stronghold. With the Soul Drinkers, you have a force that can break through the Undying and kill it. We just need to get there.'

'The *Antithesis* could do it,' said the third tech-priest. 'It's the fastest ship we have. It can't hold out forever, but we can stay ahead of the xenos fleet for long enough.'

'Do we have a deal?' asked Tyrendian.

Archmagos Voar thought for a longer moment. The tech-guard were tensed ready to raise their guns, and there was no doubt they had orders to execute the Soul Drinkers at a sign from the archmagos.

'Logic dictates,' said Voar, 'that we do.'

Tyrendian walked between the squads of tech-guard and held out a hand. Archmagos Voar shook it.

'In the name of Rogal Dorn,' said Tyrendian, 'this alliance is struck.'

Voar glanced at the huge industrial tech-priest beside him.

'That will no longer be necessary, Magos Vionel,' he said. The tech-priest's gun thudded as it unloaded the rounds back into its ammo hopper.

'Where is our enemy?' asked Tyrendian.

'Here,' said Voar. He took out a data-slate, and one of his manipulators inserted a probe into it. A star map flickered onto the screen. He handed the slate to Tyrendian.

'Selaaca,' said Tyrendian.

'You know of it?' asked Voar.

'It was the capital of the empire the Undying have destroyed. The planet beneath us is Raevenia, where the last survivors of the empire are making their final stand. Part of the fleet you are fighting is the invasion force that will complete the capture of the planet. Once Raevenia is gone, there will be no human force left between the Undying and the Imperium.'

'Then it is unlikely,' said Voar, 'that the completion of their plans in the Veiled Region will have a positive impact on the human race.'

'On that we can agree,' said Tyrendian. 'We must move quickly. Neither of our forces can hold out for much longer. I suggest that we take word back to our commander and return with an assault force. With your leave, archmagos.'

'I concur. I will position the fleet to facilitate a breakout. Primary manoeuvres will begin in two hours.'

'Until then, archmagos,' said Tyrendian. 'Soul Drinkers! Embark!'

Iktinos, Tyrendian and the Soul Drinkers of Iktinos's flock filed back up the ramp into the Thunderhawk, and the ramp swung up to seal them in.

As THE SUN went down on the space port, the Soul Drinkers loaded the last of the weapons and ammunition back onto their transports. They travelled light, and everything they needed to wage war had been stowed in a matter of minutes. The old Chapter had never fought with many heavy weapons or vehicles. Sarpedon had taught them to fight with hands and teeth if need be, up close in the enemy's face. That was how the philosopher-warrior Daenyathos had written that the Soul Drinkers should fight, and that was how Sarpedon believed an Astartes was at his most effective.

Sarpedon and Iktinos had been joined by Queen Dyrmida. She had informed the people of Raevenia, over the space port's vox-casters, that the Undying would try to take the space port, and they must be fought off before the Raevenians could be delivered from their fate. It had not been completely true, but it was closer to the truth than she had been expecting to tell.

'Chaplain Iktinos will remain on Raevenia with his flock,' said Sarpedon. 'The Undying will be

free to attack before we can succeed. You will have to fight hard before this is over.'

'My army is ready,' said Dyrmida. 'I had expected your Astartes to remain until the end of this empire, but if by taking the fight to Selaaca you can strike a blow against the Undying, I am willing to see you leave. Have you taken the fuel you came here for?'

'We will return for it,' said Sarpedon.

'There might be nothing left to return to, commander.'

'My duty,' said Iktinos, 'is to ensure that there will be. We have a defensible position and an enemy operating under a time limit they know nothing about. We will prevail, your majesty.'

'We can hold these walls if you can take down their commander,' said Dyrmida. 'If you man the gates, and if the Undying can be halted from afar, then we can hold.'

'I wish,' said Sarpedon, 'that I could give your world a better chance.'

'Remember the Raevenian way of death, commander. We will all die fighting for our home world, against an inhuman enemy. There are few in our history that can claim a better death than that. Do not fear for our ability to hold this space port, for we fight as soldiers with nothing to lose. Even in death, we shall have victory. When dying is not defeat, we cannot be beaten.' Dyrmida grasped Sarpedon's gauntlet and shook it. 'Best of luck,

Commander Sarpedon. When you return, you will find us victorious, whatever happens.'

'For Dorn,' said Iktinos.

'For Dorn, Chaplain,' said Sarpedon.

'Ready for takeoff,' voxed Brother Phol from the cockpit of Sarpedon's Thunderhawk.

'I will speak with you both soon,' said Sarpedon.

'If you do not,' said Dyrmida, 'die well.'

'I'll do my best, your majesty,' said Sarpedon, and scuttled towards the Thunderhawk, which was already obscured by the wash of heat from its warmed-up engines.

'Look into the face of the enemy, and rejoice! For to stand before him, to bask in his fury, is to tell him that you fear him not, and that he is within a sword-thrust of destruction.'

Daenyathos, *Musings Upon Extermination*

CHAPTER THIRTEEN

THE CONSTANT WENT down fighting. Her full complement of menials and tech-guard went down with her, because they were needed to work the fusion chamber. The nova cannon fired until the end, the final blast barely aimed, in the hope that the projectile would nick a necron ship and send waves of fissile material pulsing through the enemy's corridors and engine rooms.

The necron mother ship took advantage of the *Constant's* sudden lack of mobility. It turned its main gun on the cruiser, even as it absorbed a nova cannon blast that stripped away one of the spurs reaching from its central spire. The mother ship rotated majestically until its gun was in line, and then it fired, a lance of green-white power splitting the *Constant* through her prow and tearing all the

way through her stern. For a moment, the Mechanicus cruiser was impaled. Then the force of the mother ship's gun shredded what remained of her interior structure, and boiled away the hull into burning wisps of metallic gas.

The Fleet Minor threw itself as one into the mother ship's path. The necron cruisers rallied around the mother ship and blew the few remaining transport and sensorium craft apart. The mother ship itself sent out a spherical pulse of green flame that tossed the smaller craft around like ships on a storm, ripping guns and instruments from hulls, and splintering the hails of torpedoes the Fleet Minor was firing at it in desperation.

The necron fleet's command routines switched from the harrying of a determined foe to the annihilation of an enemy collapsing under the psychological pressure of battle. Some of the Fleet Minor had fled, disobeying orders to buy themselves a few more hours or minutes of life. Guided munitions and a few broad gun barrages were all that were needed to turn the fleeing ships into sprays of steel dust.

Others defied the most basic tenets of logic to charge into the enemy, sometimes aiming to ram the necron ships in some vulnerable spot. They were even easier to deal with. A few point-blank turret volleys put paid to most of them. The few that got through impacted without causing any

significant damage to the hulls of living metal in which the necron ships were clad.

The necron fleet closed in around the mother ship, as if the mother ship was the stem of a vast steel flower and the cruisers were its petals, to concentrate fire on the remnants of the Mechanicus fleet.

Only the *Antithesis* did not succumb to the breakdown the necron fleet detected in the manoeuvres of its sister ships. The cruiser spiralled away from the heart of the battle, releasing every form of countermeasure it had: short-fuse torpedoes, electromagnetic chaff, burning fuel and even heaps of refuse from spent shell casings to the bodies of its dead, to fool the necron guns for a few moments longer. Its main engines kicked in, and it powered away, forcing open a warp rift and diving in. The tactic was dangerous in the extreme; entering the warp in peaceful conditions could be dangerous enough. But the *Antithesis* made it.

The necron mother ship quickly recalculated its response to the change in Mechanicus tactics. The Mechanicus had not given up the fight as the necrons' limited intelligence on human behaviour had suggested. Instead, the *Antithesis* had sacrificed the rest of the fleet to escape.

The mother ship sent its cruisers ahead of it, folding space-time to follow the *Antithesis*. One of them, wounded by a lucky blast from the *Constant*, broke apart as it accelerated, some critical system

giving way and causing the cruiser to split in two and implode.

It did not matter. The only two enclaves of human interlopers were on Raevenia, and in the *Antithesis*, and neither had a chance of survival given the resources arrayed against them. As the mother ship joined the pursuit of the *Antithesis*, the necron transport craft began the descent onto Raevenia. They carried with them more than thirty thousand necron warriors and countless war machines, enough to subjugate an entire world.

Their lower hulls began to glow with heat as they plunged through Raevenia's atmosphere.

QUEEN DYRMIDA, STANDING at a window of the space port's command tower, watched through a pair of magnoculars as the first white streaks of falling spacecraft appeared in the sky over Astelok.

'Sighting fire!' shouted Dyrmida. One of the officers around her spoke an order into the comm-net and the crew of the anti-aircraft guns on the walls swivelled their quad-mounted cannon to aim at the falling craft. Sharp cracks of guns echoed around the space port as they sent tracer rounds up into the afternoon sky.

The reserves of Queen Dyrmida's army were stationed around the command tower ready to act as a reserve to move to any breach of the walls. The queen was in full battle-dress, heavy iridescent carapace armour over quilted flak armour, over her dark

red royal robes. She carried a repeating strikelock rifle, a finely crafted weapon with three rotating barrels and a miniature generator in the hilt. She wore the simple battle-crown, a small tiara of steel, which was the regalia of sovereignty when at war.

The population huddled in whatever shelter they could: empty fuel containers beneath the landing pads, spacecraft hangars, equipment sheds and narrow maintenance tunnels. Their fear was as obvious as the sunlight beating down on the space port, or the smell of fuel and gun oil.

Most of the soldiers were on the walls. They did not know from which direction the Undying would strike, so they were stationed all around, erecting sniping positions and makeshift battlements of empty fuel drums and spacecraft parts piled up.

The main gates were the weakest point of the walls. The space port had not been built as a fortress, and the gates would be easier to storm than the walls. That was where Chaplain Iktinos had set up, along with the thirty or so Soul Drinkers he referred to as his 'flock'.

'They're coming down in the city,' said Lieutenant Kavins, who was attending upon his queen. Dyrmida saw that he was right.

'They're joining up with the rest of the harvesting force,' she said.

'Then we know they'll be coming from that direction.'

Dyrmida scanned the sky on the other side of the space port. Bright streaks of vapour were trailing behind craft plummeting towards the woods and hills south of the port.

'I wouldn't be so sure, Kavins,' said Dyrmida.

'Incoming!' came the yell from one of the sharp-shooters on the roof of the command tower. Dyrmida followed his outstretched arm. One of the Undying landers, wounded by anti-aircraft fire, was spiralling out of control towards the space port. With a terrible sound like reality tearing, it hammered through the air, and slammed into one of the landing pads in a burst of smoke and shrapnel. The ground shook.

Troops ran from the command tower to snap fire at the shapes they saw moving among the flames and molten metal. A half-melted Undying clambered out of the flames, and its head was blown open by a well-placed round. Another was cut apart as it walked out of the fire, destroyed before it could raise its gun. Metal corpses dissolved away into nothing.

It was first blood, which meant something in Raevenian folklore of war, but in this battle, it meant nothing. There were plenty more where those Undying had come from.

A couple more landing craft were blown out of the sky. They were shaped like inverted pyramids, their lower surfaces studded with engines that glowed white as they slowed the Undying descent.

A few of them were larger, massive armoured spheres, tumbling, apparently without any means of slowing them, to impact like falling bombs in the ruins of Astelok.

Dyrmida activated the vox-bead that Iktinos had given her.

'They're making landfall,' she said. 'They're all around us, but the majority will be coming from the direction of the city. Straight towards you.'

'Understood,' said Iktinos from his position by the gates. 'May Dorn's strength be with us.'

'And the Sun Prince's blessing with us,' said Dyrmida.

Silver shapes were already gathering on the walls of Astelok, stranger-shaped enemies among the ranks of metallic warriors. They hovered or drifted, or scuttled down the walls on all fours.

More landing craft slammed into the forests to the south, within sight of the walls. The Undying gathered, and began to march.

THE FIRST SIGHT the *Antithesis* had of Selaaca was in information form, picked up by the ship's long-range sensors. The first reaction of the sensorium crew was to wonder what was wrong with their sensors. Repeated scanning showed the same results, however, and eventually they had to go to Archmagos Voar with information they were sure would incense the archmagos with its utter lack of logic.

Selaaca, it seemed, was hollow. Its core had been bored out and vented into titanic clouds of rock dust that orbited the planet in long trails of micrometeorites. And yet it had retained its mass, a fact so impossible that many of the ship's cogitators refused to accept it and spat it out in hails of punch-cards and spools of torn printout. Its interior was a lattice of steel and stranger metals, supporting continent-sized structures that pulsed with as much energy as the system's sun, caged and compressed into exotic radiation that the cogitators didn't recognise. Craft, tiny pinpricks of power, flitted over the surface and through close orbit. There was power everywhere, running through the planet's empty core, scribing glowing lines on the surface, even bleeding out into the toxic remnants of the atmosphere.

The surface was a ruin. The cities of Selaaca had been destroyed, scorched or uprooted, or pounded flat. Here and there, the monuments to the heart of the Selaacan Empire remained: the arms of a harbour wall enclosing a graveyard of sunken battleships; a great fortress in the heart of a desert, walled in by necron defences and left to starve; dozens of villages, untouched but devoid of life as they mouldered away in the hearts of forests.

Enormous wounds cut through the greatest cities. They led into the planet's interior, shattered buildings and shredded layers of history giving way to immense metallic avenues and conduits of power.

These wounds were ringed by necron facilities, landing pads and barracks, and sheets of metal, the size of islands, where gleaming necron warriors emerged to march.

Monoliths, immense menhirs of brushed steel, stood at precise intervals between the wounds, anchoring the complex webs of power that flowed across the planet. Swarms of scarabs attended to them, repairing the microscopic damage done by the particles of dust that whipped by on the burning winds that marked the death throes of Selaaca's atmosphere.

Not one living thing was detectable on Selaaca. The absence of life required by the necrons was total. Life, to them, was like death was to humans: an unimaginable aberration, a state where nothing could exist. It had to be banished before any great work could begin. Whatever the plans of the necron empire of Selaaca, of the whole necron race and its gods, it required the obliteration of life. That lesson had never been taught so bluntly as through the dead, torn husk of Selaaca.

Archmagos Voar was absorbing this information when Commander Sarpedon arrived on the bridge.

'I had not been informed,' said Voar, 'that you were a mutant.'

'It's not something that comes up in conversation,' replied Sarpedon. Tech-priests did not generally have a sense of humour, and, given Voar's silence, the archmagos was not an exception. 'It is a

complicated story, and one I am not good at telling. It does not affect my ability to lead.'

'Mutation is an abhorrence, commander, but as was made clear in our negotiations we must be willing to overlook a great many sins, given our present situation.'

'What do the xenos have waiting for us down there?'

Voar gave the printout another scan, and waved one of his manipulator units. A servitor, little more than a torso on wheels with a projector unit embedded in the dead skin of its chest, trundled over.

'I forget so easily,' said Voar, 'that not all audiences are equipped with logic circuits. Visual aids are necessary.'

The holo-unit projected a flickering image of Selaaca. Sarpedon tried to take in the implications of the scarred planet with its hollowed-out, metal-filled core visible through tears in the crust, but it just didn't seem to fit into his mind. The necrons – he still wanted to call them the Undying – must have been entombed in Selaaca since long before the humans of the Selaacan Empire had ever set foot there prior to the Great Crusade.

'The spacecraft seem to be transport and industrial ships,' said Voar, 'or the necron equivalents. The surface structures are probably power generator and capacitor facilities. The interior is opaque to our sensors, but a great deal of power is being consumed there.'

'Is there a way in?'

'Here,' said Voar, 'the planet's capital. The site of the largest surface excavation. It is likely that the necron forces first emerged from here after awakening. The signals directing the necron forces emanate from here.'

Sarpedon imagined the necron army marching from a tear in the ground, killing and harvesting as they conquered Selaaca. He could almost see the planet's cities falling, one by one, the blackout of one fuelling the fear in the next.

'What woke them?' he asked.

'Impossible to say. An excavation by the people of Selaaca. Some trigger at a necron outpost, activated by a new colony or off-world exploration. Or, perhaps, just time. Given the materiel being gathered on the surface, it seems they have yet to fully awake. What the Selaacan Empire has witnessed is the first phase of the necrons' refounding of their empire.'

'The first and the last,' said Sarpedon. 'How do we go in?'

'The *Antithesis* is designed for atmospheric flight,' replied Voar. 'I intend to pilot her into the main excavation in the capital city and deploy from there.'

'A crash landing?' asked Sarpedon with a raise of one eyebrow.

'A most precise and calculated landing, commander. There will be no crashing involved. The *Antithesis* is rather more advanced than Imperial

Naval standards. Besides, I accept the risk to my ship to fulfil our mission.'

'What forces can you bring?'

'A regiment of tech-guard. Seven hundred and thirty-three men. The tech-priest officer corps of the *Antithesis*, myself and the magi of my fleet.'

'And two hundred Astartes,' said Sarpedon.

'Given the likelihood of our being pursued by the necron fleet,' continued Voar, 'our tactics must emphasise speed over complexity. Once on the ground, we enter the main excavation.'

'And we kill everything we find until either we or they are dead,' finished Sarpedon.

'Quite. Landfall will be in two hours and fourteen minutes. If you have any preparations to make, I suggest you make them, commander, as the necrons most assuredly know we are here.'

THE FIRST RAEVENIANS to die in the last battle for Astelok were pioneers: tough, resourceful men and women recruited into the army of Queen Dyrmida from among the hunters and trappers that lived out in the wilds between city-states. A few of them were caught out by landing craft crashing through the trees almost right on top of them, in the tangled woods lining the road from the city to the space port. Undying warriors clambered out, unfolded their ancient metal limbs and immediately set about killing the pioneers, who tried to flee or hide among the trees.

The Undying guns flayed them to the bone, and left the bleeding, half-fleshed skeletons. Other pioneers were brought down by scarabs that forced their way into their mouths or burrowed through their skin with diamond-hard mandibles. The pioneer units had known before the battle began that they would be vulnerable outside the city walls, and that few of them could be expected to survive. They accepted this fate since they were fighting, not for themselves, but for the people huddled beneath the space port waiting for the Undying to claim them.

The Undying marched relentlessly through the forests, where they had landed to be safe from the Raevenian snipers and heavy weapons on the walls. It was a simple calculation for the guiding intelligence and the officer nodes of the army to make. It had also been made by Queen Dyrmida and her generals.

The traps set by the pioneers erupted just as the Undying units gathered together to march in rank. Dozens of the Undying were blown to pieces by fragmentation bombs made from fuel cells and shrapnel. Canisters of spaceship fuel exploded inside the trunks of trees, sending shards of wood and collapsing tree trunks crashing into the Undying. Some bodies self-repaired, but more phased out.

The officer nodes rapidly recalculated the angles of approach. They moved their advancing units towards the main road into the space port, and a

large area of clearer scrub on the opposite side of the space port, where the pioneers would have had a tougher job concealing booby traps.

Hidden pits collapsed, plunging Undying warriors into troughs of battery acid. Pioneers that had begged for a good death on this day manned the guns of vehicles half-buried in the ground, throwing off heaps of branches and camo-netting to blast at point-blank range into the Undying. They died soon enough, torn apart by scarabs or Undying guns, but they wiped out enough Undying to make their deaths good ones indeed.

The Undying force lost relatively few of its number, but the threat was grave enough to force it onto the open ground. Up on the walls, the men of Queen Dyrmida's army manned the guns trained on the target zones, and waited.

THE SOUL DRINKERS on the muster deck of the *Antithesis* cut a frightening enough sight that even the tech-guard units, many of whom had emotional dampening surgery, looked at them with fear. Twenty squads of ten were ranked up for Sarpedon to inspect, along with Pallas, Captain Luko, Tyrendian and Scamander. Salk and Graevus's squads had the prime places on the ends of the rank, since Sarpedon considered them the senior sergeants of his command. Techmarine Lygris was there too, for he had recovered enough lucidity to demand to be taken on this mission.

The tech-guard were being spoken to by the tech-priests who would lead them. They talked about sacred duty, obedience and sacrifice in the Omnissiah's name, and of the hateful nature of the xenos threat. Sarpedon noticed the magi among them, Vionel, a massive glowering metallic presence patched up with welded-on armour plates, and Hepsebah with extra power packs implanted into her back to fuel her lascannon. Sarpedon had heard speeches like that before, back in the old Chapter where his captain, Caeon, and Chapter Master Gorgoleon would speak to the Soul Drinkers of their position at the top of the human food chain, and of their divine right to herd the rest of the species towards the Emperor's goal.

'Soul Drinkers,' began Sarpedon, 'within the hour, we make landfall at Selaaca, and fight there against a foe with effectively infinite numbers and every reason to kill us. The necrons know we are coming. We have faced them before, and every one of you knows how unwilling they are to die. Make no mistake, battle-brothers, the necrons are the enemy of everything we have fought for. They will turn the Veiled Region into a base from which to treat the human race as cattle to kill or harvest. If we ever had a duty, it is to stop them.

'Chaplain Iktinos is relying on us, as are all the people of Raevenia. They do not deserve the fate the galaxy has placed on them. We have the power to change it. In doing so, we will change our own fate,

for we will be changing this galaxy for the better when so many have tried to use us to change it for the worse. Captain Luko?'

Luko stepped out of his squad to join Sarpedon. He looked like he would tear through the ship's hull if it would get him into battle quicker. 'Brothers! We know what we're fighting. Whatever intelligence leads the necrons, that's what we're here to kill. We've seen what these machines can do to good honest flesh, but they're not so dangerous that a couple of companies of Astartes can't turn them into iron filings. The one advantage the enemy has over us is numbers, so we keep moving. We never stop or take a backwards step. Keep charging on, forcing them back, and push on faster than they can wake reinforcements. If you get left behind, you die. Cold and fast, Soul Drinkers, and we'll kill their empire before they finish conquering it.'

'To your stations,' said Sarpedon. 'Final approach!'

The engines of the *Antithesis* screamed as the ship lunged into the toxic atmosphere of Selaaca.

A BILLION LENSES turned upwards. Scarabs paused their work on monoliths and power conduits to look at the glowing streak in the sky. Watchtower constructs, towering robots walking on spindly legs with thoraxes covered in sensors and artificial eyes, tracked it and sent its estimated landing site to the command systems in the planet's interior.

At the centre of those systems, the point at which every node connected, something vast and powerful stirred. It had slept for longer than most biological creatures could imagine. It, too, had been biological once, but that was so long ago that the memory of that time, if it could be said to possess memories in the human sense, was just a slice of information filed away among trillions of other statistics in the crystal-filled planetary core that made up its brain.

It could not move or think for long, only enough for a few key systems to warm up and a handful of milliseconds more to concoct the stream of electrons that made up its orders. The necron empire it ruled was so efficiently constructed that it need give only that single order and its will would be transmitted to every individual necron that could play a part in making it a reality.

Wake them, it said, *all of them.*

And then wake me.

'War is the only place we can be complete. Battle is the only activity at which our excellence can be meaningful. Do not believe that you can be a scholar, or a philosopher, or a leader of men. You are a warrior. When you are not inflicting death, you are not justifying your life.'

Daenyathos, *Principles of The Astartean Mind*

CHAPTER FOURTEEN

ANY OTHER SHIP would have been committing suicide, sacrificing itself and its crew to smash into the target. It had been done before by Imperial craft whose ordnance was used up and whose gun batteries were dry, or who had suffered such grave damage that the only thing they could still do was move. The necron defences assumed that this was the case, and prepared for little more than surface damage and the loss of a few thousand scarabs and other easily replaced units.

The *Antithesis's* engines were, however, up to the task of slowing it down even as its prow glowed blue-white with heat. The thin atmosphere provided just enough of a cushion for the ship to slow to a manageable speed under the massive deceleration of its forward-firing engines.

The ship crashed through a net of thread-like metallic filaments, built to keep meteorites from damaging the necron facilities in the capital city. It sheared straight through a sky-bound monorail, spilling containers and their cargoes of ore. The ship levelled out, slowing further, and roaring parallel to the ground. Its enormous prow carved through steel and stone buildings, the hurricane of its exhaust howling through what had once been the teeming streets of Selaaca. Finally, its main engines cut out, and the retro thrusters brought it down, grinding prow-first into the mass of the city.

The destruction was tremendous. Buildings were torn down like paper. The hull of the *Antithesis* split and tore, throwing chunks of metal like titanic shards of shrapnel as the keel hull was stripped away. Broadside guns were torn off and tumbled through ruined streets. The beak of the prow rode up through the remnants of an amphitheatre, scattering chunks of pale stone.

The *Antithesis* shuddered to a halt. Its artificial gravity had been stressed to breaking point to absorb the lethal deceleration that would have turned any living thing inside it to paste. Systems failed and power cells burst, throwing showers of sparks from the tears in the hull. Fires broke out along the stricken ship's length. Fuel poured from a ruptured fuel tank and ignited, blowing out a section of the engine housing in a tremendous tongue of flame.

The *Antithesis* would not fly again, but if the Astartes could do what they claimed, it wouldn't need to.

LUKO WAS FIRST out. Sarpedon couldn't have stopped him if he had wanted to.

'Go! Go!' shouted Luko, and hauled himself up through the exit hatch before it had fully opened.

Toxic air rolled into the *Antithesis*, foiled by the respirators in the helmets of the Soul Drinkers and the gas masks worn by the tech-guard. The Soul Drinkers had mustered in maintenance chambers near the upper hull, where the impact would not cause so much damage, and Luko had taken the first place beneath the hatch that would let them out.

The first impression Sarpedon got of Selaaca was of a sky the colour of night, scattered with stars and obscured by steel-grey wisps of corrupted cloud. He clambered out, his talons anchoring him to the upper hull of the spaceship. The fallen city was metal and stone, edged in silver by the unfiltered light of Selaaca's sun: half a fallen column, a collapsed wall, a statue of some Selaacan noble, standing in a field of rubble.

Metal had spread across the ruins like a stain, deep pools of it, and thick webs of it like the cocoons of metal beasts. Dark steel towers made up a skyline that had once been dominated by monuments and civic buildings, spewing exhaust gases

into the air. There was even metal in the sky, orbital installations like spindly new constellations.

The city that had once stood here had been smothered by the webs of steel. Here and there, it fought to the surface as a collapsed wall or a heap of rubble that might have been some great palace or basilica. The impressions of streets still remained, and a skyline of fractured towers. It was losing, however. It would not be long before the scarabs finished spinning their metallic caul, and Selaaca decayed away to nothing. Only the alien would remain.

Was this what the necrons wanted to do to the universe? Smother it in steel, and crush the life out of it?

Then there was gunfire.

Luko caught a blast on the shoulder. He didn't break stride as the blast sliced a chunk out of his shoulder pad, and he dived out of Sarpedon's eyeline, scrambling down the torn hull of the *Antithesis*. His squad followed him, their bolters opening up before they hit the ground.

'Deploy!' yelled Magos Hepsebah, who led the first unit of tech-guard. They were assault specialists with grenade launchers and plasma weapons, looking almost as inhuman as the magi with their gas masks and the heavy ribbed cables connecting their weapons to sensor packs plugged into their spines. The tech-guard emerged from hatches a short way along the hull, Hepsebah in the front rank.

Sarpedon followed the tech-guard down towards the city streets. Graevus, power axe in his mutated hand, was leading the first of the assault squads beside him.

Sarpedon scurried down the hull, and hit the ground running. Emerald blasts streaked around him, boring cores out of the stone and metal of the wreckage surrounding the *Antithesis*.

Behind the ship was an immense valley of ruins, torn by the ship's crash-landing. In front of it was a yawning chasm in the ground, ringed by ruins leaning poised to collapse over the edge. The ground sloped down into the chasm, where the darkness was studded with pulsing green lights. The ruins were infested with necron warriors, their metallic shapes just visible among the destruction. Luko's squad was running for cover among the ruins surrounding the chasm.

'There!' shouted Hepsebah. 'That's the main shaft.'

'Soul Drinkers!' yelled Sarpedon. 'Forward!'

The Soul Drinkers piled out of the *Antithesis*, firing as they ran. Necrons fell, skulls blasted open. More emerged from the ruins as if they had been roosting there, clambering over broken stone to close to firing range. Sarpedon saw Luko jumping a ruined wall and slicing a necron into ribbons with his power claws, as bolter fire cut down another that lurched up at him. Sarpedon followed in Luko's wake, and fired a bolter volley into movement that approached through the darkness.

Streaks of crimson light erupted from Hepsebah's lascannon, the barrels spinning as raw energy pulsed from the power cells mounted on her back. The walls of a nearby building disintegrated, and charred robotic limbs clattered to the ground among the debris.

Sarpedon dived into cover alongside Captain Luko.

'Lots of them out here,' said Luko. 'And there'll be more.'

'Hepsebah!' shouted Sarpedon. 'Think you can keep up?'

'Mock me not, mutant,' replied Hepsebah.

Sarpedon charged on, Luko beside him, leading the Soul Drinkers into the maw. He saw one Soul Drinker falling, leg sheared off by a blast that tore up into his abdomen. Another was being dragged along by his battle-brothers, one arm stripped away to bloody bone. Pallas was supporting another who had lost a part of his leg, blood pumping from the wound in his greave.

Sarpedon reached the edge of the shaft, and his eyes adjusted to its darkness. It curved downwards into the planet's crust, a metal-shod spiral tunnel like the lair of an immense mechanical worm. It was wide enough to act as a thoroughfare for huge vehicles like the necron harvesters. The *Antithesis* could have wedged itself inside if it had stopped a few hundred metres later.

Behind the Soul Drinkers, the tech-guard were covering the rear, sending gouts of plasma pouring into

the ruins around the maw. Grenades blew necrons off their feet or brought buildings collapsing around them, and Hepsebah's lascannon arm reaped more wreckage among the necron warriors. The other magi were further back with the rest of the tech-guard, and some of the Mechanicus soldiers were stranded, pinned down by fire and left behind by the speed of the assault.

They would be left there. There was no way the attack could stall to rescue them. If they stopped, they would all die. Many of the tech-guard had simple logic implants, and they would understand. The others would die alone and terrified, cursing the Soul Drinkers. That was the way it had to be.

Up ahead, swarms of scarabs were emerging in shimmering streams from holes in the walls of the metal shaft. Soul Drinkers carrying flamers ran to the fore, spraying a curtain of fire ahead of them. Scarabs ran into the flames and were immolated in the burning fuel, painting streaks of fire across the walls and ceiling as their systems went haywire. Tech-guard units made it to the front, and hosed the walls with their own flamers.

'Lygris,' voxed Sarpedon, 'are you still with us, brother?'

'I can feel it,' replied Lygris, who was towards the rear of the Soul Drinkers formation. 'I can hear its voice.'

'Not for much longer,' said Sarpedon.

The scarabs dispersed, many of them clattering to the floor as husks of smouldering metal. The tech-guard were catching up, and Sarpedon spotted Magos Vionel clutching a dismembered necron corpse in one of his huge industrial paws. Vionel threw the body to one side, and it phased out.

'Forward!' ordered Sarpedon. 'Archmagos, we cannot tarry here.'

'Then we leave the wounded,' said Archmagos Voar over the vox. 'They are commended to the Omnissiah. Tech-guard! Advance!'

Sarpedon led the way down into the dark metallic throat. It curved down beneath the city, its walls threaded with glowing green channels of power. The Soul Drinkers and tech-guard advanced at a run and covered the distance quickly, every man and Astartes well aware of the necrons that would be converging on the city to hunt them down if they hesitated.

Dim light shone from below, and, after a final kink, the throat ended in a circular opening, beyond which was an enormous excavation deep into the earth.

The necrons had not invaded. They had always been there, waiting beneath Selaaca for whatever signal the Selaacans had inadvertently given them to wake up and reclaim their empire. For a moment, Sarpedon could only stare at what they had created.

The necron tomb-city stared back.

* * *

'I AM MINDED to pray,' said Chaplain Iktinos, 'for all of us. For our brothers on Selaaca. For the people who face death around us. For ourselves. But also, for our future.'

Iktinos knelt before the gates of the space port. Gunfire was cracking from the walls on either side as the Raevenian snipers in the gatehouses took ranging shots at the Undying warriors advancing in ranks down the road from Astelok.

Iktinos's flock, numbering more than thirty Soul Drinkers, knelt around him. Only Iktinos truly understood the change that had come over them since they had numbered themselves among his followers. They were not just remnants of ravaged units looking for a leader. They were not even spiritually enthusiastic Astartes, who attended to Iktinos as an expression of their faith. They had become something else. In a sense, they were not even Soul Drinkers any more, for they did not follow Sarpedon and his ideals, but Iktinos and his plans. Which, though Sarpedon did not know it, were very, very different.

'It is an honour,' said one of the flock, 'to die for this future.'

'It is a greater honour to live for it,' said Iktinos.

'But to live to see his plan completed,' said another, 'is a blessing too great for me to beg.'

'Do not fear to ask to serve,' said Iktinos. 'Many of you will fall, and you will have done more for mankind than any other in the ten thousand years

of misery the Imperium has suffered. Those who live will honour the fallen with every step they take beyond. Cherish the life that fate may grant you, and welcome death! Praise the day that gives us this fight! Praise the death and the dealing of it! Bless every bullet you fire and every wound you take, for it is all part of the same fate. Think not of failure if you die, or of shame if you live. Think only of the future.'

Iktinos took out his crozius and laid it on the rockcrete of the gate road.

'This weapon is an instrument of my will,' he said. 'This will is victory. This victory is to build a future for the human race. If my will is undone, the victory will be lost and the future will die. This is what lies on our shoulders.'

Every battle-brother of Iktinos's flock laid his weapons – bolters, combat knives, flamers, plasma guns – on the ground. They echoed Iktinos's words in an intense murmur. It was not a prayer that could be found in any sacred work of the Soul Drinkers' Chaplains, or in the *Catechisms Martial* of the legendary Daenyathos. It was Iktinos's prayer. This was his fight. His will was being done, and, through him, the will of his master.

Iktinos's prayer was finished, and he looked up at the sky of Raevenia. Undying landing craft were still searing down through the sky, and the dull thuds of the anti-aircraft guns opened up again, spitting red-black clouds of burning flak into the air.

A commotion up on the walls beside the gate reached his ears. Something had alarmed the men up there, and it took a lot to faze men that had seen their home city torn to shreds by the Undying.

Iktinos headed to the gatehouse, a watchtower built into the support on one side of the massive double gates. Makeshift barricades had been piled up in front of the gates, welded with spikes and hooks to snag the Undying as they clambered over. Iktinos wove a path through them and reached the gatehouse door. He ran up the stairs inside, pushing past snipers stationed at windows along the stairway.

Two more snipers were stationed at the top of the watchtower. They started as Iktinos climbed up into their roost. The Space Marine barely fitted into the small room.

'Astartes,' said one of the snipers.

'What have you seen?' asked Iktinos.

The view from the gatehouse was enough to sap most men's wills. Thousands of Undying were trooping along the road, so vast in numbers that they trailed almost to the gates of Astelok. They were in strict formation and in perfect step, all holding their guns at ease, all with the same unmoving grimace on their metal skulls. The air vibrated with the impacts of their metal feet on the dirt. Iktinos quickly calculated there were at least ten thousand in the forward mass, and who knew how many more approaching from other angles or

still hidden by the forests. It was an army large enough to subjugate a world, and it had been arrayed against the single space port that still resisted them on Raevenia.

The sniper pointed to the edge of the wood that bordered the road. The woods were still smouldering from the booby traps that had funnelled the Undying towards the gates.

A vehicle was crashing through the trees. At least, a vehicle was the best description that Iktinos could think of. It was a steep pyramid, several storeys high, carried along on a crackling bed of energy that scorched the grass beneath it. A huge green crystal was embedded in its pinnacle, from which arcs of power were playing down the sheer black sides. Around it were the barrels of four energy weapons, dripping with the energy barely contained in their glowing capacitors. One side of the monolith slid open, revealing a liquid black pool suspended impossibly vertical, rippling with energy. Undying warriors marched alongside it like an honour guard. Iktinos could see that these warriors were the elite of the army, bigger and less humanoid with armour plates, not of dull metal, but of deep crimson covered in glyphs picked out in gold. This was the royal guard of whatever called itself the monarch of the Undying.

Another of the huge machines was crunching through the trees on the other side of the road. The dark paths carved through the forests further away

suggested there were more still, advancing slowly, but relentlessly.

'What is it?' asked the sniper.

'We will find out soon enough,' said Iktinos. 'What is the range?'

'We've had a few sighting shots. Their front ranks are still past rifle range. The... war engines, whatever they are, will be in range a lot later than that. We know how far the warriors can shoot, but those machines might out-range us.'

'Do not fire upon the Undying in earnest,' said Iktinos, 'until they are three ranks in. You cannot kill them all. Sow confusion instead.'

'Yes, sir,' said the sniper. His voice was shaking, and it was impossible to tell if he was more afraid of the Undying or of Iktinos.

Iktinos examined the approaching Undying more closely. A few of the flying warriors were hovering along the edge of the treeline, many of them with long-barrelled cannon that looked like they had the range to strip the gatehouse away at any moment. The elite, the immortals of the Undying horde, were falling into step alongside the warriors, dwarfing them with their hulking size.

A few among the warriors were taller than those around them, walking fully upright in a grim echo of a man. They carried staffs instead of guns, and their metallic forms were wrought into more elaborate shapes like ornate armour. Their

eyes burned brighter with intelligence, and energy crackled around them like emerald haloes.

'Note their leaders,' said Iktinos.

'We… we kill them first, right?' said the sniper.

'If you can,' said Iktinos. But the truth was, he did not think the snipers had much chance of inflicting anything more than nominal losses on the Undying. Killing as many as possible would not win this battle. Raw shock and devastation would be the key. The Soul Drinkers, and the Raevenians before them, had assumed that the Undying were immune to such things, that they had none of the mental weaknesses of men. Iktinos saw that their weaknesses simply had to be exploited.

'There are leaders among them,' voxed Iktinos to his flock. 'Leaders means a chain of command. And a chain means it can be broken. The soulless ones are not immune to the terror and confusion of war; a Space Marine is. That is how we will win, my brothers. The xenos need logic to function, but an Astartes can achieve victories that defy all logic. When they see the certainty of their victory breaking down, they will become as vulnerable as any other enemy.'

Iktinos headed back down the stairs to join his battle-brothers behind the gates.

'Sir,' said the sniper, 'when the Undying get here… where do we go?'

'You stay here,' said Iktinos, 'until you die.' Then he ducked out of the watchtower and left the snipers to their hopeless fight.

A CITY OF tombs stretched so far it disappeared into the horizon, where the metal-clad sky met the ground.

Every tomb was a masterpiece. Crafted from brushed metal, stone and gold, they were the resting places of the necron army's generals, places of worship, monuments to a future without biological life. Some were like temples, their columns surrounding sarcophagi carved with the images of the regal, skeletal things inside. Others were blocks of steel carved deeply with stylised images of conquest and genocide, subjugated xenos and alien eyes picked out in gold. One was an enormous hand of black stone bones, holding a necron form, curled up like an obscene foetus, in its palm. One was a steel skull with its inhabitant just visible in its mouth, wide open as if in mid-scream. There must have been thousands of tombs, arranged in a grid to form avenues between the sepulchres.

Techmarine Lygris pushed to the front of the Soul Drinkers as they formed a gun line at the entrance to the tomb-city.

'Get me to an interface,' he said. 'I can lead us through.'

Sarpedon couldn't see Lygris's face because the techmarine wore his helmet, but the strength an

Astartes carried in his voice was gone. Lygris was a wreck, broken by whatever he had seen when he interfaced with the necron information network. Sarpedon knew that if his old companion were ever to become as he once was, it would not happen on Selaaca.

'Stay back, Lygris. Keep alive. Luko! Lead us forward. The xenos will be close behind.'

The Soul Drinkers advanced in a tight formation, Luko taking the far right of the line as it made its way between the first rows of tombs, the tech-guard following. Scamander, as was so often the case, was beside Tyrendian as they moved. His eyes were smouldering.

'Power spike,' voxed Voar.

'I don't like the sound of that,' said Luko's voice over the vox. 'Tighten up, Soul Drinkers! Mutual cover! Graevus, you're fast response!'

'Yes, commander,' replied Graevus, whose assault unit was just behind the main gun line. Half the Soul Drinkers squads advanced with the other half covering them, training their bolters down the long avenues between tombs.

'We'll need to get one of these open,' voxed Luko. 'They look solid enough.'

The tomb just in front of Luko, shaped like a chunk of battlement from an iron fortress, split open down the middle. Freezing vapour poured out, clinging to the ground like liquid. Green light bled from the darkness inside.

'Damn,' said Luko.

Luko dived to the side just as a blast of emerald light tore out of the sarcophagus towards him.

'Close up and cover!' yelled Sarpedon, watching from the centre of the line.

Luko's squad leapt into cover as blasts of power shredded the walls of the tombs beside them.

Sarpedon heard the grinding of metal on stone. The tomb next to him was opening, slivers of ancient stone flaking away from a stylised face sculpted as if it was half-buried in the floor. The golden sphere of the face's single eye rolled out of the fractured socket and thunked to the floor. Light bled from the socket, stuttering as something moved inside.

The stone split open, and the necron inside unfolded with an ancient majesty.

Its skeleton was tarnished gold inlaid with deep blue. Its eyes flashed green and crimson, and its skull was set into a headdress like coiled snakes cascading down over its shoulders. A cape made of linked panels of gold and steel clanked around it. It carried a staff topped with a blade, inset with a fat green jewel.

Sarpedon reacted first. He ducked beneath the edge of the split sarcophagus and heard the hiss of a blade cutting through air. He came up, bolter blazing, hammering shots into the necron's torso.

The necron turned on him and lashed out with his staff again. Sarpedon turned it aside with his

forearm, but the staff fired a shard of brilliant green energy that threw Sarpedon off his feet.

Sarpedon slammed into the tomb behind him, splintering abstract carvings. The breath was knocked out of him and his head swam. Instinct took over, and he fired at the blurry gold shape advancing on him, rolling to the side and springing up on his arachnid legs.

The necron wrenched the bolter out of Sarpedon's hand and crushed it in its powerful metal fingers, flinging it away. Sarpedon drew the Axe of Mercaeno from his back, and, for an instant, barely a passing of time at all, it showed hesitation when it saw the force weapon in Sarpedon's hand.

It had no face to express emotions with, just a leering skull, but its body language suggested an apprehension that was beyond the scope of a machine's emotions.

The necron struck again and again. Sarpedon caught the blows on the haft of his axe, and flicked the butt of the weapon up into the necron's face, snapping its head back and sending it reeling. It was taller than him, perhaps twice as tall as a necron warrior, and it was stronger and more resilient by far, but it had a weakness that they did not.

'You were alive,' snarled Sarpedon. 'You used to have a soul.'

The necron might even have understood him. It didn't matter. It would get the message sure enough.

Sarpedon let the force well up inside him, spiralling around the aegis circuit built into his armour. It burst up into his mind like a volcano, and flowed out of him, hot and violent.

For the first time, the necrons bore witness to the Hell.

SARPEDON DID NOT even remember when he had first discovered the Hell.

It might have been when he was a child, before the Chaplains of the Soul Drinkers ever found him. Or, more likely, it was a refinement of raw, formless powers he had demonstrated back then, and had first come to be in the Librarium of the Soul Drinkers, flagship, the *Glory*, as Sarpedon was being tested and trained by the Chapter's Librarians.

It was a form of telepathy, but a brutal, uncontrolled one, a raw mental bludgeon. It was rare indeed among psykers, but as a weapon it was formidable. Tyrendian's lightning and Scamander's fire were weapons in the simplest sense, implements of destruction. The Hell attacked its enemy's minds just as other Librarians attacked their bodies.

The key was fear. The hardest lesson Sarpedon had learned was that fear did not make itself. He had to find it in the enemy, draw it out and give it form. It was a strange thing for a Space Marine to think so deeply about fear, which the Emperor had

created him to control and ignore as an unwanted sensation, but Sarpedon had to understand it.

What did a necron fear?

THE NECRON WRAPPED its arms around Sarpedon, and, unable to crush him through his power armour, threw him against the tomb behind him. Sarpedon struggled to his feet. He could hear gunfire everywhere, and glimpsed more of the ornate necrons battling the Soul Drinkers all along the line. More were emerging from their sarcophagi. Some were being battered back by bolter volleys, but some had emerged among the Soul Drinkers and tech-guard, and were throwing bodies aside as they killed.

Sarpedon kicked out with his front legs, but the necron held firm. Sarpedon ripped the Axe of Mercaeno up into its torso, and felt the blade bite into unnaturally hard metal, gouging a furrow up to its throat. The necron hauled him into the air, and slammed him down on the roof of the tomb.

A spike of dark steel was driven through Sarpedon's backpack, through the back of his armour and out through his chest. He was impaled there, stuck like a pinned insect with his legs kicking out in every direction. The pain hammered through him, and he felt one of his lungs deflate, bubbling blood out into his chest cavity.

Like fear, pain was something a Space Marine might feel, but never bow to. Pain was the

Emperor's way of reminding him there was work to do. An Astartes' duty overrode pain. It even overrode death.

Death. The necrons were death, the death that had descended on Selaaca. That was how the Selaacans must have seen them: an army of oblivion marching through their cities to snatch them away.

There was only one thing that death might fear.

The Hell took form. It was life, infinite, seething life, an avalanche of fecundity. A steaming spectral jungle unfolded, thousands of predatory eyes glinting. Every surface was covered in ravenous life. Insects swarmed in dark masses in every corner. Vines split the ancient stone of the tombs. They wrapped around the legs of the ornate necron, bursting into flower or seed. Slimy limbs reached up from the swampy floor and tried to drag the necron down.

It had a soul. Or at least, it used to. It had once been alive, and it still remembered some of what that meant. It still retained some of the personality of whatever damned creatures had become the necrons. That was all the Hell needed to take a hold.

'What is the alien? It is more than merely a creature of non-Terran origin. Such a thing would hold no holy disgust for us. The alien is an idea, a concept, deadly by virtue of its mere existence. The very possibility of the alien becoming a dominant force among the stars is corrosive to the human soul.'

Daenyathos, *A Thousand Foes*

CHAPTER FIFTEEN

NORTH OF THE space port gates, the advancing Undying crossed rifle range. The snipers yelled a warning, and the officers of the Raevenian army gave the order to fire.

Raevenian guns opened up in such numbers that the view from the walls was blurred, as if through heavy rain. The sound was appalling, like an earthquake, an endless exploding din.

Undying fell. Some were shredded beyond self-repair, smashed into shards of metal that phased out before they hit the ground. One of the lords, the tall, regal Undying with ornate carapaces, held up an onyx sphere that pulsed with black light, and the fallen Undying around him clambered to their feet, even scattered shreds of metal flowing back together like quicksilver to re-form into warriors.

One of the flying warriors crashed into the trees, a neat hole punched through its skull by a sniper's bullet. A rocket battery opened up on the walls, and a chain of explosions ripped through the front ranks of the Undying, throwing shattered warriors into the air.

There were so many of them. A man could not count them, and the destruction around them did not slow them down.

Death meant nothing to them, because they were death.

The Undying broke the cover of the trees to the south of the space port and met a similar curtain of fire from the southern walls, where the Raevenians had set up most of their heavy weapons: machine-gun nests, missile launchers and vicious mortar-like devices, which fired clouds of razor wire that turned the approaches into near-impossible terrain. The Undying warriors were slowed down by the wire that draped over them like silver spiders' webs, catching limbs and gun barrels. They tore their way through it with metallic hands, but they could only advance at a crawl, and the guns battered into them. The Undying nobles issued their silent commands, and the Undying broke formation, heading this way and that to make for less tempting targets. One noble was caught in a missile blast and was sheared in two, its lower half clattering to the ground, dead and useless. Its upper half was picked up and dragged along by the Undying around it.

* * *

QUEEN DYRMIDA WATCHED from the balcony of the space port's control tower, from where she could just see the tops of the monoliths approaching behind the main Undying line, and the shuddering of the trees to the south as they were battered by stray fire. It sounded like the air itself was tearing.

'You should take cover, your majesty,' said Kavins.

'I know,' said Dyrmida, 'but when they reach us, I will fight.'

'As shall we all. But your part in this battle has been played. Your plan has been put into motion, and you can do nothing now to change its course.'

'I can go to them and show them I am willing to earn my throne by fighting alongside them.'

'If we lose you,' said Kavins, ' more harm will be done than good.'

Dyrmida looked at Kavins, who had the face of a veteran that had been through plenty of wars and come out the other side with his zeal and aggression replaced with weary experience.

'I know all of this,' she said, 'but at least down there I would know I was doing something to aid my citizens.'

'Your majesty,' said Kavins, a note of urgency in his voice, 'I suggest you retire to the situation room. The Undying may have longer-range weapons than we expect, and you will be a prime target.'

Dyrmida followed the officer into the command centre. There were officers everywhere, coordinating the actions of the troops on the walls and on

the landing pads. Raevenian soldiers stood guard to protect them, and Dyrmida knew how much they would rather be in the battle than waiting for the Undying to break through. The gunfire was loud, even here, making it impossible to concentrate on anything other than the approaching destruction.

'They're going through ammunition like it's water,' one officer was saying. 'We'll have to send runners.'

'Hold,' said another into a field telephone. 'Damn it, hold them at the west! I'm not having these things climb over undefended walls when our backs are turned!'

Officers saluted Dyrmida as she passed, and she returned their salutes almost unconsciously. The rear echelon detritus of war littered every surface: maps spread out on tables and floors or pinned to the walls, sidearms and ammunition crates, mess tins and furniture pushed out of the way to make room for impromptu conferences. Everything smelled of gun oil and sweat.

'Your majesty!' said a junior officer clutching the receiver of a field telephone. 'Another monolith spotted.'

'How many is that?' asked Dyrmida.

'Four. This one's to the south.'

'Then they will put up a fight there. Redeploy some of our anti-tank reserves. We must keep it from the walls if we can.'

'Yes, your majesty.' The officer began relaying her orders into the telephone in the abbreviated speech typical of her soldiers.

'Do we know yet what they do?' Dyrmida asked Kavins.

'The monoliths? Siege engines probably, but we won't know for sure until they get in range.'

'Keep me updated if any more emerge. Make their destruction a priority.'

'Already done.'

The queen and the officer reached the situation room. It was a flight control room hurriedly set up as a nerve centre, with a number of the control consoles removed and replaced with a map table. The map of the space port on it was covered in pins and annotations showing where the various units were stationed. A number of communications officers sat at the consoles relaying orders and reports.

'You,' she said to the officer watching the pict feed from the northern gates, 'what news from Iktinos?'

'None,' the officer replied. 'The Soul Drinkers have gone quiet.'

'Let us hope they find their voice when the gates fall,' said Dyrmida.

Situation reports were coming in on the size and composition of the Undying force. Dyrmida was soon overwhelmed by it all, the enemy seeming to get more numerous with every moment, even as their warriors were shot down.

* * *

IN A CORRIDOR on a lower floor of the control tower, where an impromptu triage station had been set up to handle casualties from around the tower, a pair of medics looked up at the shouting nearby. Two soldiers approached, supporting a third. The wounded man was covered in blood, deep wounds in his chest and face.

'Over here!' shouted the medic.

The soldiers half-dragged their wounded comrade to the triage station and laid him down.

'What happened?'

'Looks like a mortar blew up or something,' said a soldier. 'Proper shredded him.'

The medic's partner opened a trauma kit, a bag packed with all the bandages, dressings and stimulants needed for a typical battle wound.

'He's messed up,' he said.

'Will he make it?' asked the soldier.

'Sure,' said the second medic without much conviction as he cut open the wounded man's fatigues.

'Damn it, that's a perforated bowel,' said the first medic, wrinkling his nose. 'You guys, get back to the walls. We'll deal with him.'

'Right.'

'What's his name?'

The soldier shrugged. 'Don't know. We found him wandering around outside. Must've come down off the wall.'

The soldiers left, wiping the blood off the fronts of their uniforms.

'Forget it,' said the first medic as the second took out a bundle of sutures and dressings. He was holding the wounded man's wrist. 'No pulse.'

'Then this is how it starts,' said the second. 'We decided where the bodies go?'

'Maintenance room, one floor down,' said the first. 'Lucky guy,' he said to the body. 'You get a body bag. They're gonna run out soon.'

The second medic headed to the other side of the corridor where a supply of black body bags was piled up against the wall.

Neither man noticed the green glow breaking through the dead man's eyelids.

THE TOMB-CITY GAVE the impression of having been silent for aeons. Now, it was filled with the din of gunfire, lasguns and bolters hammering, necron weapons hissing as they tore through stone, armour and flesh. The tech-guard were pinned down by the emergence of the necron lords, their advance cut into knots of soldiers and tech-priests, finding what cover they could before it dissolved around them.

Archmagos Voar noticed the masses of ghostly jungle spreading across the tombs, but he did not care much. He was concentrating on more immediate matters.

Another tech-guard died beside him, sliced in two. The men around Voar were yelling, running from cover to cover as they tried to outflank the pair of necron lords that were sowing carnage through

them. Lascannon fire from Magos Hepsebah streaked around them, but a shimmering energy field leapt up and dissipated the torrent of crimson energy.

'Device Gamma,' said Voar. One of the tech-guard behind him handed Voar a metal sphere, with a transparent section revealing twin hemispheres of metal wrapped in wire. Voar ran his hand over the activation panel and the device hummed to life.

He threw it like a grenade past the columns of the tomb behind which he was sheltering. It rolled along the ground between the two necron lords, and burst, throwing out a shower of white sparks: electromagnetic chaff, similar to the counter-measures used by the Mechanicus spacecraft, but crafted to interfere with the wavelengths that Voar had detected coming from the destroyed necron in his lab.

'Forward!' yelled Voar, his voice amplified to maximum.

Tech-guard charged forwards around him. Green flame danced around them, but it was wild and unfocused. Half-blinded and deafened, the necrons couldn't aim properly at the advancing tech-guard.

Fire poured into the two xenos. Plasma bursts crashed against their power fields, spitting globs of liquid flame everywhere. Two tech-guard hauled a multimelta into place beside the tomb, one slamming a fuel bottle into its side as the other opened fire.

The power field around one of the necrons overloaded with a white flash. The lord was plated in
pitted rose gold, its skull covered in deep scroll-
work and its hands in silver blades. Each palm was
fitted with a crystal from which it fired bolts of
green fire, but, in its blinded state, it was shooting
at random.

The multimelta recharged and the tech-guard
hammered fire at the shieldless lord again, the air
rippling as pure heat radiation thrummed from
the weapon. The necron's torso melted and
shifted, revealing layers of circuitry beneath. The
lord stumbled back, molten metal dribbling from
its wounds.

Voar moved with rapid precision past the tomb
and into range of the stricken necron. His manipulator units slithered from his shoulder, striking
like snakes to implant their metal hooks in the
necron's molten chest. Voar accessed his internal
capacitor, and delivered a massive blast of power
into the xenos machine, tailored to the exact frequency that would shatter its circuitry.

The necron lord's torso burst open, throwing
chunks of metal ribs and spine. The remnants of
the necron clattered to the floor. Its wounds covered over with quicksilver as it began to self-repair.
Voar stood over it, snapping a manipulator into
each of its eye sockets. He forced the remaining
charge into it, and its skull exploded.

The second necron lord was similarly confused by the interference from device Gamma. Magos Vionel broke cover and stomped up behind it, grabbing the lord around the waist and hurling it against the closest tomb, splintering marble and bronze. Vionel's other arm fired three rivets into the lord, pinning it to the tomb through its neck and one arm.

The lord struggled. It was strong, but the fat rivets piercing its metallic frame held fast. Its senses were still scrambled, but it couldn't have missed Magos Vionel putting his enormous steel shoulder down and charging towards it.

Vionel impacted so hard that the tomb collapsed, and the lord was crushed down into a mass of broken stone. Vionel reared up and crashed down again, slamming his shoulder into the lord. He beat enormous metal fists against it, throwing out clouds of dust and shards.

The lord tried to drag itself to its feet, but there was nothing left of its motive systems. Its arms and legs were smashed and its torso split open. One eye had popped out, a flickering green lens dangling from a wire. It looked like a crushed insect, fluttering with the last sparks of life.

Vionel reached down and twisted the lord's head off. A couple of sparks flew from the stump of its broken spine, and then it died. Vionel dropped the battered metal skull and stomped it flat under an ironclad foot.

'It works, then,' voxed Magos Hepsebah.

'Forward!' ordered Voar again. The tech-guard advanced through the tombs, pausing to glance at the wrecked remains of the necron enemy.

SARPEDON PULLED THE Axe of Mercaeno from the necron's ribs and threw the thing aside. The Hell had worked. It had given him the opening he had needed to kill the alien machine.

'Here!' voxed Techmarine Lygris. Sarpedon saw that Lygris was clambering through the remains of the wrecked tomb. 'It was connected.'

Lygris had found an interface into the rest of the necron network, in the remains of the lord's tomb. It was a cluster of black crystals on the sarcophagus floor, like an obsidian flower, that would have fitted into the back of the necron lord's skull.

Sarpedon looked up to take stock of the situation. The nearest necrons had been destroyed or disabled by the Soul Drinkers and Voar's tech-guard, but more were waking, and their honour guard – the larger, less humanoid warriors the Mechanicus had codenamed the Immortals – were marching into the tomb city from outside.

The Soul Drinkers had to move quickly. If they were pinned down in the tombs, they would be swamped by necrons. Lygris had recovered much of his lucidity since the harvester, but he was still not the Astartes Sarpedon knew. Lygris would be risking his soul as well as his life if the necrons assaulted

his mind once more. If Lygris gave the Soul Drinkers a chance to turn the battle, however, Sarpedon had to take it.

'Go,' said Sarpedon. 'Shield your soul, my brother.'

A dataprobe extended from Lygris's finger and spun like a drill bit. He bored into the crystal with it, slumping down as his consciousness slipped into the information landscape inside.

'Perimeter!' shouted Sarpedon. The Soul Drinkers moved up to form a cordon around Sarpedon's position, loosing bolter volleys at the necrons just visible advancing between the tombs.

Captain Luko slid into cover beside Sarpedon.

'I hope he gets out intact this time,' he said.

IF THERE HAD been a soul in there, a mind that could think and comprehend, then it was so utterly alien that a human mind could not encompass its nature.

Lygris could feel nothing, see nothing. His mind would not let him. It was shielding him, closing like a pupil in a bright light, to protect him from being overloaded.

Lygris did not remember what he had seen when he bored into the crystal that had controlled the necron harvester. His memory, like his consciousness, had closed ranks to keep him safe from it. He had only the vaguest of impressions: of immense age, beyond human imaginings; of things born

before mankind had crawled from whatever primal ocean had spawned it on ancient Terra; of power, and of hate.

Pure, mechanical, soul-crushing hate, as powerful as a supernova and as cold as the dead star that remained, that was what could kill him. That was what could take everything human in him and flay it away until there was nothing left of Lygris.

He could hide from it forever. He could shut himself off and save himself from that fate, but an Astartes had a duty that demanded everything from him, even unto death. Lygris had made that oath every time he had walked into battle for his Chapter and his Emperor. He would not back down from it now.

Lygris opened his mind, and let the hatred in.

LYGRIS WAS THROWN clear of the shattered tomb in a shower of green sparks. Sarpedon caught him and dragged him into cover.

Necron fire was coming from every direction. The tech-guard had linked up with the Soul Drinkers, and together they formed an entrenched position among the tombs. They were holding well, but more necrons were arriving at the far end of the tomb-city, and emerald fire was stripping away the cover of the remaining tombs.

'We've got more coming in behind us!' voxed Luko, who was directing his squad's fire nearby.

'Keep them busy!' replied Sarpedon. He looked down at Lygris. He was unconscious, but alive.

Pallas arrived beside Sarpedon.

'He's out,' said Sarpedon. 'We need him.'

Pallas extended an injector from his medicae gauntlet, and stabbed it into a port in the neck joint of Lygris's armour. Lygris's system flooded with stimulants. He bolted awake, coughing up a clot of blood.

'Are you with us, brother?' asked Sarpedon.

'I am, commander.' Lygris's speech was slurred, and his movements were uncoordinated.

'Where do we go now?' asked Sarpedon.

Lygris struggled to his feet.

'Nowhere,' he said.

The ground shook. In the centre of the city, necron tombs sank into the ground, and an enormous square pit was revealed, taking up a good third of the city's area. Chunks of masonry and steel fell as titanic engines ground away beneath the city with a sound like an earthquake. The whole chamber shifted to accommodate it, the ground sloping towards it, the ceiling rising.

'Hold position!' blared Archmagos Voar's vox-unit. 'Steel yourselves! The Omnissiah wills the human soul to prevail! Before no xenos trickery shall we falter!'

The pit deepened and became a shaft of blackness. The dim light glinted on the tip of a structure emerging from its depths.

'Sweet spires of Mars,' whispered a tech-guard nearby.

Level by level, with a slow and alien majesty, a pyramid emerged from beneath the tomb-city.

'Death holds no fear only for the fool. An Astartes' duty is to control that fear and to turn it into a blind hatred of the end of his life, for it brings with it the inability to fulfil his duty to the universe.'

Daenyathos, *Tome of Universal Truths*

CHAPTER SIXTEEN

THE PILE OF bodies had started out as a single bagged corpse thrown into the command centre's storeroom. The room had been chosen because it was equipped with air-scalable doors, and no one wanted the stink of the dead filling the command centre.

There were about a dozen bodies there. Most of the dead from the unfolding battle lay where they had fallen, or in heaps below the walls. The bodies in the store room represented those who had made it to the tower for treatment and had succumbed to their wounds, or who had died closer to the command centre as weapons exploded or chunks of shrapnel flew from fire on the walls.

The pile settled again, a rattle of air escaping dead lungs. One of the corpses wriggled, like a shiny black worm, out from underneath the other bodies.

It was the first body that had been thrown in there. Unlike most of them it had been zipped up in a body bag before being dumped in the room.

The seal on the bag split open. A bloody hand reached out and pulled the bag apart. The body inside, a Raevenian soldier caked in blood, clambered to its feet. It was half-bent over in a position that a human spine could not maintain for long, its head thrust forward like an animal's. Its wounds were so disfiguring it was impossible that it was still alive. Its eyes flickered green.

The corpse opened the door with the hiss of a breaking air seal. No one had thought to bar the door from the outside, since the idea of a corpse walking out was ridiculous.

The dead Raevenian shambled down the corridor, passing storerooms full of abandoned equipment. Its gait became surer as it went, as if it was rapidly relearning how to walk. The corpse room was in the command centre's basement, and was not being used by any of the commanders and support staff of Queen Dyrmida's army. The muffled thunder of gunfire was the only sound aside from the clicking of metallic heels on the floor.

Footsteps came from up ahead. A soldier emerged from a bend in the corridor. He was wearing the uniform of a medic, and was dragging a body bag along behind him. His uniform was smeared with blood, and his hands were red with it.

The soldier saw the corpse and stopped.

'Hey,' he said. 'Hey, you're a live one, right? Stay there, don't move. I'll get you help.' He dropped the bag and hurried up to the corpse. 'Listen, sit down, and I'll get someone from upstairs. Got it? Speak to me, pal. Come on.'

The corpse grabbed the back of the soldier's neck and slammed him against the wall. Its other hand punched into the soldier's back and closed around his spine. It ripped out a handful of vertebrae.

The soldier gasped, and flopped to the floor, his legs useless. Before he could scream, the corpse reached down and slit his throat with razor-sharp fingertips. A whisper of breath gasped out of the wound, followed by a spray of blood.

The corpse stepped over the body bag as it left the soldier to die. It found the maintenance door it had been searching for. It was locked, but it rammed the palm of its hand into the door just below the lock and it burst open. A chunk of bloody palm was torn off and slipped to the floor. The corpse did not seem to notice. Blood-slicked metal glinted through the wound.

The room contained shelves of tools, lubricants, paints and other maintenance supplies. Set into the floor was a large metal hatch with a wheel lock.

The corpse knelt down and hauled on the wheel lock. Flakes of rust broke off, and the lock squealed as the corpse forced it open. With a boom, the lock snapped open and the corpse hauled the hatch up.

Burning green eyes looked up from the darkness of the maintenance space below.

The Undying climbed up through the hatch. They were skinnier than the warriors, lacking the broad carapaces over their shoulders, and they didn't carry any weapons. Instead, long silver claws folded out from their forearms, fitting over the ends of their fingers.

The corpse led them out of the room. One of them knelt down beside the dead soldier and slit his back open with its blades, removing bones and organs with inhuman speed and accuracy. Another opened the body bag and began doing the same to the dead soldier inside. A neat pile of organs and bones was piled up beside the bodies, arranged as precisely as the pieces of a machine. In less than two minutes, the soldier the corpse had killed was hollowed out, and the Undying pulled its still-clothed hide into it, fitting its limbs and torso inside. It pulled the dead man's face over its skull. The third Undying finished its dissection and did the same. The soldier it wore had been killed by a blast that tore away one side of his chest, its bloody metal ribs visible through the wound.

More Undying were coming up from the maintenance space where they had been waiting patiently for the infiltrator to let them through. They followed the corpse towards the stairwell leading up into the command centre. The three wearing the skins of the dead took the lead. The others went

naked and undisguised, but it did not matter. Soon there would be enough bodies to go around.

THE PYRAMID WAS immense. Its pinnacle tore into the ceiling, and its base had dislodged almost half of the tomb-city. Chunks of rubble tumbled down its sides like rain. The pyramid was made from glossy black stone, deeply inscribed with glyphs and patterns that echoed circuitry.

The pyramid was stepped, and on each level stood black menhirs, like the standing stones erected all over Selaaca, channelling information across the planet's surface. Somewhere in its vastness and majesty was a very recognisable arrogance, the proportions designed to awe, the triumphal pictograms of stylised necrons marching across wasted planets. The necron warriors were soulless, but the intelligence that had caused the pyramid to be constructed had enough of a personality left to want to proclaim its superiority.

A wide staircase hundreds of steps high led to the upper levels. The top quarter of the pyramid was a columned temple, its entrance flanked by obsidian statues of necron Immortals permanently at guard. Patterns of gold spiralled around the columns, pulsing with energy.

The rumbling stopped. The pyramid had forced its way fully into the tomb-city.

Techmarine Lygris, being helped along by Apothecary Pallas, looked up at the pyramid.

'It's another tomb,' he said.

'The intelligence?' asked Sarpedon. 'It's in there?'

'I can taste its thoughts,' said Lygris.

If Lygris had still been able to speak with his own tongue, thought Sarpedon, would he have detected a note of fear in the Techmarine's voice?

'Archmagos,' voxed Sarpedon, 'we need you to hold the base of the pyramid. Keep the necrons off our backs.'

'Very well, commander,' replied Voar. The tech-guard were just behind the Soul Drinkers, moving to take up positions among the tombs. Necrons were already emerging from the tunnel that led back up to the surface, the vanguard of the force that had pursued them through the ruins above. 'The time you have shall be bought with the blood of the Omnissiah's faithful. Do not waste it.'

'All squads!' ordered Sarpedon. 'Assault units to the fore! Soul Drinkers, advance!'

The Soul Drinkers broke cover and made for the base of the pyramid. The necrons that had survived the pyramid's emergence opened fire, but they were in disarray. The Soul Drinkers were as fast and ruthless as any Astartes, Graevus leading the assault units up front that leapt obstacles on their jump packs and brought down the necrons in their way with chainswords and bolt pistols. The tech-guard engaged the necrons on their flank, swapping fire with the aliens to tie them down and keep them from blunting the advance. Sarpedon glimpsed the

fat bursts of laser from Magos Hepsebah, and even spotted a broken Undying being hurled aside by the industrial strength of Magos Vionel.

Lygris was on his feet, and snapped shots off at the necrons between the tombs. The Soul Drinkers had almost reached the pyramid.

'Heavy resistance,' voxed Graevus from up ahead. 'They're throwing warriors at us.'

'Open us up a path,' replied Sarpedon. 'Luko! Salk! With me! Up the steps!'

Sarpedon ran forwards at full tilt, Lygris struggling to keep up as Sarpedon scrambled over the ruined tombs in front. Pallas and Tyrendian were there, too, Tyrendian scorching the shadows between the tombs with a bolt of lightning that blew an Immortal to burning pieces.

The assault units were battling with the necrons up ahead. Sarpedon ran past them, leading the rest of the Soul Drinkers onto the steps.

'Support fire!' shouted Luko as his squad made it onto the steps. His Soul Drinkers turned and aimed down into the tombs, where dozens of necrons were massing to march on Graevus's embattled assault troops. 'Fire!'

Squad Luko raked the tombs with explosive fire. Necrons fell, clambered back up self-repaired, and fell again with massive wounds blasted through their metal carapaces. Squad Salk joined in, and a unit of tech-guard made it onto the bottom level of the pyramid to lend the weight of their las-fire to the battle.

Tyrendian and Scamander joined Sarpedon and Lygris at the front.

'How do we kill it?' asked Tyrendian. 'Assuming we even know what it is?'

'I don't know,' said Lygris. 'But we have to do it now.'

'Heads up!' shouted Scamander, looking towards the pinnacle of the pyramid. Hundreds of black motes were swarming from inside the temple entrance.

'Scarabs,' spat Lygris.

'Guns up! The xenos are upon us!' ordered Sarpedon. More and more Soul Drinkers were making it onto the pyramid steps, forming a firing line of bolters that was sweeping the ruined tombs of necron defenders. Many of them turned to see the new threat from above.

'Unless we are to shoot them all, one by one,' said Scamander, 'I suggest you all get down.'

Tyrendian looked at the young Librarian. 'Can you do it?'

'I can.'

'Then commander,' said Tyrendian, 'I suggest we all do as he says.'

'Everyone,' ordered Sarpedon, 'down!'

The Soul Drinkers threw themselves onto the steps. Scamander stood and walked forwards. The swarm descended: scarabs, hundreds of them, buzzing down on steel wings, their jaws glowing molten red as they prepared to bore through power armour.

Scamander raised his arms. His hands glowed orange. Ice formed around his feet, crackling across the black stone.

Scarabs flowed around him in a black cloud, eager to force their way through the joints of his armour and eat him alive.

Scamander yelled, and a wave of fire exploded from around his hands. Billows of flame radiated out from him, like a red storm with Scamander at its eye. Scarabs flew haywire, circuits burned out and wings on fire. The fire rippled over the heads of the Soul Drinkers, scorching the backpacks of their armour as it licked up the stairway and across the ornate slabs of the pyramid.

The roar of the fire died down. Burning scarabs were everywhere, pinging against the sides of the pyramid as they flew blinded and out of control. A metallic hail of dead scarabs fell, trailing smoke.

Scamander fell back onto the steps. His arms and shoulder pads smouldered. The rest of him was caked with ice, hissing where it touched the heated armour. Scamander began to roll down the steps, unconscious. Tyrendian hurried forward and supported him, hauling him into a seated position, and propping him up against a terrace of the pyramid.

'Apothecary!' called Tyrendian, but Pallas was already there. Scamander's mouth lolled open, and his eyes were rolled back.

'Keep moving!' ordered Sarpedon. The Soul Drinkers advanced up the pyramid, the tech-guard reaching the lower levels below them. Sarpedon could see Hepsebah's cannon raking the ruins below.

Only the temple remained before Sarpedon: the temple making up the top of the pyramid. Between the black stone columns of its entrance there was a darkness so profound that his enhanced eyesight couldn't penetrate it.

'I can feel it,' said Lygris. 'It's watching us.'

'Not for long,' said Sarpedon, and scuttled into the temple.

Unnatural dimensions assailed him. Space did not fold up correctly in the temple. Even in the darkness, the angles of the walls did not add up correctly, and even up and down seemed skewed, as if reality was being distorted through a lens. Sarpedon struggled to keep his footing as his equilibrium told him that left was right.

He was in a chamber of brushed steel, that much he could tell. But it was not a chamber, it was an intersection of a larger structure, one that could not possibly fit into the temple at the top of the pyramid. The necrons had folded this place to fit inside the structure, blaspheming against the basics of physical reality.

Above was a sky composed of information: half-formed chains of numbers and commands, flickering images of blueprints, chains of data

streaming off into infinity. It hurt Sarpedon's eyes just to look at it. It didn't want to fit into his mind. He looked down at a floor, inlaid with the skulls and carapaces of necron warriors, beaten flat, perhaps damaged warriors recycled into building materials or some grand sacrifice of the alien machines to their leader.

Sarpedon clambered up the wall of the chamber, and reached the top to give himself a better view. A labyrinth of machinery led off as far as he could see: enormous engines, half-formed as if in the process of melting into slag; forges churning out necron warriors and scarabs; forests of captives, nothing more than skeletons wrapped in tendrils of bleeding muscle; grand tombs, their sarcophagi lying open, waiting to receive lords yet to be built; an immense spire of glowing steel with warships suckling power from it; oceans of inky black information, infested with hunter-programs that writhed and darted like translucent sharks; ziggurats of pure carbon, and monoliths of obsidian.

Sarpedon's mind whirled with the impossibility of it all. It could not be real, this patchwork of tech-heresies.

Lygris pulled himself up onto the top of the wall. Sarpedon could see that the Techmarine was exhausted. Some of the datavaults built into his armour had melted.

'It's information,' said Lygris, looking out across the hellforged labyrinth. 'This is what they want,

what they plan to build. This is what they will do with the galaxy if they get their way. The wall between information and reality is thin here. Their designs and their plans, they… they break through.'

'Where is their ruler?'

'In the labyrinth, at its heart. I can take you to him. I can feel him watching me in every interface I have.'

'We must hurry,' said Sarpedon. 'This place could kill us as surely as the necrons.'

'Agreed,' replied Lygris. 'Follow me.'

The Soul Drinkers advanced into the temple behind Sarpedon, through the shadowy gateway that marked the temple threshold. They were thrown into disarray by the sudden shift in reality, but their officers ordered them forwards. Tyrendian supported Scamander, who looked semi-conscious and drained, his hands still smouldering, and his feet leaving icy prints on the mosaic of dismembered necrons on the floor.

'This just gets better and better,' snarled Captain Luko. 'Where's the thing we're supposed to kill?'

'Near,' replied Lygris.

'Good,' said Luko. 'Dismantling these machines has left me thirsty for a proper fight.'

Ghosts drifted through the walls of the labyrinth. They had the faces of necrons, emotionless skulls with burning eyes, but they drifted above the ground, trailing long whipping tails of cables and probes. Their hands were bundles of syringes and

glowing blades. They were broader and far quicker than a necron warrior, and, most disturbingly of all, they were only half-there, transparent and shimmering as they flickered in and out of reality. A dozen of them emerged from the walls, moving swiftly to surround the Soul Drinkers. More of them were diving down from the information sky like spectral comets, a whole host of them, almost matching the hundred or so Soul Drinkers in numbers.

'Then drink your fill, captain,' said Sarpedon.

WHEN THE UNDYING had come to Raevenia, and even before, when the worlds of the Selaacan empire were winking out, one by one, tall tales of the aliens' capabilities had been swapped between the fearful citizens of Astelok. Among them were stories that echoed gruesome fairy tales of skeletal creatures that came invisible in the night and wore the skins of those they killed. No one really believed them, of course, for who could be left alive to pass them on? But still they spread, and became embellished with stories of glowing green eyes and blades for fingers, and a death that crept from the shadows unnoticed.

The officers and troops manning the command centre's situation room learned, in that moment, that the stories were true.

'Sentries to the situation room!' yelled General Damask, who was overseeing the command centre. 'Now! Gods, now!'

The door burst open, revealing the bloodstained machine beyond it. The room beyond the machine was in ruins, the communications officers inside cut to ribbons, lying in foul gory shreds on the floor, or draped over their switchboards.

Damask drew his sidearm and snapped shots into the Flayed One. Shots hammered into its torso, and it fell backwards. Two more took its place, darting into the room.

Raevenian troops burst in through the far door. One of them swore and raised his gun immediately, spraying fire at the Flayed One. Bullet holes stitched across the doorway. The Flayed One hurtled through the fire and slammed into Damask.

It was heavy, all metal and blades. Bright slashes of pain opened up in the general's arms and hands as he fended off the blades that snickered down at him.

'Kill it! For the crown's sake get this thing off me!'

There was more gunfire as more troops burst in. A Flayed One fell, skull blown open. Another clawed its way along the ceiling like a huge metal spider, and dropped down on top of the first soldier, carving through his throat with its finger blades.

A metal hand closed around Damask's throat. It sliced shut, and his head came away, his neck cut to ribbons. His gun clattered to the floor, and the last sound he made was the long gurgling breath escaping from his severed windpipe.

'Infiltrators!' someone shouted. 'Undying! Seal them off!'

The soldiers in the room turned as the door behind them was hauled shut, a loud booming indicating that map tables and document cabinets were being piled up behind it. They yelled and swore and hammered on the door, but it stayed shut. They tried to kick it in and shoot the hinges off, but the half-dozen men in the situation room were trapped.

A Flayed One skewered a soldier through his ribcage from behind, lifted him up, and dashed his brains out against the edge of the map table in the centre of the room. Markers indicating the Raevenian positions around the space port scattered onto the floor, and blood spattered across the diagram of the space port's walls and landing pads. Another soldier backed against the door, and yelled as he fired on full-auto, emptying his gun's magazine at the Flayed Ones entering the room. The gun's movement clicked on an empty chamber, and bladed hands reached for him. He fought them off, screaming, even as his fellow soldiers were dragged down and butchered. Finally, his abdomen was slit open, and the scream caught in his throat, drowned in the blood gurgling up from a wound in his lung.

The Flayed Ones seemed barely to notice the barricaded doors. One of them, still wearing the tatters of the medic's skin, reached up and pulled down a ceiling tile, revealing a cavity between the ceiling

and the floor of the level above. With inhuman ease, it slid into the space, followed rapidly by half the other Flayed Ones. The others turned to the metal shutters on the situation room's windows and began to tear them from the walls.

'YOUR MAJESTY, THEY'RE here,' said Kavins.

Queen Dyrmida looked up from the field radio with which she had been trying to get an explanation for the din coming from the lower floors. She had set up her quarters on an upper floor, where she could have a good view of the unfolding battle, near the landing control room with its banks of communications consoles and monitors. 'They?'

'The Undying. Flayed Ones.'

Dyrmida stood up. 'How?'

'We don't know.'

Dyrmida drew her sidearm. She was well-practised with it, as good a shot as any of her soldiers, but skill at arms had not saved the men undoubtedly dying beneath her feet. 'Can we get out through the lower floors?'

'No,' said Kavins. 'We're sealing all the ways up. A cargo lifter I had detailed to ferry ammunition to the walls is landing on the control tower roof.'

'Can we contain the Undying in this building?'

'Please, my queen, do not let that concern you. We must get you out of here.'

Kavins led her towards the exit leading to the stairwell. The other troops in the control room,

mostly communications officers, were hurriedly disengaging their comm systems and checking their guns.

The sound of tearing metal came from the floor. One of the officers screamed and disappeared through a hole in the floor. Dyrmida caught a glimpse of bloody silver through the flesh of the soldier's legs before he was gone.

'Move!' shouted Kavins, spraying fire from his sub-machine gun at the hole.

Bullets flew in every direction. One soldier was caught by a stray round. A Flayed One dragged itself out of the hole and was shot to pieces. Another hole opened up, and another man died, blades slicing up into his abdomen and through his spine.

Dyrmida ran for the door, the officer close behind her. He slammed the door behind him and hauled its lock shut. The stairwell was white-painted and narrow, made to serve as a maintenance access to the roof of the tower. The door boomed with the stray gunshots hitting it, and Dyrmida heard the men trapped in there screaming.

Kavins had shut them in there to die so that there was more chance of the queen escaping. She knew that she should be ashamed of that fact, but the feeling was drowned out by her heart hammering in her chest.

She ignored the thought and pushed upwards. Gunfire echoed from below, mingling with the

sounds of the guns on the walls. She hauled on the wheel lock on the door in front of her, and the door swung open to the roof. It was scattered with antennae and receiver dishes.

The smell of gun-smoke hit her. It was thick in the air, drifting in a pall from the soldiers on the walls. Across the landing pads, she could see her soldiers manning the defences, keeping up a hail of fire against the two columns of Undying approaching from the north and south. The massive black pyramidal vehicles, the monoliths, were drifting towards the main gates, apparently immune to fire, thousands of Undying teeming around them. The Soul Drinkers knelt on the other side of the gate, waiting. Hundreds of soldiers had flocked to hold the walls to the south, and heavy weapons thumped as they sent anti-tank shells and missiles into the Undying advancing through the smouldering remains of the forest's edge.

Kavins slammed the door shut and readied his gun.

'Hold here, your majesty,' he said. 'We'll get you off here soon.'

'Do not risk your life for me, Kavins,' said Dyrmida. 'Too many have died that way already.'

'It will not come to that.'

Kavins pointed as the lifter rose above the edge of the command centre roof. It was a stubby box-like craft with short stabiliser wings, and it rose on a pair of vertical jet engines on a column of rippling

hot air. It was a small craft, big enough for perhaps half a dozen passengers. Through the cockpit windshield, Dyrmida could see the pilot, brow furrowed as he held the craft steady.

The rear access ramp of the lander opened, and the craft swivelled to bring the ramp over the roof. Metre by metre, the craft descended, until Kavins was able to run over and grab the lip of the ramp. He held his hand out.

'Your majesty,' he said.

Dyrmida put her foot on Kavins's hand and pushed herself up onto the ramp. Her upper body was on the ramp, and her legs were kicking out over the roof. She pulled herself towards the safety of the crew compartment.

Dyrmida heard gunfire over the roaring engines, and looked back to see Kavins firing at something on the edge of the roof.

It was an Undying, one of the Flayed Ones, still wearing the scraps of skin it had worn as a disguise. Bullets sparked against its skull, and it fell, but more followed it, clambering onto the roof.

Kavins paused for a moment to wave at the pilot, indicating that the lander should take off without him.

'No!' shouted Dyrmida. 'We can save you! Turn back!'

One of the Flayed Ones was scaling an antenna. Dyrmida, still clinging to the ramp, aimed her sidearm at the Flayed One and fired, but the shots

snapped wide. She knew what it was going to do, and she couldn't do a thing to stop it.

The Flayed One leapt from the antenna onto the front of the lander. Dyrmida could just hear, over the roar of the engines, the sound of the lander's front windshield shattering.

The lander lurched suddenly, almost throwing Dyrmida out. The cockpit door burst open, and the pilot flew back into the crew compartment in two pieces, his body carved apart from one shoulder to the opposite hip. The sundered corpse tumbled past Dyrmida as the lander pitched backwards. The blood-slicked Undying looked at Dyrmida through the open cockpit door, the gore from the pilot's death running thickly down its grinning skull.

Kavins looked up as the lander's shadow passed over him. He dived out of the way as its bulk flopped down onto the roof of the command centre. Half the roof collapsed into the control room below. Debris shattered up into one engine, and it exploded in a storm of fire and metal, throwing torn Flayed Ones off the roof. Flame billowed across the roof, and torn fuel lines sprayed through the fire.

Queen Dyrmida didn't know where she was or what was happening to her. All she knew was that one half of her world was agonisingly hot and the other was not. She rolled away from the flames, too confused and shocked to register the pain from broken bones in her leg.

She was still holding her gun, for her hand had closed around it in a lucky reflex. She wiped her other hand across her face, getting some of the blood out her eyes. Behind her was the wrecked lander, explosions shaking it as fuel cells cooked off inside. The spatters of blood on the lander's nose were blackening in the heat.

She saw Kavins in front of her. He was lying on his back, and a Flayed One stood over him. It squatted over his chest and punched its blades into his eyes. Kavins spasmed, and then he wasn't Kavins any more, but just another body laid low by the Undying.

Dyrmida tried to get to her feet, but her leg collapsed under her. The pain threw her into a white place of agony, and she nearly blacked out, forcing herself to stay conscious for a few moments more.

Flayed Ones were clambering over the edge of the roof and walking towards her. There was little hurry in their movements. They didn't need their speed now.

Their blades were so sharp that their edges glowed orange with the light of the flames, like slivers of fire. Dyrmida imagined them cutting through her, slicing her apart into bloody chunks.

She would not go through that. They would not carve her up while she was alive.

Queen Dyrmida of Astelok, Regent of Raevenia, put the muzzle of her pistol to the underside of her jaw.

The Flayed Ones advanced on her, fixing her with their burning green eyes. Their faces didn't change from the impassive rictus of metal. Somehow, it would have been better to see their hate.

Blades touched her skin.

Dyrmida pulled the trigger.

'How many have died? None but the Emperor knows. How many of their stories are remembered? Barely a drop in that ocean. Strive to overcome not only the standards of your heroes, but of everyone who has died forgotten.'

Daenyathos, *The Bullet
and the Skull*

CHAPTER SEVENTEEN

THE BLAST RIPPED right through the ruins of the tomb, and sheared through Archmagos Voar's legs. Voar hit the ground, tech-guards running to his aid. One of them was shredded to atoms by another fat eruption of green fire, but two more grabbed Voar by his shoulders and dragged him clear, spraying las-fire at the necron destroyer that had fired on them.

Voar's auto-senses rapidly took stock. His legs, simple but sturdy motivator units, had been completely destroyed, one flayed off at the knee, the other fused and useless. They held no vital systems, and he could function at almost full capacity, save for the ability to move under his own power.

'You,' he said to the tech-guard kneeling beside him, firing rapid las-fire at the destroyer, 'Carry me.'

'Yes, archmagos,' said one of the tech-guard, and pulled Voar's arm over his shoulder so he could half-carry, half-drag Voar around.

The vox-net opened up. It was barely possible to make out voices among the distortion. Voar engaged his logic circuits and rearranged the static-filled snippets of sound into recognisable words.

'This is Sarpedon!' said the voice over the vox. 'We're under attack from some necron machines that can phase in and out. Bullets pass right through the damn things. Advise!'

'I had anticipated this application of their phasing technology,' said Voar. He amplified his vox-unit to address the tech-guard around him. 'Device Epsilon! Now!'

One of the tech-guard ran forwards carrying a second weapon similar to the device Gamma: a metal sphere wrapped in circuitry and wires. This one contained a power source that turned the metal translucent as it pulsed.

'Crystavayne,' voxed Voar. 'I am inconvenienced. Deliver device Epsilon to Commander Sarpedon.'

'Yes, archmagos.' Crystavayne ran through the ruined tombs and knelt beside Voar. The inferno pistol that Voar had given him was still in his hand, its muzzle glowing a dull red with the constant fighting.

'Archmagos, be still. I can fix the–'

'I am in no danger,' snapped Voar. 'The same is not true of Sarpedon. Deliver the device Epsilon. That is an order.'

'Very well,' said Crystavayne, taking the weapon from the tech-guard.

'And be quick,' said Voar. 'Ancient they may be, but the patience of the necrons has run out.'

THE LABYRINTH WAS twisting again, warping space to throw the ghost-like necrons in greater number into the Soul Drinkers' position.

Sarpedon slammed the Axe of Mercaeno into the chest of one of the machines, and the power field split deep into its torso. The machine shifted out of phase with reality again, turning transparent, and the axe slipped through the apparition harmlessly. One of its limbs solidified, and stabbed a bundle of knives and injectors at Sarpedon. He was a fraction of a second quicker than the machine anticipated, and grabbed the limb with his free hand. He drew back his arm and hurled the necron at the wall, but, just in time, it shifted again and passed right through it.

'Give me a whole company of Traitor Marines to fight,' spat Luko, who was fighting back to back with Sarpedon, lightning claws blazing. 'At least when you hit them they stay hit.'

Soul Drinkers were dying to the necron ghosts. One lay, throat opened up, his helmet wrenched back off his head. Another was dragging himself along, trying to hold in his entrails as they spilled through the triangular hole slashed open in his armour.

One of the ghosts had been destroyed, phasing out a moment too late to avoid the volley of bolter fire that slammed into it. It lay half-shifted, flickering like an image on a faulty pict screen, back blown open and spilling ghostly circuitry across the floor. Another had been skewered through the head by a chainblade, and had fallen like a metal puppet with its strings cut. The others were faster, materialising to strike, and then becoming ghosts again faster than the Soul Drinkers could target them.

They functioned naturally in the abnormal dimensions, too, shifting in and out of folds in space, warping from one place to another. This was their home ground. The Soul Drinkers were the intruders, and the necrons had them trapped in their labyrinth.

One of Voar's tech-priests stumbled over the threshold into the midst of the Soul Drinkers. He looked mostly human, with only a medicae gauntlet on one hand and cranial interfaces in his scalp to suggest his augmentations. In one hand he held an inferno pistol and in the crook of his other arm was a device like an oversized grenade. Sarpedon remembered him as Magos Crystavayne, one of the officers of Voar's fleet.

'Commander!' shouted Crystavayne.

It was the only word he got out before the necron ghost behind him shimmered into reality and speared him through the back with both sets of blades. Injectors pumped to fill him with acids that

would eat him away from the inside, and blades vibrated to slice easily through his bones and organs.

Magos Crystavayne slumped to his knees, still impaled on the ghost's blades. The ghost shifted back into spectral form, as twin fountains of blood sprayed from the magos's back.

With his last moment of life, Crystavayne thumbed an activation catch on the device he held. His inferno pistol dropped from his hand, and he slumped down onto his back.

The device split open. A glowing orange-white core was revealed, and it pulsed, flaring up to fill the labyrinth intersection with painful light.

The light died down, Sarpedon's auto-senses fighting to adjust. A necron above him shuddered as if its image was obscured by static, and suddenly it was real. Its skull split apart as its jaws opened, wrenching a tear across its face like a ragged grin, and it screamed.

'They're real!' yelled Sarpedon. 'Kill them!'

Most of the Soul Drinkers dropped to one knee and fired, blazing full-auto at the ghosts suddenly locked into their physical forms above them. Sarpedon saw one Wraith materialise halfway through the wall, writhing as its innards fused with the wall, sparks bleeding from its eyes.

Luko killed another, leaping over Sarpedon to grab the necron's tail of cabling and spine, dragging it down and slamming it into the floor. He leapt on it, and slashed its skull into three slices with a sweep of his claws.

Sarpedon saw something like panic in the movements of the necron ghosts. They were darting around at random, throwing themselves out of the way of angles of fire. It didn't work. Forced to stay in physical form by the Mechanicus device, they were little more than target practice for the Soul Drinkers.

'They're fleeing from us, commander!' voxed Sergeant Salk, who was kneeling, directing his squad's fire. One of the necrons clattered to the ground behind him, its head and one limb missing. With its capacity to phase out gone, the wreck stayed there, smouldering.

'More will follow,' said Sarpedon. 'Lygris? Can you lead us on?'

Lygris stumbled up to Sarpedon and leaned against the wall, breathing heavily enough to distort the vox-unit that Pallas had fitted him with.

'I can,' he said. 'It is far through the labyrinth, but I can lead us through… through the broken space. It will not be long before we reach it. It is talking to me.'

'What does it say?'

'That we will all die.'

Sarpedon pulled the Axe of Mercaeno from the body of the necron he had killed.

'For a creature of such intelligence,' he said, 'it has little imagination.'

'Follow me,' said Lygris.

* * *

IT WAS SURPRISINGLY quiet by the main gates in the northern walls of the space port where Chaplain Iktinos and his flock waited for the real battle to begin. The gunfire from above was muffled by the walls and the gatehouses, and the Undying made little sound save for the grinding of their feet in the dirt and the occasional falling tree, knocked down by the advancing monoliths.

A few soldiers were running, here and there, to collect ammunition or carry wounded comrades to triage stations. Reserves waited nervously in a maintenance hangar, wishing, at the same time, that the Undying would not breach the walls, and that the aliens would hurry up and force their way in so they could get the fight over and done with.

The command centre was burning. Flame-shadowed smoke billowed from its tower, and the fire was spreading through the building. Communications from the centre had ceased.

A soldier ran from the direction of the reserve. He was wounded, one of his hands half blown off and the stump of his wrist wrapped in a bloodstained bandage. He had evidently been pressed into service as a messenger because he could no longer hold a gun. He was young, his face and short blond hair smeared with gun residue and blood.

'Chaplain!' he shouted as he ran. 'Chaplain! The centre has fallen. Queen Dyrmida is lost.'

Chaplain Iktinos knelt before the gates. The thirty or so Soul Drinkers with him knelt too, their heads

bent in contemplation. Iktinos looked around at the messenger's approach.

'I see,' he said. 'Thank you.'

'We… we don't have anyone in command. Her generals are gone too.'

'That will be all,' said Iktinos, and turned away again.

The messenger stood for a moment, unsure what to say. Then he backed off, turned, and ran towards where the reserved were stationed, perhaps to see if there was anything else he could do.

'Soon,' voxed Iktinos quietly to his flock. 'Remember, my brothers. It matters not who survives, so long as there is one of us.'

The drone of a monolith's engines reached Iktinos's ears. It was on the other side of the gate.

'Nothing matters,' continued Iktinos, 'but the Salvation.'

Enormous energy weapons tore at the gate with a sound like industrial saws grinding through plascrete. The gates shuddered, and cracked lines appeared, describing a massive rectangular shape like another doorway set into the surface of the gates. The ground shook, too, thrumming with the scale of the power being unleashed.

There was panic on the walls. Men were running, some away along the top of the walls, others into the cramped stairways leading down. Some were standing clear of the defences,

heedless of the danger, because on Raevenia a good death was as meaningful as a good life, and there were good deaths to be won defying the aliens, even now. Green fire rippled along the walls. Men fell, half their bodies flayed away. Some stood and defied for a few seconds more, yelling their anger and firing their weapons even as their bodies were flayed away into gnawed skeletons.

The cracks in the gate deepened into molten-edged furrows. A huge section of the gates fell inwards, slamming into the ground with a sound that deafened men. The Space Marines' auto-senses protected them.

The monolith, the size of a building, loomed over them, suspended a metre above the ground on a shimmering field of energy. Two more glided behind it. Undying warriors marched alongside it, hundreds of them in strict formation. Many of them had patches of bright silver where they had been shot down, self-repaired, and rejoined the advance. Closest to the monoliths were the Immortals, the larger warriors with twin-barrelled weapons, their carapaces inscribed with ornate patterns as if to acknowledge the majesty of the monoliths.

'Charge!' yelled Iktinos. The Soul Drinkers leapt to their feet and ran forwards, chainblades whirring, bolters stuttering fire into the Undying.

Some of the flock died there, immolated in the green flare that raked through them from the guns

mounted at the pinnacle of the monolith, but it did not matter.

Only the Salvation mattered.

LYGRIS HAD BEEN right. The short sprint through the labyrinth had been an unholy few moments of mutilated space and obscene dimensions, the soul-pollution of reality deformed by an alien will. Nevertheless, Lygris led them to the labyrinth's heart, and to what lay there.

Sarpedon saw the tomb of the necron overlord and wondered if there was anything in the galaxy that could truly be holy if such a thing could exist at the same time.

It was an enormous beating heart of grey flesh the size of a tank, a biomechanical mass surrounded by a tangled nest of cabling and wires, power conduits that dripped pure energy and chunks of alien machinery in glossy black slabs.

A conveyor system sent mechanical arms rattling overhead on tracks. They carried human bodies, captive Raevenians, and dropped them into vats of black metal from which ran thin cables glowing bright with their life force. The cables ran into the heart, and every time it took a revolting, fleshy beat the cables shone brighter and another body fell.

The Soul Drinkers ran into position behind Sarpedon and Lygris. They were too fine a cadre of soldiers to fall dumbfounded at the sight, but their shock was still obvious, engendering muttered

oaths at its size and foulness, and growls of anger that such a thing should exist. Quite apart from its appearance, the heart emanated such a profound sense of wrongness that it made the labyrinth around it seem mundane.

'The necrons are advancing towards your position,' said Archmagos Voar over the vox. 'They are reinforced in greater numbers. We cannot hold and are falling back. We are slowing their advance, but they will be upon you soon.'

'Acknowledged,' replied Sarpedon. 'We've found it.'

'The intelligence?'

'Its tomb.'

'Then Emperor's speed, commander,' voxed Voar, 'and let the word of the Omnissiah speak of your wrath.'

'Graevus,' said Sarpedon, 'cut that thing open.'

Graevus led his squad towards the heart. Freezing vapour coiled around their feet as Graevus took his axe in his mutated hand.

'Steel your souls,' he said.

The Soul Drinkers behind him levelled their bolters at the heart.

The heart split open, and a gale of ice and chemicals roared out. Graevus was thrown off his feet along with most of his squad. The billow of white vapour was blinding.

Sarpedon drew breath, but his throat felt as if it was closing, so cold was the air. His ears were full of noise.

By his feet, Graevus was rolling onto his back and drawing his bolt pistol.

'Report!' shouted Sarpedon.

'Got nothing,' voxed Luko from behind.

'Sounds from behind,' said Salk. 'Covering.'

'Hold position!' ordered Sarpedon. 'Graevus, did you see it?'

'No,' said Graevus. 'Squad! Advance!'

Visibility was zero. Sarpedon could barely make out his own lower limbs reaching out before him. The faint glow of Graevus's power axe through the icy gloom was the only sight he had of his brother Astartes, and then it was gone. Sarpedon scuttled a few paces forwards, the Axe of Mercaeno heavy in his hands.

Green fire glimmered ahead: two eyes, burning.

'Contact!' shouted Graevus over the vox. 'Get down! Squad, down! Covering fire! Now!'

Sarpedon hit the ground, ready for the volley of bolter fire to tear over his head from the Soul Drinkers behind him. A few fingers squeezed down on triggers. Most did not have the chance.

The gale came again, a hundred times stronger. Graevus flew backwards and slammed into Sarpedon, almost throwing Sarpedon along with him. Sarpedon's talons dug in to the metal of the floor and he held on. Graevus bounced past, and two of his squad followed.

The vapour was whipped into a whirl, like a white-streaked tornado. Sarpedon could see Soul

Drinkers being caught up in it, picked up off their feet or slammed into walls. Several tumbled away down the corridor through which the Soul Drinkers had advanced, their armoured forms clattering away through the labyrinth. Some were thrown right over the labyrinth walls.

Sarpedon gritted his teeth and dug in harder. Chunks of metal were swirling, smacking against him like shrapnel. Through the vapour, he could see the heart had split open, but it was still beating, slabs of torn muscle like immense petals of dead flesh pulsing obscenely.

The necron overlord that emerged from the storm was three times Sarpedon's height. Its skull hung low in its chest, its shoulders huge slabs of curved steel. Its torso was a sarcophagus, an ornate casket shaped like a scarab, inset with a fat black gem of datacrystal. Its arms were long enough to touch the ground, but its hands were, in spite of their great size, somehow elegant, the fingers like articulated knives.

Instead of legs, it had a hovering motivator unit like one of the floating necrons. Unlike them, its abdomen was equipped with dozens of limbs, like the legs of a centipede, wriggling underneath it as if searching for something to grab.

It held a scythe, wrought in twisted gold, as ornate as the average necron warrior was plain. Green flame rippled up the blade, matching the flame in the overlord's eye sockets.

Its skull was so long and gaunt that it lost any similarity to a human form. It had no mouth, as if the horizontal slit in a necron skull had been judged surplus to requirements. It was just a long, teardrop-shaped mask of metal, its eyes the only hint of the human form about it.

Its metal was dull red, flecked with gold, and it was gleaming. It had not slept under the earth of Selaaca, stained with age. It had been kept pristine in its obscene heart, perfectly preserved, waiting to wake.

Cables glowing with life force snapped off sockets in its thick spine, whipping around in the wind. Its fuel was the life force of the Selaacan captives being drained away in the vats.

Its burning eyes focused on Sarpedon, narrowing to emerald slits.

'*Die*,' it said.

'BROTHERS! FOR THE future!'

Iktinos bellowed at the top of his voice, and perhaps some of his battle-brothers could hear him over the chaos erupting before the space port's ruined gates. The Chaplain's crozius carved down again, shattering through the metal torso of the Undying immortal in front of him, its head smashing through the glowing barrels of its weapon, spilling liquid power over the collapsing remains.

The monolith loomed over him. Iktinos's flock was setting about it with bolters and chainswords,

the metal rents in its surface rippling and closing up as if the metal was alive.

They were surrounded, and they were dying. Five of the flock lay dead already. It was magnificent, this sight, for it meant that those brothers had died for the Salvation. A time would come when Iktinos would enter their names in a roll of honour, and they would become legends.

The monolith turned, and a rectangular pool of shimmering blackness that drank the light dominated the side facing Iktinos.

'Brother Vozh!' called Iktinos. 'Melta-bombs!'

Vozh had been in an assault squad before joining the flock, and a pair of large cylindrical melta-bombs were clamped to the sides of his bulky jump pack, explosives that burned hot enough to bore through armoured vehicles. Vozh ran through the chaos to Iktinos, handing the Chaplain the melta-bombs.

Vozh was surrounded by bedlam, hundreds of Undying, crowding around the Soul Drinkers. Their remains lay thick on the floor, only to phase out, one by one, making the ground undulate like the surface of a metal sea. The gatehouses on either side were crumbling and aflame, raked by fire from the monoliths. Without the Soul Drinkers, the Undying would have swarmed into the space port, and the whole place would have fallen in short order. Only the sheer ferocity of the Soul Drinkers was plugging the gates, for every Undying who made it

through had no choice but to turn and fight them to avoid a bolter shell through the back of the skull or a limb lost to a chainblade.

The monoliths had been brought forwards to grind through the Soul Drinkers, to simply roll over them and crush them. That was not a fate that Iktinos accepted.

Iktinos shouldered his way past one Undying, and ripped the arm off the Immortal between him and the side of the monolith. He tore the pins from the melta-bombs, and hurled them both into the vertical pool in the monolith's side. Undying were emerging from the pool, the shapes of their skulls and carapaces forcing through the film of blackness.

The melta-bombs detonated. The surface of black liquid disappeared, and with it any parts of the Undying that had come through. Neatly severed skull sections and limbs clattered to the ground. The space beyond, deeply inset into the monolith's interior, was spattered with white-hot bolts of superheated matter boring through the metal.

Iktinos threw himself to the ground. Something inside the Undying vehicle ruptured, throwing chunks of burning coils and knives of living metal. The monolith groaned like a wounded giant, and listed to one side as anti-grav units burned out. Purplish flames licked from its wounds.

The stricken monolith blocked the gates more effectively than any makeshift barricade could. The

vehicles behind it were trapped outside, and turned their weapons on the gatehouses to bring them down and force a gap open.

'Take it to them!' yelled Iktinos. 'My brothers, to me! Give them not one foot inside!'

The flock closed ranks, dragging the wounded. They crammed back to back, a tiny island of purple armour in the mass of tarnished steel that surrounded them.

It was the kind of fight a Space Marine was created for: face-to-face, brutal and lethal, where strength and determination counted for everything. The Undying might be relentless, they might feel no pain, but that counted for nothing in the face of the sheer killing power of Astartes with orders to stand their ground.

Brother Vozh died, half his head and one shoulder flayed away, even as he spitted an Immortal through the torso with his chainblade. Another Soul Drinker followed him, his legs blown out from under him, disappearing beneath the clubbing gun butts of the Undying that crowded over him.

The circle of Soul Drinkers shrank. More Undying were torn apart.

The future that Iktinos imagined would be worth every drop of Astartes blood.

SARPEDON HIT THE wall hard.

His mind was divided in two. One half, the human side, was full of pain and shock, battered

against the inside of his skull and barely sensible. The other half, the Astartes mind, stepped back from the pain and panic, and coolly took stock of the situation. One of his rear legs was shattered, twisted and useless underneath him. His skull was fractured, and slathering blood down his face. His bolter was gone, clattered away somewhere in the labyrinth where Sarpedon knew full well he would not find it.

He was alive, and he was still holding the Axe of Mercaeno. The overall assessment, then, was positive.

Sarpedon had come to rest a short distance from the overlord's heart. The overlord had hurled him there, picking him up with one outsized metal claw and flinging him into the winds it conjured around it. Broken power conduits hung, dripping life force. Chunks of biomechanical machinery rolled along the ground, picked up by the ice-cold wind.

Sarpedon looked up. The overlord was drifting over the wreckage of its heart towards him, its scythe in its hand. Sarpedon forced himself to his remaining legs, the ruined one dragging behind him, spraying ichor from a ruptured artery.

'One day...' snarled Sarpedon, 'One day we will scour this galaxy of everything like you.'

The wind sounded something like laughter.

The overlord darted forwards and reared up, insect legs wriggling. Sarpedon tried to roll out of the way, but his rear leg buckled, and he slumped

to two knees. The overlord was on him, the weight of its body slamming into him.

The legs on the overlord's underside wrapped around Sarpedon, and held him tight, lifting him up off the ground as the overlord reared again. Pincer-tipped limbs dug into the chitin of Sarpedon's legs. A metal hand pulled his head back, and the scythe blade passed in front of his face as it was brought down to the level of Sarpedon's throat.

Sarpedon forced an arm out from the overlord's grasp. He grabbed the scythe blade a finger's breadth from the skin of his throat.

The blade cut through the ceramite of his gauntlet. A line of red pain opened up along his fingers, and he knew that, in a few moments, he would lose them to the blade. He closed his fist around the blade and wrenched it down, trying to force it from the overlord's grip.

The overlord's grip held firm, but Sarpedon continued to pull the blade down. Seeing his opening, he twisted it around and used it to cut through one of the insect arms that held him. The overlord's limb clattered to the floor, picked up by the howling winds and sent spinning away.

Sarpedon's other arm was free. He tore the Axe of Mercaeno out of the overlord's grip, and ripped it up into the side of the overlord's abdomen. The blade sliced through the living metal of its carapace, and Sarpedon twisted, feeling circuitry and power coils crunching.

Sarpedon threw himself free of the overlord. The gales hit him again, and he stabbed his talons into the floor to keep himself from being carried away on the wind.

He tried to find his fellow Soul Drinkers. Most of them were scattered, unable to come to Sarpedon's aid as they were battered against the walls or thrown helplessly along the corridors of the labyrinth. He could hear gunfire, and knew that others were fighting the necron warriors that had made it through the tech-guard and into the temple.

He was on his own, but he did not feel frustrated or betrayed by that fact. He could leave the defence to his battle-brothers. He had made the decision to come to Selaaca and face the overlord, and in a way it was right that he should face the alien alone.

The overlord's scythe came down. Sarpedon ducked to the side, still keeping his purchase on the ground. He sliced up with the axe, burying it in the lower lip of the overlord's chest, and ripping it up through layers of metal. The overlord reared up, its eyes flaring in anger, and slid backwards on its antigrav.

Sarpedon and the overlord faced each other, both wounded, separated only by a few metres of freezing vapour. The rent in the overlord's chest silvered over, closing up as its self-repair systems kicked in. It lowered its skull like an animal preparing to charge.

Sarpedon set his remaining back leg, anchoring himself to the ground, and drew the Axe of Mercaeno up into a guard.

He knew the overlord would charge, and the overlord knew he would drive off the first few strikes of the scythe with speed and strength well beyond any human the necrons of Selaaca had ever encountered. Faster than an unaugmented eye could see, Sarpedon parried the great curved blade as it arced down at him, throwing it back in the hope of forcing an opening to the overlord's torso or skull. The overlord, however, was as fast as Sarpedon was, and opened up paths of its own: a strike with the butt of the scythe to the side of Sarpedon's head, a lash with a lower limb that threw Sarpedon onto three knees, and a backhand slap that slammed into Sarpedon's chest-plate and drove shards of rib further out of position.

Sarpedon was going to lose. He was going to die.

He saw a bundle of cables glowing with life force, spraying liquid green power like a severed artery. It was whipping down from its mountings above the remains of the biomechanical heart.

Sarpedon ducked down low and sprinted along the floor, forcing his way against the wind. He rolled under the overlord, barely registering the scythe whipping down and slicing off his broken back leg. He scrabbled upright again and ran for the heart, expecting, any second, for the scythe to fall point-first and impale him like an insect on a pin,

transfixing him wriggling to the floor while the overlord set about murdering the rest of the Soul Drinkers.

It did not come. Sarpedon was a split second too fast.

He grabbed the cable in one hand. It burned with power. Drops of life force spattered onto his armour and burned like molten metal.

He turned to see the overlord above him, scythe raised to cut him in half.

Sarpedon turned every drop of strength inside, and unleashed the Hell.

Light and life filled the biomechanical chamber. A sun burned overhead, a thousands suns, their brilliant light in every colour of the spectrum. Life boiled like a churning sea underfoot, swarms of insects, coils of vines and soaring trees, an endless landscape of life rolling out on a seething carpet. The light was burning, the raw anger of the stars fuelling a terrible mass of relentless life that boiled over and rose in a flood of limbs and organs.

The overlord reeled. Everything the necrons despised, everything that still held some meaning in what was left of its soul, flooded its alien senses.

It would only last a second. It was all Sarpedon needed.

Sarpedon leapt, letting the howling wind catch him and throw him towards the overlord. He drew back his arm, and drove it forwards as he fell onto the overlord.

His fist, clutching the bundle of cables, punched into the overlord's chest. The scarab split down the middle, and Sarpedon's fist drove deep into the machinery inside.

The life force still flowing through the cables discharged in a tremendous blast of raw energy, directly into the overlord's body. Systems overloaded, and capacitors burst with the sudden flood of power. Sarpedon was thrown by the force of the shock, clattering along the ground, his senses full of light and noise.

The overlord's anti-grav units ruptured, spraying green fire, and it tipped onto one side as it fell. It dropped its scythe and clawed at its chest, metal coming away under its claws.

Sarpedon learned that even a face with no features, with just a pair of burning eyes and an expanse of blank silver, could still register panic.

The overlord's chest exploded. Green liquid fire sprayed from the ruptured stump of its spine. Chunks of carapace banged off the walls, trailing flame.

Sarpedon shook the static out of his head. The overlord's body flickered with flame. One hand, still attached by a bent length of metal, flopped to the floor.

The overlord's skull had come to rest nearby. Sarpedon hauled himself to his feet and stamped on it, slicing it in two with the talon of one foreleg.

The wind had died along with the overlord. The other Soul Drinkers were making it into the heart chamber, bolters trained on the overlord's remains.

'Is it dead?' asked Captain Luko, his lightning claws unsheathed just in case.

'Yes,' said Sarpedon.

'What's going on back there?' came a vox from Sergeant Salk. 'The Undying just broke formation. It's as if they're blind.'

'The intelligence is dead,' said Sarpedon. 'There's nothing guiding them.'

'In that case, advancing,' replied Salk.

The bolter fire became thicker as Salk and his men advanced through the labyrinth, shooting down the necrons whose resistance suddenly fell apart, their tactics reduced to individual random movements.

Sarpedon looked back at the ruptured heart. Tangles of flesh-ribbed cabling lay around the cradle in which the overlord had slept, shaped something like a number of metal hoops, slick with greyish gore, strung with the wires that had held the overlord curled up like the larva of some giant insect. The freezing winds had left the flesh dead and whitish, caked in flecks of ice.

A thousand tiny silvery spiders swarmed from the dead petals, scurrying like a carpet of blades. Sarpedon hurried back as they approached, their tiny pin-like legs clicking along the metal floor.

They flowed over the body of the overlord. A group of them broke off and picked up the skull, and, before Sarpedon could reach it, they had brought it over to the rest of the body.

'Flamers!' shouted Sarpedon. 'Flamers forward!'

The head was back on the body. Sarpedon tried to grab it and wrench it back off, but the overlord's hand shot up and gripped his wrist.

The flame of its eyes lit up again. Liquid metal flowed into tentacles that reached from the overlord's ruptured breastplate. Its ruined, lopsided skull seemed to grin as it self-repaired and yanked Sarpedon off his feet again.

'When the battle is won, your work is not done. Your duty is not a destination. It is a journey. Victory is merely a landmark on that road. You will never reach a time when your work is done and you can leave the fighting to another. You will die with the road still to be walked.'

Daenyathos, *Examinations Upon Duty*

CHAPTER EIGHTEEN

LYGRIS RAN ACROSS the chamber just as the gunfire started.

He had seen the ruined body of the necron overlord, and had known that it was not over. A creature like that would not place the future of its existence in the fallible hands of a single physical vessel. The overlord that Sarpedon had fought was just a weapon, a machine under the creature's control. Its mind was something else entirely.

The Soul Drinkers opened fire, but the overlord dripped with bright silver liquid metal, and every bullet scar healed instantly. Sarpedon was held in close, the overlord trying to crush him or twist his head off. The Soul Drinkers were good enough shots not to hit their Chapter Master, but the overlord was shielding its head and torso, just waiting

for its weapons to solidify from the mass of shimmering quicksilver growing from its back.

They would keep it busy. That was all Lygris needed.

Lygris reached the overlord's open sarcophagus, his feet crunching through layers of frozen flesh. The dataprobe slid from his finger. Inside the sarcophagus, nestling between the torn petals of muscle, was a column of black metal that ended in a complex shape like an open hand with clawed fingers, each claw ending in a jack that fitted into the back of the overlord's skull.

Lygris glanced back at the battle behind him. The overlord was a mass of silver tentacles, the resources of the cradle waking up just in time to arm him with more weapons every second. Sarpedon would be dead soon.

Lygris inserted the probe and let his mind drop away from his body.

THE HARVESTING MACHINE had been a crude cage of simple orders. The tomb-city had been a towering ziggurat of unholy light. The overlord's mind, the intelligence that commanded the necrons of the Veiled Region, was something that could not even fit into a metaphor conjured by Lygris's mind. There was no way it could make sense.

It was a storm of knives; a sea of hate; an erupting star of time, spewing the future, cold and metallic, into aeons to come.

There was just enough left of Lygris's soul to scream out a last note of defiance. Then, he let it take him over, and he prepared to spend the last moments of his life causing as much damage as he could to the overlord's mind.

THE GRIP ON Sarpedon's throat tightened.

The silvery limb wrapped around his neck, choking the life out of him. Other limbs, like silver snakes, snared his waist and arms. He was about to die.

Then, suddenly, its strength was gone.

Sarpedon turned around and planted a foreleg in the overlord's chest. He pushed off it, ripping silver tentacles away, and landed free of its grasp on the floor.

The light in the overlord's eyes was going out. The fresh bullet holes in its carapace were not self-repairing. Silver spiders fell from between the joints of its body, shedding like scales that plinked onto the floor.

The anti-grav motors died down, and the overlord's body sank to the floor. The final lights went out in its eye sockets, and its limbs and skull hung limply. It toppled over, and clattered onto one side.

There was no sound, save the faint hiss of the overlord's capacitors cooling down. Even the cables and conduits carrying the Selaacans' life force were turning dull.

Sarpedon watched the overlord for a long moment. Soul Drinkers advanced to stand beside him, guns trained on the machine's corpse.

Out of the corner of his eye, Sarpedon noticed movement. It was Lygris, lying in the remains of the biomechanical sarcophagus. He was convulsing. Sarpedon ran to him, and pulled his dataprobe out of the interface the overlord had used to direct the necron armies.

'Lygris! Brother!'

Lygris did not reply. Sarpedon turned his head over. The Techmarine's eyes had rolled back and were blank.

'Lygris,' said Sarpedon, 'it is done. The foe is dead. Share in this victory. Speak, brother! Speak!'

Pallas was at Sarpedon's side. His medicae gauntlet snickered open and a needle emerged. He inserted it into the port in the neck of Lygris's armour.

'His heart has stopped,' said Pallas. The gauntlet hissed as it injected a hefty dose of adrenaline into Lygris's veins. 'Nothing.'

The other Soul Drinkers were gathering. They were all battered by the overlord's onslaught. Some had broken limbs, or were clutching bloody rents in their armour. They stood in a circle around Sarpedon and Lygris, and none of them spoke.

Pallas's gauntlet injected Lygris again. He pulled off Lygris's helmet and held one of the Techmarine's eyes open with his finger, but it had rolled back and was blank. Blood ran from the tear duct.

Sarpedon watched.

'Brother,' he said. 'Do the Emperor's work. Stay alive.'

Sometimes, an Astartes could stay dead for a long time without a heartbeat, far longer than a normal man, and survive, sitting bolt upright and spluttering back to life with a new reason to seek revenge. Lygris did not.

'The necrons have broken off their attack,' voxed Salk from the labyrinth. 'They're in disarray.'

'Hold position,' voxed Sarpedon. He looked from Lygris to Pallas.

'Our brother,' said Pallas, 'is gone.'

Sarpedon closed Lygris's eyes.

'Take his gene-seed,' he said to Pallas.

The Soul Drinkers were silent. They had lost brothers before, friends and fellow warriors, irreplaceable and much missed, but they had never known a loss like this. Lygris had been there from the start. He was part of the Chapter's soul.

Luko stepped forwards from the assembled Soul Drinkers.

'He will join the Emperor at the end of time,' he said, 'and fight on.'

'We will join him there,' echoed Tyrendian. 'No brother is ever lost. He fights on a different battlefield now.'

'We all will,' said Sarpedon. He closed Lygris's eyes. 'In death he has avenged himself on these aliens. There will be time to mourn our brother

when we have left this world. I will carry him. We must make haste back to the *Antithesis*.' Sarpedon switched vox-channels. 'Sarpedon to Voar. What is your situation? The xenos leader is dead. Come in, Voar!'

He heard nothing in reply but static.

'The tech-guard may have been overrun. Luko, Graevus, take the point. The rest, stay close. We're breaking out.'

Sarpedon hefted Lygris's body onto his shoulder, and the Soul Drinkers advanced.

CHAPLAIN IKTINOS STOOD surrounded by the bodies of his flock. The Undying had kept coming, thousands of them, but the flock had held firm and sold their lives for a price the Undying could not pay. The Soul Drinkers that still lived at the gate breach were a tiny island in the sea of alien steel, but they had not taken one step back.

The aliens faltered. Their relentless advance stumbled, in many cases literally, the warriors losing all coordination and sprawling uncontrollably onto the bloodstained ground. The monoliths ground to a halt, and their guns lowered and fell silent.

Iktinos clambered on top of the bodies and looked through the gates. The whole Undying army was milling aimlessly, its individual warriors reverting to crude placeholder programs that had them patrolling at random, firing ill-coordinated blasts up at the walls.

One of the surviving flock clambered over to Iktinos. His name was Brother Sarkis, and he had lost most of his leg, flayed away to the thigh. He changed the magazine of his bolter as he paused to draw breath.

'Chaplain,' he said. 'What has happened?'

'Sarpedon has been victorious,' said Iktinos. He switched to the vox-net of the Raevenian army. 'Sons of Raevenia! The Undying have been broken. Their minds are addled and their wills broken. Strike now, for Raevenia! Strike for your queen!'

The reserves broke cover and ran forwards, the foremost shouting war cries to spur their fellow soldiers on. The men taking cover on the walls emerged from shelter and brought their guns to bear on the Undying again. The few survivors of the command tower, bloody and ragged officers forming a crowd of walking wounded at a triage station, decided, as one man, to join in the final routing of the Undying.

For the sons of Raevenia, it must have been a glorious moment, one they would speak of for generations, and that would adorn works of art and fanciful histories long into their future.

None of that mattered to Iktinos.

They swarmed past Iktinos and his surviving flock. Gunfire hammered relentlessly, and the Undying fell in their hundreds, like cattle penned in to be slaughtered by Raevenian fire.

Less than a dozen of Iktinos's flock lived. They gathered around him now, most of them wounded, some hauling themselves up from beneath the bodies of the dead. They had all once been battle-brothers of the Soul Drinkers, but now they were something else, their personalities subsumed to Iktinos's. They served him now, and, through him, his master.

'I have brought us here,' said Iktinos, 'and we live. Thus has our victory been won. On this dismal and distant soil, we have sown the seed of mankind's future. We may not live to see the future unfold, but have faith, my brothers, that it will come to pass! The words of the prophet will out! His will shall be the truth!'

Iktinos's flock bowed their heads and knelt among the dead, the ground beneath them consecrated by the blood of their fallen brothers.

Iktinos took his copy of the *Catechisms Martial*, the manual of war written by the philosopher-soldier Daenyathos, from where it hung by a link of chain from the belt of his armour. He held it up to his chest, over his primary heart, and bowed his head in prayer.

'We may not survive what is to come,' said Iktinos. 'Those we once called brothers, the hunting dogs of the corrupt Imperium, may not see fit to spare our lives. It matters not. For him, what we have sought here will be found. He who has directed us, who has written out the future history of the galaxy for

us to read, his will shall prevail. We have served! And so we, too, shall prevail!'

The Soul Drinkers at the gate clutched their own copies of the *Catechisms Martial* as they chanted.

'We shall prevail!'

THE SOUL DRINKERS advanced at a run through the tomb-city. Gun smoke was heavy in the air, tinted by the unnatural haze of burned alien metals.

The necrons had scattered. They fell before volleys of bolter fire and a few well-placed chainblade thrusts from Graevus's squad. They were roaming at random through the remains of the tomb-city, even the ornate necron lords stumbling blind. Like those in the labyrinth before them, they were unable to mount a defence against the Soul Drinkers.

There was no sign of Voar and his magi, save for the bodies of the fallen tech-guard, draped in pools of blood over the wrecked tombs.

'Where in the hells are the Mechanicus?' snarled Luko. His body language suggested he would rather the necrons mount a proper defence, so he could get his claws into some metal.

'They fled,' said Sarpedon, still carrying Techmarine Lygris's body on his shoulders. 'Or were captured.'

'No survivors?' asked Graevus up ahead. 'No communications?'

'Let us hope,' said Tyrendian bleakly, 'that they did not take the *Antithesis's* transport craft with them.'

The Soul Drinkers crossed the threshold of the tunnel leading up from the tomb-city. The tunnels were similarly devoid of decent resistance. Graevus's squad cut down the few necron warriors that came towards them out of the blackness, or shot isolated scarabs off the walls.

'Voar,' voxed Sarpedon. 'Come in! Where are you?'

There was still no reply. Even as the Soul Drinkers approached the surface, the tech-guard's vox-channels were empty.

Sarpedon watched the battle-brothers around him as they covered the tunnel ahead of them and behind them. Every Astartes was battered, and many were wounded. There was not one who did not have a chunk of his armour flayed or sliced away. A few could not move on their own, and were supported by their battle-brothers. The force that marched towards the opening that led to Selaaca's fallen capital numbered barely one hundred Soul Drinkers. Even if Iktinos's force had survived on Raevenia unscathed, Sarpedon commanded little more than one-tenth of the Chapter's original strength. A Chapter under the Imperial yoke could expect to be disbanded with such irrecoverable losses, and added to the long list of Chapters that had been destroyed in the long war since the Age of Imperium began.

Sarpedon would not let the enormity of that hit him, not yet. There would be time to consider the

Chapter's future later. For now, they had to ren-dezvous with Voar, if he was still alive, and get off Selaaca.

The ruins of Selaaca's capital became visible at the end of the tunnel. A few bursts of bolter fire shattered the scarabs still clinging to the walls and ceiling. The deep wound in the earth and the pall of smoke from the crash-landing pointed towards the resting place of the *Antithesis*, which Voar had assured Sarpedon contained enough transport craft and fast fighters to get the Soul Drinkers off the planet.

Sarpedon directed the Soul Drinkers to a ridge overlooking the stricken spacecraft, several hun-dred metres away. The battle-brothers formed up along the ridge, watching the approaches to the spaceship warily.

'Voar, come in,' voxed Sarpedon again, tapping into the ship's vox-net. 'We're making our approach to you. Acknowledge.'

'Still nothing?' asked Luko.

'Nothing.'

'Then we go in?'

'Yes. All Soul Drinkers,' ordered Sarpedon, 'approach in line! Expect resistance!'

As if in reply to his words, a blue-white lance of energy tore down from Selaaca's sky, and speared the *Antithesis* amidships. The sound was appalling, a shriek of superheated air ripping through the city. The ground shuddered, and ruins tumbled,

bringing down necron structures, and revealing the raw stone of the fallen city through the wounds that opened up.

'Down!' yelled Sarpedon. 'Take cover!' He threw himself down on the reverse slope of the ridge, rolling Lygris's body off his shoulder to the ground by his side.

Chain reactions ripped through the hull of the *Antithesis*. The ship was hundreds of metres long, and, though double that length lay between it and the Soul Drinkers, the ground beneath them shook like an earthquake. Fissures opened up in the ruins, sending the remnants of Selaacan buildings and necron structures alike falling into the networks of tombs and warrior forges below. A flare of plasma ripped up into the sky from the ship's engines, and another chain of explosions tore right through the heart of the ship, rippling up the side of the hull and bursting its sides. Broadside guns and chunks of deck flew trailing flames. Bolts of molten metal fell in a searing rain, sizzling against the ceramite armour of the Soul Drinkers. The sound was tremendous, like the roar of a stormy ocean amplified a thousand times.

The din died down, but the heat rolled over the ridge, hot enough to scald the lungs. Sarpedon pulled himself up to the edge of the ridge so that he could see.

Over the course of several minutes and hundreds of explosions, the *Antithesis* was utterly torn apart.

The final chain of detonations blew off its prow, and molten metal flowed from its severed neck in a red-black torrent, like thick gore from a massive wound. The ground below it sagged with the heat billowing out of the wreck, and, as it dissolved away, the huge charred hull sections began to sink.

Sarpedon looked up at the sky. The afterglow of the attack still flickered in the thin atmosphere. Only one force could do that to the wreck of the *Antithesis*. It had been an orbital strike, from a spacecraft flying high above them.

Sarpedon didn't have to say anything. All the Soul Drinkers knew what the loss of the *Antithesis* meant. They were stranded on Selaaca.

Sarpedon clambered back onto the reverse slope, and slid down onto his back.

'The necrons?' voxed Captain Luko.

'I don't think so,' said Sarpedon. 'That was a lance strike. Imperium tech.'

The sound of engines broke Sarpedon's concentration. He looked up to see three Thunderhawk gunships circling around the mushroom of smoke pumping from the wrecked spaceship. They were not Soul Drinker craft. They were painted a deep golden yellow, with the image of a clenched fist stencilled on their sides and tail fins.

'Blessed Throne,' hissed Luko. 'What are they doing here?'

'Draw back! Defensive positions!' ordered Sarpedon.

The Soul Drinkers moved rapidly, Sarpedon pausing only to heft Lygris's corpse back onto his shoulder. The ruins of a civic building rose from the bottom of the slope, half-buried in debris from the necron excavation of the tunnel. Statues of the planet's dignitaries, missing heads or limbs, stood guard outside an empty doorway that lead to a half-collapsed dome. Soul Drinkers took up positions in the doorway, and behind the drums of fallen columns half-buried in the earth.

The Thunderhawks' engines got louder as they came down to land, vanishing just out of sight of the Soul Drinkers' position.

Salk was beside Sarpedon, in cover behind a length of fallen wall.

'We are betrayed, commander,' he said.

Sarpedon looked at the sergeant.

'We are,' he said.

Yellow-armoured Astartes were advancing into sight. Each Thunderhawk had carried about thirty Space Marines, so, an almost company-strength force surrounded the Soul Drinkers' positions with their bolters levelled at the ruins.

'Fists,' snarled Luko.

The Imperial Fists had once been a brother Chapter of the Soul Drinkers, both having been created from the Imperial Fists Legion following the Horus Heresy. They had the same primarch, Rogal Dorn, and many times before the Soul Drinkers had broken from Imperial rule, the two

Chapters had fought, feasted and planned campaigns together.

'Give the order,' voxed Luko.

'Hold your fire,' ordered Sarpedon. 'All Soul Drinkers! Hold your fire until my order!'

'They will surround us,' said Tyrendian. 'Strike at them, cold and fast, as Daenyathos wrote!'

'No!' snapped Sarpedon over the vox. 'I will not die down here, not after all we have achieved! An Astartes' bolter is not a fit weapon to take the life of a Soul Drinker! Do not give your lives so cheaply!'

'We can take them, commander,' said Luko.

'Hold your fire!' barked Sarpedon again over the vox. 'That is an order!'

The air split and crackled in front of the main force. With a sound like tearing silk, reality burst open for a moment, and, suddenly, twenty Astartes in golden-yellow Terminator armour were standing in front of them: First Company Astartes, elites, wearing the ancient suits of Terminator armour their Chapter had carefully maintained since the days of the Great Crusade.

Their leader was bare-headed, a giant brute of a man with a blunt, solid face, a shaven head and several metal studs in his forehead. His ornate armour was emblazoned with images of stylised fists and lightning bolts. In one hand was a thunder hammer too large for even most Soul Drinkers to wield, and on the other was a shield bearing the heraldry of the First Company.

'Damnation,' said Sarpedon as he caught sight of the officer.

'You know him?' asked Luko.

'By reputation.'

The officer strode forwards, covered by the bolters of more than a hundred Imperial Fists.

'I am First Captain Lysander of the Imperial Fists,' shouted the Terminator officer. 'I am here to take you and your men into custody. I have the entire Third Company and half the First at my disposal, and guns in orbit trained on your position. As a fellow Astartes, I am willing to give you death in battle if you so choose, but if you resist, you will die. Make your choice.'

Lysander was a legend among the Astartes, especially the Imperial Fists and their successor Chapters, of which the Soul Drinkers were one. He was relentless and stubborn. When the battle needed a man who would stand firm and never break, and force the same out of his men, the Imperium had few better than Lysander.

He was also a man of his word. If he said he would wipe out the Soul Drinkers, he would do it.

Sarpedon looked between the Soul Drinkers sheltering in the ruins. If he ordered them to fight, they would fight. They would all die if he did that, to a man, for the wrath of betrayed battle-brothers was too powerful a force to spare any of them. At least then it would be over, and they would all have the peace that Luko had spoken of.

'It will not end like this,' said Sarpedon, but he was speaking to himself.

'Sarpedon!' shouted Lysander. 'Traitor and mutant! Show yourself!'

Sarpedon strode out of the doorway, his mutant form plain to see for the Imperial Fists whose guns focused on him. He saw their sergeants and captains, the Astartes carrying heavy bolters and missile launchers among their ranks, the dozens of bolters trained on him, all of them ready to turn him into a cloud of burning ceramite at Lysander's order.

'You are a disgrace,' said Lysander, 'to your Imperium and to your primarch.'

'It is the Emperor and the primarchs who are disgraced,' replied Sarpedon, 'by the corruption of the Imperium that has come to be.'

'Still you blaspheme!' retorted Lysander. 'Still you defy! My orders are to take you and your renegades in alive, but there will be few angry words spoken should I bring you in dead. One final time, down arms and surrender, and you will live long enough to appreciate that your deaths will be quick.'

Sarpedon scanned the troops behind Lysander once more. Among them, he spotted a figure dwarfed by the terminators, flanking the Imperial Fists captain, a normal-sized human, wearing the red robes of the Mechanicus.

'Voar!' shouted Sarpedon. 'You have betrayed us!'

'Did you expect anything less?' replied Voar calmly. He stepped forwards from between two of Lysander's

Terminators, and pulled his hood back to reveal his almost-human face. 'Our alliance was a matter of expediency for both of us. As soon as I learned that we faced the Soul Drinkers, I contacted their fleet, which helped secure our journey to the Veiled Region. The path we forged through the Veiled Region was theirs to follow. Did you truly believe that a servant of the Omnissiah would not have seen the consequences of our alliance, and prepared accordingly? Do you think a servant of the Imperium and a scion of Mars could ally with renegades and mutants on your terms?'

'I expected nothing less,' replied Sarpedon, 'but my hatred of the xenos overcame that. What galaxy is this where I and my brothers are despised even more than the alien?'

'Enough words!' roared Lysander. 'Make your choice, Sarpedon!'

Sarpedon switched to the vox. Lysander would not hear him.

'Luko,' he voxed. 'If I fall, down weapons and surrender.'

'Surrender?' replied Luko. 'Commander, what are you…'

'Captain,' said Sarpedon, 'I trust you with what may be my last order. As an Astartes, as my battle-brother, execute it as I command.'

Sarpedon unfastened the seals on his helmet and took it off his head, casting it into the rubble and dust at his feet, so that he was face to face with Lysander. He took the Axe of Mercaeno off his back.

'If you want my Chapter,' he said, 'you will have to come and take it.'

Lysander smiled.

'There is some shadow of honour in you yet, mutant,' he said.

Lysander strode forwards, and Sarpedon advanced to meet him. The toxic atmosphere of Selaaca was raw in Sarpedon's throat, his augmented lungs fighting to make it breathable. It was worth it to look into Lysander's eyes.

'Hold your fire,' voxed Lysander to the Imperial Fists. He closed off the vox-link. 'What possessed you?' he said. 'What could make an Astartes forsake the Imperium he is sworn to defend?'

'I saw it for what it truly was,' replied Sarpedon.

'Duty to the Imperium,' said Lysander, 'must blind a man to its ills.'

'If you believe that,' said Sarpedon, 'then you will always be my enemy.'

Lysander hefted his hammer over his head, and roared as he slammed it down. Sarpedon jinked back, smacking the haft of the hammer aside with his axe. The impact of the hammer hitting the ground and discharging its power field threw Sarpedon onto his back talons, and he stumbled back as he tried to bear his weight on the leg he had lost to the necron overlord.

Lysander saw the opening. He swept the hammer in a massive arc, and slammed the head into Sarpedon's chest. Sarpedon was lifted off his feet

and thrown back, tumbling end over end in the dust. Lysander darted forwards to finish him off, and the hammer arced down again.

Sarpedon rolled to one side, and the hammer pounded the ground beside him. Lysander rammed his shield into Sarpedon, and threw him back again. Sarpedon rolled to his feet, and the two Astartes faced one another again.

The breastplate of Sarpedon's armour was dented and smouldering. He had fought his way into the tomb and out again, and the mauling from the necron overlord had left him slower and weaker than before. His limbs felt heavy, and every movement hurt. Lysander was fresh to battle, and had come ready for a fight. Sarpedon could tell from the look in the Imperial Fist's eyes that he was enjoying this.

The two Astartes circled, sizing one another up for the next strike.

'Half the Second Company is arriving at Raevenia as we speak,' said Lysander with relish. 'If your Chaplain lives, we will have him in custody within the hour, your space hulk, too. It is over, Sarpedon. Your Chapter ceases to exist on this day.'

'Then you will have the Soulspear, too,' replied Sarpedon. 'It is in a void-safe in the armoury of the *Brokenback*. I trust you will take better care of it than the Mechanicus.'

'Blasphemer!' yelled Lysander.

Sarpedon ducked under the arcing blow of Lysander's hammer, and drove the axe up into Lysander's chest. The head of the axe tore through the ceramite of Lysander's armour, throwing sparks of power.

For a second, the two were locked together, Sarpedon fighting to wrench the axe from Lysander's armour. Lysander forced Sarpedon closer with his shield, and headbutted Sarpedon on the bridge of the nose.

Sarpedon reeled. He fell, leaving the Axe of Mercaeno embedded in Lysander's breastplate. He tried to get to his feet, but the hammer knocked his many legs from under him, and he sprawled to the ground again.

Lysander planted an armoured foot on the backpack of Sarpedon's armour, forcing him down into the dust. The lower edge of Lysander's shield pressed down on the back of Sarpedon's neck. Sarpedon could not move, pinned to the ground.

'If you expected an execution here and now, Sarpedon,' said Lysander, 'then I am pleased to disappoint you. Your death will serve as an example to the Imperium of the wages of betrayal. My Chapter's executioners will extract their debt in full view of Rogal Dorn, when we take you to the *Phalanx* and proclaim your crimes to the galaxy.'

Sarpedon could not reply. There were no words left. He looked up at the ruins where the Soul

Drinkers were sheltering, and he prayed silently that Luko would do the right thing.

Lysander raised his shield, and slammed it down on the back of Sarpedon's skull. Blackness fell over his eyes and consciousness left him.

The last thought Sarpedon had was of his Chapter in chains, and of the sentence of death that would fall on them when the Imperium found them guilty.

WARHAMMER
40,000

Contains the novels *Soul Drinker*, *The Bleeding Chalice* and *Crimson Tears*

THE SOUL DRINKERS
OMNIBUS

BEN COUNTER

ISBN 978-1-84416-416-5

WARHAMMER
40,000

THE
SPACE WOLF
OMNIBUS

Buy these
omnibuses or read
a free extract at
www.blacklibrary.com

WILLIAM KING

SPACE WOLF • RAGNAR'S CLAW • GREY HUNTER

ISBN 978-1-84416-457-8

WARHAMMER
40,000

DAWN OF WAR

BLOOD RAVENS

THE DAWN OF WAR OMNIBUS

Contains the novels *Dawn of War*, *Dawn of War: Ascension* and *Dawn of War: Tempest*

C S GOTO

ISBN 978-1-84416-535-3